Sarah Meyrick studied Classics at Cambridge and Social Anthropology at Oxford, which gave her a fascination for the stories people tell and the worlds they inhabit. She has worked variously as a journalist, editor and PR professional. Alongside her day job, she is Director of the Bloxham Festival of Faith and Literature. She lives in Northamptonshire with her husband. *Knowing Anna* is her first novel. For more information, see <www.sarahmeyrick.co.uk>.

Sarah
MEYRICK

*Knowing
Anna*

Marylebone House

First published in Great Britain in 2016

Marylebone House
36 Causton Street
London SW1P 4ST
www.marylebonehousebooks.co.uk

British Library Cataloguing-in-Publication Data
A catalogue record for this book is available from the British Library

ISBN 978–1–910674–36–9
eBook ISBN 978–1–910674–37–6

Typeset by Graphicraft Limited, Hong Kong
First printed in Great Britain by Ashford Colour Press
Subsequently digitally printed in Great Britain

eBook by Graphicraft Limited, Hong Kong

Produced on paper from sustainable forests

For my parents, Jeremy and Elizabeth,
in gratitude for their unending love and support

THE PILGRIMS

Theo, Anna's husband
Beth, their daughter
Sam, their son
Ruth, Anna's mother
William, Anna's father
Tom, Anna's brother
Father Stephen, parish priest
Tamsin, Anna's friend
Milo, Tamsin's son
George, Milo's friend
Mary Anne, Anna's friend
Lucy and Ella, Mary Anne's daughters
Catherine, Anna's friend
Chloe, Catherine's daughter
Jackie, Anna's colleague
Celia, Anna's colleague

Prologue

Anna is running. Light as fluff, she is fairly flying along the towpath, enjoying the wispy autumn mist rising off the river and the nip of cold air at the back of her throat. A magnificent heron swoops over the water and she feels her heart soar.

She is heading away from Farmleigh towards the woods, and can just glimpse Aston church spire in the distance. On and on she flies, faster and faster, blissfully aware of the oxygen in her lungs, the lifeblood coursing around her body. It is good to be alive on a morning like this. To her surprise, she notices that she's wearing an unfamiliar sprigged summer dress; not ideal for running, perhaps, but pretty and light and short enough that it doesn't restrict her movement. Glancing down, she sees that at least she has on her familiar purple running shoes.

'You see?' she says to her unknown companion. 'Everyone said I couldn't do this any more, but I can! They all seem to think I'm dying. I must tell Theo – he'll be so relieved!'

Even as she speaks she can hear her words being snatched away by the breeze. The firm surface of the towpath melts beneath her feet and the river fades from view. She is still in flight, but unanchored now, and the fierce joy of a moment ago is giving way to panic. She strains to stay put, to keep her foothold on the ground, to resist the upward pull away from the riverbank. If she can only hang on, she knows she'll turn the corner, discover some vital piece of information that hovers just out of reach.

Resistance proves futile. The fleeting relief as she wakes and finds herself in the familiar surroundings of her bedroom gives way to a stab of disappointment when reality hits. *Here we go again*, she thinks. There's that crack in the ceiling, and the stained patch where the gutter overflowed last winter. The cool air she's breathing is actually coming through the window she insists is left open, to minimize the smell of the sickroom. She's back in the foggy world of illness, engaged in the delicate dance between pain and stupor. The exhausting struggle to eat the treats the family carry upstairs for her, to ask Sam about his latest football match, and Beth about her GCSE coursework. To watch the grey hollows in Theo's beloved face deepen with tiredness and fear.

She reaches out to the bedside table for her phone and glances at the time. 14.08. Tamsin will be coming out of the studio at the end of her lunchtime show. Good timing; she may go straight into a production meeting to plan the next day's programme, but she'll probably pick up a text. Anna summons her strength.

Come round 2day or 2moro? Can't hang on much longer. Dreamt I was running. Running out of time? A xxx

Almost at once a reply pings back. *Running, huh? Thought u meant 2 b sick. 2moro after show ok? T x*

Anna smiles. *Between 2 and 3 safest. Bring kit? A x*

Course. Chocolate or gin? T x

Booze + morphine = bad combo, she taps. *Choc always good.* Though that's not really true any more, she thinks; but Taz can eat it. *Just not flowers. Remind me of graves. C u A x*

Lilies in the bin, then. Be there. Love u. T xx

12 miles
Theo

Theo finally ran out of excuses to avoid the loft just before supper on Friday. He played for time until the lasagne was safely in the oven, the table laid and the salad mixed, before reluctantly going upstairs to locate the long metal hook and opening the hatch.

In terms of firsts, a visit to the loft barely counted. Compared with the first parents' evening in a post-Anna world (Beth's; petrifying), the first family birthday (Sam's; wretched) or the first wedding anniversary (still to come), it hardly rated. Nonetheless, he realized he was approaching what should have been a mundane task with a sense of dread. As the ladder rattled down towards him, he steeled himself for what he would find overhead: all those clear plastic boxes with their coloured lids firmly clipped into place, meticulously stacked and neatly labelled in Anna's precious handwriting. BABY CLOTHES, PHOTO ALBUMS, SCHOOL REPORTS, SHEET MUSIC (CELLO), SHEET MUSIC (PIANO) awaited him. And with it, the unbearable impression that all the loose ends of the life he'd loved more than his own had been tidied up and filed away. So utterly over.

He hovered on the top step, and almost without thinking found himself calculating the distance to the floor below. It was a habit he'd slipped into after the funeral: the odds on achieving a swift and merciful death. If he fell, would he break his neck? Could he be sure of dying? Or would he simply fracture a wrist, end up bruised and embarrassed? *See*, his father's voice hissed in his ear. *You haven't got the guts. Call yourself a man?*

'What are you doing up there, Dad?' By the sounds of it, Sam was standing in the bedroom below.

'Looking for Mum's walking boots,' he called down. 'I know I put them up here somewhere when ... when we first found out she was ill.' As he spoke, he caught sight of them in the far corner under the skylight, next to a box marked CAMPING KIT. He remembered the day he'd carried them up here. The pair of them had come home from the hospital appointment, appalled by the unexpected news the oncologist had delivered, kindly, but clearly, in her clean white office. He could still see the bland British landscapes on the walls, selected presumably in the faint hope of offering comfort to patients caught up in the maelstrom of personal catastrophe. Something to focus on as the unreal words *advanced*, *inoperable* and *terminal* floated in the hospital-scented air.

At the time they had been almost too shocked to speak. Much later, in the middle of the night, he would awake in a sweat, swamped by a wave of white hot anger, of sheer fury, of utter *outrage* that the insatiable maw of death was threatening to rip apart his family. Was this some kind of divine punishment by a vengeful God? Returning home from the hospital, though, Theo sought solace in habit and made a cup of tea, simply for something to do. How pathetically British! They sat at the scarred pine kitchen table, clutching their chipped blue and white mugs in silence.

There seemed almost nothing to say. The truth was quite literally unspeakable. Anna was chalk-white, trembling and staring bleakly at the leaflets the doctor had given her.

'Can I ... shall I ... phone anyone?' he asked.

'No, not yet.' She whispered so quietly he could hardly hear. 'Can't face it.'

'Your mum? The schools? Stephen, perhaps?'

'No!' The word shot out like a bullet. She took a deep breath to regain her composure. 'Let's just ... keep it to ourselves for now. For today, anyway. Then at least we can begin to make some plans.' And Theo recognized that this was how it would be: Anna would write lists, make rotas for childcare, fill the freezer, buy Christmas presents she might not be there to give, constructing a raft of careful arrangements in a futile attempt to outwit time. What was the phrase? She would put her affairs in order.

4

In practice that meant a sudden frenzy of tidying, organizing and swooping around the house with black bin liners, clearing away everything that Anna now deemed surplus to requirements. He'd rescued her walking boots and taken them up to the loft, unsure why, but knowing simply that he couldn't bear to see them binned, just because she had no further use for them. Now, picking them up, he put a hand inside each boot, feeling with his fingers the places where she had stretched the fabric out of shape, where the lining had worn threadbare, the contours that represented the unique imprint of her beloved feet. He lifted the boots to his face, rested his cheeks against the leather and breathed in the earthy smell. *Anna, Anna, Anna.*

'Dad, I can smell burning!' Sam shouted this time.

Theo wiped his wet face on his sleeves. Damn the lasagne! It was his failsafe dish, and he couldn't even do that properly. He had to get a grip. With a huge act of will, he pulled himself together and unfolded his long body down the ladder to see whether supper could be rescued.

The lasagne was just about acceptable, once he'd scraped off the black edges. Sam made the best of it, with all the discrimination of most eleven-year-old boys. Beth, on the other hand, picked desultorily at the helping on her plate. She sat scowling, curling a strand of her crop of dark red curly hair – Anna's hair – round and round her finger. Finally she dropped her fork with a dramatic sigh.

'It's not that bad,' he said, fighting a rising bubble of irritation.

'*Whatever.*' She stood up to clear her plate to the sink.

'Where are you off to?' he said. 'What about pudding? There are chocolate brownies.'

'Uh, gross, Dad. I don't know how you two can eat so much.' She glared at Sam accusingly.

'I'll have yours, then,' said her brother, untroubled by her disdain. He was swinging his feet, kicking the table leg.

'So where are you going?' repeated Theo. He could hear the tension leaking into his tone.

'To *pack*, of course. If I've got to come on this ridiculous trek I'm going to need, like, *stuff*, aren't I?'

'Wait! I've got something for you.'

Beth hovered at the kitchen door. Theo could feel her indecision. Slam the door or ... or what? Could her father possibly have anything to pique her interest? His own father wouldn't have tolerated such defiance, that was for sure. Malcolm would have roared at him, grabbed his collar, reached for the strap. Theo felt a sudden stab of love for his sulky, stroppy fifteen-year-old daughter. Without getting up, he reached behind him. 'Here. Take these,' he said, holding out the boots. 'Try them on.'

Beth stared, as if suspecting a trick. 'Are they ... like ... Mum's?'

'Yes. But you're a six, too. Better than trainers, that's for sure. Worth a shot?'

Beth stood motionless for a beat. Then she stepped forward, took the boots, gave him an awkward half-hug, and left the room in silence.

Saturday morning was unseasonably cool and breezy. Spring had come late, and brought with it blustery winds that had lasted right until the end of May. Looking out at the garden, Theo could see the apple blossom sprinkled like snowflakes across the lawn. He wondered if the late frost had been enough to jeopardize the autumn crop. No pies, no crumble, no chutney, to see them through the winter. But with no Anna — and this was more her territory than his — that was one less thing for him to worry about. He sighed as the doorbell rang.

'Beth? Sam? You ready? Derek's here,' he called up the stairs. 'Time we were off.'

Derek, their neighbour, whose own wife Doris had died two years ago, had kept an avuncular eye on the family ever since Anna's diagnosis. He was always offering Theo help, but in terms too vague to be much use. Theo had seized with some relief on the idea of asking him for a lift into Guildford. Now, as they all piled into his ancient Skoda, the exhaust hanging on by a thread and the seats gritty with biscuit crumbs, he wondered if this had been entirely wise. But Derek's rheumy eyes had filled with tears at the suggestion. 'It would be my pleasure, Theo. An *honour*,' he said.

It was still early, barely nine o'clock, but a small crowd had already gathered in the Cathedral car park. People were pulling on walking boots, filling water bottles and packing rucksacks.

'God, Dad, who *are* all these people?' Beth demanded as Derek pulled over. Theo suddenly realized that he had been so focused on filling his rucksack, supervising Sam's packing and shutting up the house for a week, he'd given the other walkers little thought.

'Well, Granny Ruth and Grandpa William, for starters,' he said, spotting his in-laws. As Derek switched off the engine, Theo saw the compact figure of Father Stephen striding purposefully towards them, a clipboard under his right arm, his left hand smoothing his thick silver hair. How could the man look so *dapper*, even in walking togs?

'Theo! Bethany, Samuel. Good to see you all!' The heartiness of the priest's greeting grated on Theo's nerves. 'Do you kids want to stow the bags in your granddad's car?'

'How are you, Theo?' he continued when they were alone.

'Bearing up,' he replied, busying himself with the zip on his fleece. *Stupid expression.*

'Everyone here?' Theo cast vaguely around the car park, avoiding eye contact.

'Not far off,' said Father Stephen. 'I think we're expecting eighteen today. Some people are coming and going over the week, of course. How about we meet and greet together? Perhaps you can introduce me to anyone I don't know. I'm sure everyone's waiting to say hello. It's your gig, after all.'

'Hardly!' Theo said shortly. 'But I suppose I'll have to do.' He forced as much of a smile as he could muster, waved goodbye to Derek, and allowed himself to be carried along on the tide of the priest's bonhomie.

With his parents-in-law he found Anna's brother Tom. He was touched; he hadn't been sure that Tom would make the effort. But that was unfair: Tom worked long hours in IT which took him out of the country a great deal. Of course he was busy with his own life. At least he was here. Ruth kissed him warmly in greeting.

'You persuaded her out of the house, then?' she said, nodding in Beth's direction.

7

'By the skin of my teeth. She's missing a party. Someone's sixteenth. I hope she'll last the course.'

'Trust me; she will. And if not, I'm here with the car.'

Mary Anne, the natural leader of the group of women who'd appeared out of nowhere when Anna was pregnant ('our head girl', said Anna), was there with her two blonde daughters. So too was kind Catherine, who had quietly left casseroles and cakes on the doorstep during those dreadful few weeks. Both women appeared to have left their husbands at home. Catherine's daughter (Cleo? Clara?) was deep in conversation with Beth, their heads bent over a phone.

There were a couple of Anna's colleagues. Jackie, a large Afro-Caribbean woman with a wide white smile, and Celia, whose dark-rimmed glasses and cropped grey hair gave her an eager, owlish look. Celia, as it happened, was also a keen gardener and a loyal customer at Greene Fingers. Which reminded him: he hoped to goodness Sharon was coping at the garden centre without him. It was late in the planting season, but a bank holiday weekend always brought out the punters in force. Thank heavens Mike had been persuaded out of retirement – yet again – to lend a hand. He'd give them a ring later.

Out of the corner of his eye, Theo caught sight of Tamsin pulling up in her old red banger. Instinctively he glanced at his watch. She wasn't quite late, but he suspected that was more a matter of luck than judgement. Out of the car spilled Milo and another boy of a similar age, snorting with laughter, and struggling to keep their dog Smith under control. That didn't bode well. And did Tamsin *really* imagine that she could walk a hundred miles in those sandals?

Anger welled up, a frighteningly physical response, acidic in the back of his throat. Why the hell had it been *Tamsin* – not him, not the children, not even Ruth or William – who had shared Anna's last conscious hour? If only he'd realized that the end was so close. But how could he have known? He even remembered smiling at the sound of soft laughter rolling down the stairs to the kitchen where Sam was half doing his homework, and he was making a start on supper.

8

There'd been no sign that death was poised to pounce. Yes, he knew the pain was worsening, but they'd sorted out the morphine, got it under control. But even before Tamsin left, Anna had fallen asleep. From sleep she slipped into unconsciousness, and twenty-four hours later it was all over. Somehow he imagined there'd be more time, the chance to say goodbye. How was it fair – how could it *possibly* be fair – that a wife and mother could be snatched from her family *six miserable weeks* after diagnosis?

'Theo!' William laid a hand on his shoulder. 'You all right, old boy? You're white as a sheet! Chin up.'

Theo shook himself. He could see Father Stephen heading in his direction. 'Sorry, William. I was miles away. Are we ready to go?'

'I think everyone's here,' said Father Stephen, consulting his clipboard. 'Shall we move over to the Cathedral now? Unless you think there's anyone still to come?'

'I'm sure you've got it covered,' said Theo. 'Happy to move. I'll round up my two.'

Father Stephen shepherded the party into the Cathedral with the authority of a well-disciplined sheepdog. Theo brought up the rear, Sam in tow. Beth and Cleo/Clara had been joined by Mary Anne's girls, Lucy and Ella. Theo could hear their laughter and felt marginally better. Beth had known these three since they were all in nappies; she'd survive the week.

As they entered through the great west door, after a word with the duty steward, Father Stephen ushered everyone forward through the main body of the church into a small side chapel. There was a brief flurry of protest when Milo realized that Smith might have to stay outside, but Theo could see Tamsin assessing the situation, before turning the full force of her charm on the elderly steward. '*Thank* you,' she was saying as he approached. 'You've been so very understanding.

'Now, Smith, *behave.*' She fixed the dog with a hard stare. 'One strike and you're out, mate.' As she looked up, Theo found himself exchanging a brief conspiratorial smile with her. His earlier fury seemed to have dissolved. She'd changed her shoes, he noticed. He mustn't forget: she was Anna's closest friend.

9

'Friends, do all come in. Come in, sit down,' urged Father Stephen. The party distributed itself uncertainly, squashing onto the wooden seats and along the bench underneath the window.

'Thank you, everyone. And may I thank you for coming here today? I think it would mean a lot to Anna. I know there are people here from all parts of her life. Her family, of course. Her friends and colleagues. For myself, I can only say that it's a great privilege to be asked to lead this venture. I've been on other pilgrimages, but none quite like this one. I'm sure some of you are wondering what you've let yourselves in for.' Nervous laughter rippled around the chapel. Theo saw Mary Anne and Catherine exchange glances. William took Ruth's hand. Beth was staring at the floor.

'Well, let me explain. Nine years ago, Anna went on a pilgrimage to Santiago de Compostela in Spain. Perhaps you were one of those who wondered what on earth possessed her to spend a month walking almost three hundred miles. But if you knew her then, you'll no doubt remember that she came back profoundly moved by the experience.'

Stop, thought Theo. *Enough already. Leave it there. I don't want to think about it.* He concentrated hard on the pile of children's books on the windowsill.

'But that was Anna's journey, and her story,' continued Father Stephen. 'This week you'll have the chance to discover your own.' Theo exhaled.

'So what are we going to do? Well, Anna's suggestion was that some of her friends and family might walk the Pilgrims' Way to Canterbury in her memory. It's a route that's been walked by thousands of pilgrims over the centuries. They often set out from Winchester. We've cut a corner to fit our pilgrimage into the half-term week, which is why we're starting here in Guildford. Actually, I think that's rather fitting. This is a building where Anna often performed, so there's a happy association.'

Father Stephen paused and looked around. 'I know that some of you are probably uncertain about the whole notion of pilgrimage. Perhaps it's not something you ever imagined yourself doing, and you're not quite sure why you're here. Or you're just plain worried about managing the hundred and four miles!'

He beamed at them. 'Please don't worry. All sorts of people go on pilgrimages for all sorts of reasons, not necessarily religious ones. It's a matter of allowing ourselves time and space away from the relentless routine of everyday life, in the hope of discovering something new. So can I encourage everyone to approach this week with open hearts and minds? Open to God – or at least the *possibility* of God – and all that he might have in store for us? Let me get the ball rolling with one of my favourite prayers for pilgrims. Wherever you stand on belief, I think it can speak to us all.'

He put on his glasses and began to read from a small paperback.

> 'Set out!
> You were born for the road.
> You have a meeting to keep.
> Where? With whom?
> Perhaps with yourself.
> Set out!
> Alone or with others –
> But get out of yourself.
> You have created rivals;
> You will find companions.
> You envisaged enemies;
> You will find brothers and sisters.
>
> Set out!
> Your head does not know
> Where your feet
> Are leading your heart.
> Set out!
> You were born for the road –
> The pilgrim's road.
> Someone is coming to meet you,
> Is seeking you
> In the shrine at the end of the road,
> In the shrine at the depths of your heart.
>
> Go!
> God already walks with you.'

Father Stephen closed the book, and let the silence sit for a few moments. Then he continued. 'Our journey this week is also about honouring Anna, a woman everyone here loved or admired. It's a chance for us to share our stories about her, to give thanks for her life and all she meant to us.' Theo was aware of the familiar taste of salt as tears welled up. He felt Sam's sticky hand reach out to find his.

'And with that in mind – Mary Anne, Catherine – your turn, I think?'

The two women stepped forward, a little hesitantly, with a black canvas sports bag. Mary Anne cleared her throat. 'Catherine and I had an idea. I hope you'll approve,' she said. Undoing the zip, she pulled out a bundle of purple T-shirts, and shook one out. On one side #walkforanna was printed in white, on the other, a web address and the logo of a cancer charity.

'We've set up a website, so that people can make donations,' said Catherine. 'I don't know about you, but I'm not sure I can walk a hundred miles without a bit of encouragement. So for anyone who wants one, help yourself to a T-shirt and take a handful of these little cards, which explain what we're doing. We can give them out on the way. The idea is to get people to sponsor us and help raise money to stop other families from losing their lovely mums.'

'I'll have one,' said Beth, just too loudly, and stood up from her child-sized chair. There was a gentle round of applause, as she pulled on a T-shirt far too large for her slight frame. Others followed, until most of the group were wearing them.

'Right!' said Father Stephen. 'Before we go, a couple of practicalities. This isn't a route march – we're not an army! We'll be walking at a group pace. That's part of what it means to travel together. We may find ourselves stopping from time to time, if someone in the group needs a drink or a plaster for a blister. And that's part of pilgrimage, too – helping to carry each other's burdens. If anyone gets into real difficulties, we've got a back-up car, courtesy of Ruth.

'Second, each day will be marked with a short pause for reflection. Everyone is welcome. Take part in any way you can. I'm also going to suggest we spend some time each day in silence. Some of us will probably find that harder than others,' he added with a smile directed at Sam and Milo. 'But I'll try to help by offering some ideas to think about as we walk. And now, as we set off, I'd like you to hear again one of Anna's favourite poems, by John Donne, which you may remember from her funeral. William – would you?'

Theo watched his father-in-law stand in his seat, ramrod straight. He pushed his glasses up his nose, cleared his throat, and began to read in his sonorous voice.

'Bring us, O Lord God, at our last awakening, into the house and gate of heaven, to enter into that gate and dwell in that house, where there shall be no darkness nor dazzling, but one equal light; no noise nor silence, but one equal music; no fears nor hopes, but one equal possession; no ends nor beginnings, but one equal eternity; in the habitations of thy glory and dominion, world without end.'

Theo stumbled out of the Cathedral, dazzled suddenly by the unexpected sunlight. The early cloud had lifted, and although there was still a nip in the breeze, the sun was shining out of a cheerful blue sky dotted with occasional cotton-wool clouds. Glancing at his watch he saw that it was just after ten o'clock. They had twelve miles to cover today. Three or four hours on his own probably amounted to at least six as a group.

He looked round for Sam, who was holding Smith's lead while Milo stowed his water bottle in his rucksack. Was a six-hour walk going to prove too much for these two, and for Milo's friend George? Sam, at eleven, was a good few inches taller than Milo, and these days his limp was, if not quite invisible, rarely a hindrance. He'd taken him to the clinic for new supports to go into his walking boots a fortnight earlier, and had mentioned, as casually as possible, the impending walk. The orthotist, who had looked after Sam since the beginning, had been equally casual in her response.

'That sounds fun, Sam. Better than spending half-term on the Xbox?'

And Sam had dutifully smiled in return, and shrugged his almost adolescent shoulders insouciantly, as if walking a hundred odd miles was an everyday occurrence.

Milo, on the other hand, was to all intents and purposes still a little boy. How old was he? Eight? Nine? Anna's department again. She would have known; just as she would have known which birthday card to buy, what he'd like as a present. Luckily, he had always been an inexhaustible ball of energy, determined to keep up with Sam, whom he adored.

Would it be better if the boys were at the front or the back? Would the sight of walkers ahead in the distance discourage or motivate them? Theo wasn't sure. Knowing the two of them, they would probably scoot up and down the line, wearing themselves out in the process. He hoped George was as energetic. But perhaps he underestimated them. Maybe they'd find their rhythm during the week. *You mollycoddle that boy*, said his father's voice. *He needs to toughen up if he's ever going to be a farmer.* But he *isn't* going to be a farmer, thought Theo irritably. *So you can shut up about that, Dad.*

At that moment he caught a call from Father Stephen, at the front of the line of walkers, signalling the off. Theo waved back, marshalled the boys and set off in pursuit.

For the first half-mile or so, the route wound downhill from the Cathedral into the city centre and over the railway bridge before descending to the river bank. It hugged the river for another mile or so before meeting the Pilgrims' Way in a large open park just to the south of the city. Within half an hour, the walkers had emerged onto a track that climbed up steeply alongside a wooded hillside. Theo felt his heart lift a little as they ascended. To their right lay a vast tract of woodland, to their left a rolling chalk ridge.

'A triumph of the people over the planners,' said William, falling into step beside him. 'There was a scheme to build houses on Pewley Down after the First World War, but it was defeated. And then a local brewery stepped in. Bought the land and donated it to the people of Guildford in memory of the fallen. Can't argue with that. Masterstroke.'

'Cheers to that brewery!' said Theo. 'What are our other highlights today?'

'St Martha's church, at the top of this hill. Glorious spot. Panoramic views. Victorian rebuild of a Saxon original. Said to be the site where Saxon pagans burned a clutch of early Christian martyrs. In fact, there's some suggestion that the name St Martha's is a corruption of "martyrs". No idea if that's actually the case. But here's a true story. During the last war the church was disguised to look like a clump of trees to save it from bombing. Like something out of *Macbeth*.'

'Sounds more like *Dad's Army* to me,' said Theo.

William gave a gruff bark of laughter. 'Speaking of the Home Guard, look out for pillboxes. Amazing to think what a serious threat the German invasion seemed at the time. Assuming we're taking the North Downs Way, there're about a dozen of the things along the route. We pass at least half of them today.'

'Would a concrete pillbox really have been any cop in the face of an invading army?' asked Theo. 'That reminds me of a story my grandfather told me. He spent most of the war patrolling a beach in Kent, armed with nothing more than an old rifle and five rounds of ammo. In the end he persuaded his godfather to post him a revolver as back up. Luckily, Hitler never showed up.'

He enjoyed William's company. He was a fount of knowledge, but wore his learning lightly. A gentle man, he tended to take a back seat in family gatherings. Ruth was the organizer, the dynamo in the marriage. Or was that just how it looked? You never really knew. How was his father-in-law coping with Anna's death, he wondered? He had been so paralysed by his own pain that he'd scarcely noticed.

'How are you, William?' he asked, aware of the inadequacy of the question.

'Mustn't grumble.'

'But . . . really? Deep down?'

For a moment he thought William hadn't heard, or was pretending not to have done. Theo glanced sideways at him. He was striding purposefully enough, using the gnarled thumb stick he had leaned on for half a century. But had he always stooped so much? Been quite so gaunt?

'Harder for her mother,' he said eventually. 'Hard to get over the loss of a child, even an adult one. Hardly need tell you that. But we soldier on. Same for us all, of course. Best foot forward and so on. Kids OK?'

Theo looked ahead up the track. The boys were sharing dog duty, and looked cheerful enough. Beth's purple shirt was just visible near the front of the group, but he couldn't read her body language at this distance. How on earth did you define 'OK' anyway?

'I don't really know, to be honest,' he said. 'As well as can be expected, I suppose.'

By lunchtime, the group was beginning to find its tempo. Conversation bubbled up and down the line of people. Sometimes the path was wide enough for them to walk as pairs or even threes. At other points, it was single file only. The boys had kept up a barrage of chatter from the outset and so far showed little sign of fatigue.

Theo at least was glad to stop for lunch. As the party gathered in a grassy picnic area on the edge of a nature reserve, he looked round for his daughter. 'Beth!' he called. 'Sandwiches? Drink?'

Beth looked up, raised her eyebrows, and called back: 'Dad, don't fuss. I'm fine. I've got a cereal bar.' And that, he realized as she turned back to her friends, was the last he'd see of her for now. Was it a good thing, that she was so absorbed in conversation with the others? They'd all known each other since they were babies, in some case bumps. And surely it was healthier that a fifteen-year-old was in the company of people her own age, rather than clinging to her father's every word. Mind you, he'd seen her deep in conversation with Tamsin, earlier. But that was to be welcomed; Tamsin was her godmother.

Theo sighed. Anna would have known how to handle Beth, when to worry, when to tease and when just to let things go. And if she'd been here, he would have had someone to talk to. In almost two decades they had never run out of things to say to each other. There was still so much more he wanted to share. The day-to-day trivia, as well as the profound. Those moments when you know that only one person in the whole world would appreciate why something was funny, or shocking or surprising. The things that you saved up to tell each other, because you knew they would bring delight or amusement. A dozen times a day he caught himself thinking, *I must remember to tell Anna that* ... But all those thoughts would now go unsaid. *Enough*. Ruth had just arrived in her car. He picked up his sandwiches and headed squarely in the direction of his mother-in-law.

'I promised you silence!' Father Stephen's loud voice broke through the hubbub. 'As I said earlier, we're going to try walking in silence for a while every day. My thought is that today we'll see if we can manage half an hour. If that goes well, perhaps we'll extend the time tomorrow.' He looked around the uncertain faces, and smiled broadly.

'Trust me on this one, please. I promise it's going to be worth it. Silence can be alarming, I know, but it gives us a chance to *think*. Now, our theme for today is going to be "gathering". Today, at the start of our venture, we've gathered for the first time. Most of us know our fellow pilgrims, and I hope you've had the chance to say hello to those you don't.

'But whoever you walk with, when you go on pilgrimage, you tend to form a bond with your fellow travellers. And that can be something precious. There's a bit in the Bible where Jesus says, "Where two or three of you are gathered in my name, there will I be also." So in the next half-hour, shall we think about our gathering? What or who have we left behind? Why have we come? What's our part in this pilgrimage?

'This next part of the walk is a chance for us to *gather* our thoughts a little. You might like to offer that up in prayer, but that's up to you. Shall we say five minutes to pack up your picnics, and then we'll be off?'

For Theo, it was almost too obvious. He was here because Anna had asked him to come. At the time, he would have promised to walk to the moon, if he thought it would bring her comfort. In fact, he realized now, the prospect of the pilgrimage had brought *him* comfort since her death. It was a physical task, which had always been his forte. It was something to keep Beth and Sam occupied during half-term. The Easter holidays had been grim; he'd been totally unable to plan anything. Apart from Easter Day itself, when he'd thrown himself on the mercy of Ruth and William, it had been unutterably bleak. The walk had been something to look ahead to, to keep on the horizon on days so black that even the effort of getting out of bed in the morning felt beyond him. Was this perhaps why she'd suggested it?

As for what he'd left behind, that was quite simply the horrible emptiness of life without her. It all happened so fast. One minute they were going about their lives, and the next, it seemed, Anna was having tests for the nagging discomfort that she'd insisted was a pulled muscle from dragging home a sack of organic potatoes from the farm shop. Then came the deadly diagnosis. He'd just about got his head round the fact that she wasn't going to recover, and that the prognosis meant weeks not months, when all of a sudden it was into the hospice and then back home to die.

It was, frankly, a relief to be away from home, because everywhere he turned the house was full of memories. It felt like a home with the heart torn out. How they'd poured love into that house! For the first four months of their life together they'd lived in a non-descript property on the edge of Farmleigh, in a cul-de-sac just off the Aston road. ('Ugh!' said Anna. 'I'm far too young for a bungalow!') He'd rented it from the family of an elderly client, who had moved into a care home. The house was tired, the decor threadbare and the carpets swirly and unpleasantly full of cat hair that no amount of vacuuming seemed able to remove.

'The garden's the only thing that's not stuck in the 1970s, and that's because you look after it,' said Anna.

'It's cheap and it's ours,' he replied, burying his face in her apple-scented hair. 'I'd put up with a lot worse for that.'

To this day, he marvelled at their outrageously good fortune in finding each other. He'd been at work, trying to jazz up a tray of slightly bedraggled bedding plants on the trestle tables outside the garden centre on a perfect June day, when she'd driven up in her battered blue Morris Traveller. Absorbed in the task at hand and only dimly aware of the sound of a car, he hadn't looked up until she was almost upon him. She stood, a slight figure in a lilac dress and a floppy off-white cotton hat shading her from the midsummer sun. The dress was sleeveless and her arms were peppered with freckles. She hovered with indecision, shifting her weight from one foot to the other, almost *shimmering* in the sunlight, it seemed to Theo.

'Can I help you?' she asked.

'Sorry?'

'Isn't that what you're supposed to ask me?' she said. Her smile revealed a slight gap between her front teeth. Tiny beads of sweat glistened on her upper lip.

'Sorry! I was miles away,' he stumbled, suddenly aware he'd been staring. 'Can I *help* you, madam?' he continued with exaggerated politeness, bowing slightly.

'I think it's just possible you could save my life,' she said gravely, picking up his tone.

'Oh? No pressure then.' She was hovering again, he noticed, glancing anxiously back at her car. 'You don't look in imminent peril, if you don't mind me saying. What exactly seems to be the problem? And how do you think I might be able to help?'

'My normally rational friend is getting married on Saturday and she's in serious danger of turning into Bridezilla. The florist has cancelled with two days' notice and she's distraught. I thought ... well, I wondered if you could supply me with a dozen olive trees? You see, she's Palestinian and I thought they'd make a statement.'

'A dozen? By Saturday?'

'There's more ...' she said, looking down at her sandalled feet. The pink varnish on her toenails was chipped. 'I don't have much money. Is there any chance ... any *at all* ... that I could borrow them?'

'Baby? Grandma? Shopping that might be melting?'

The shimmering girl looked up, flummoxed. 'I'm sorry?'

Theo seized the advantage. 'You keep looking at the car. I couldn't help wondering what's even more important than your friend's wedding.'

The girl let out a great gurgle of laughter. 'None of the above! It's just Chuck. The trouble is that I can't afford to get the lock fixed and I absolutely daren't let him out of my sight. It's more than my life's worth.'

'And who's Chuck when he's at home?'

She laughed again, and pinkened prettily. 'I'd better introduce you. I must seem terribly rude.'

By the time Anna had returned, carrying not a dog, as he'd expected, but a cello ('Chuck the cello ... it's my worst nightmare when I fly anywhere,' she explained), Theo was already half in love with her. He rashly promised to find the trees – knowing it would probably mean a 5 a.m. dash to his supplier in Southampton tomorrow – and even agreed to let her hire them for a sum so paltry that it would barely cover his petrol.

And then, joy of joys, he discovered that Anna's friend Nadia was marrying his cousin Tim, and he therefore had a cast-iron excuse to see her again. He didn't let slip that he hadn't been planning to go to the wedding. His mother, he knew, would be glad of his company. Any inconvenience his last-minute appearance might cause the family seemed trivial in comparison with the unthinkable prospect of letting her slip through his hands.

The wedding completed the spell she wove over him. He arrived, uncomfortable in a suit he'd pulled from his father's wardrobe, and strained for a glimpse of her. Someone had arranged the olive trees to good effect: there were two in the church porch, two up near the altar, and the rest lined the aisles. Their simple terracotta pots were offset by plain white ribbons woven among the leaves.

When Theo couldn't at first spot her he panicked briefly, then leapt with relief to the conclusion that she would appear with Nadia, as her bridesmaid. What he hadn't anticipated was that Anna would play the bride into the church. He was so busy watching the door for the arrival of the bridal party that he overlooked her entirely until the very moment the music began. There were two violinists, and Anna on the cello. He had no idea what the piece was: only that it was beautiful, and she was its source.

To his delight she sought him out at the evening reception, after he'd packed his mother safely home in a taxi. 'Thank you for the trees,' she said shyly. 'I think they worked, don't you?'

'I loved them,' he said, unable to keep the smile from his face. 'And it was good to hear Chuck in action.'

'Oh,' she said. She breathed out a deflated sigh, and plonked herself in the chair next to his.

'What's the matter?'

'I'm sorry,' she said, recovering herself. 'It's just all a bit of a mess.' And she told him that the musicians in the church made up three-quarters of the Montague Quartet. Nadia, the viola player, was the fourth. They had met as students and for the last couple of years had enjoyed modest success touring and performing.

'You may not have heard of us, but we've been on Radio Three a couple of times. And we're pretty big in Eastern Europe, for some reason. But I'm leaving,' she continued miserably. 'It's agony.'

'Why are you leaving, if you love playing so much?'

'How do you know I love playing?'

'I was watching you,' said Theo, realizing that he hadn't taken his eyes off her for a single second of the service.

And Anna had explained that what had once been a happy relationship with Laurence ('as in Montague, our glorious leader') was in its death throes.

'Why are you breaking up?'

'Artistic differences.'

'Seriously?'

'Well, only if you think "artistic temperament" equals licence to cheat.' She was teasing him again. 'I found out he's been playing the field as well as his fiddle. Again. And I've finally come to my senses and given him the elbow. But now he's so angry with me that he never misses a chance to humiliate me during rehearsals, in public too if he can. It's poisoning the quartet for everyone. We just can't make music any more. So I'm out, but I'm scared stiff.'

All the time she was speaking, Anna was glancing in the direction of one of the other musicians, who was flirting with the prettier of the two bridesmaids.

'That's him? The good-looking git doing his best to charm the pants off the schoolgirl?'

'Uh-huh.' She nodded unhappily.

'So that's why you're over here with me? Because you're trying to avoid your ex?' asked Theo.

'Only partly,' she answered, blushing again as she had at the garden centre.

For a fraction of a second, Theo hesitated. *I have nothing to lose but my pride*, he thought. 'Then let's give Laurence bloody Montague a dose of his own medicine,' he said, looking straight into her dark blue eyes. 'Come and dance with me.'

21

And that was it. Six weeks later she moved into the bungalow with him, and by Christmas they were married. They spent a cold but blissful week's honeymoon in a damp cottage near Whitstable. Meanwhile Anna set herself up as a freelance musician: a combination of dashes up to London for orchestral session work, and peripatetic teaching in a handful of local schools. Helped by a small legacy from his aunt, they scraped together just enough money for a deposit on a house of their own.

They'd fallen on their feet with the Brew House. A narrow, dark-red brick building spread over three floors, it was tucked into a corner next to the old brewery, which had been abandoned a decade earlier and allowed to sink into dereliction. It was in the least attractive part of Farmleigh, next to a down-at-heel garage and an empty warehouse. But Anna, at least, had immediately seen the potential. True, the house had fallen into disrepair and smelled of hops, but it had good bones, she insisted, and someone had clearly once loved the garden. They put in as low an offer as they dared and to their surprise the harried estate agent practically bit their hands off.

There followed a year of intensive DIY: sanding and painting and repairing the Brew House, reclaiming the garden from the jungle of ground elder and brambles, until Anna, pregnant with Beth, finally admitted defeat and put her feet up. By then they had turned the ground floor into a single open-plan living space, with a kitchen one end and two squashy sofas the other. Upstairs they had a decent double bedroom, a serviceable nursery, and a bathroom.

By the time Anna was pregnant for the second time, Theo had transformed the top floor into another bedroom, and somehow squeezed their double bed up the narrow stairs into the space under the eaves, leaving the children the run of the floor below. They could lie in bed and look out of the skylight over the higgledy-piggledy roof lines of Farmleigh, which had come to life around them while they were almost too busy building their own nest to notice. An imaginative developer had bought the old brewery, and it now housed a trendy graphic design company on the top floor, and an art gallery and café on the middle and ground floors. The garage had been bulldozed and replaced by three new townhouses, and the warehouse behind them was being redeveloped as a community centre.

'You're smiling,' said Catherine, walking alongside him. 'Penny for them?'

The silent period had flashed by, he realized. They'd doubtless been walking through beautiful scenery, but he'd noticed none of it.

'I've been gathering my thoughts, as instructed,' he said. 'You?'

'It made me realize what a noisy world I live in. You know: work, children, radio, TV . . . I don't know about you, but I felt very self-conscious to begin with. I'm not used to peace and quiet. It was like being in an assembly at school and being desperate to giggle. But then I got into it. I rather enjoyed the sensation.'

'That's what Anna used to say about running,' said Theo. 'She used to go out with her iPod and of course I assumed she was listening to music, maybe even learning a new piece she was working on. She admitted one day that she only took it so that if she met someone she knew, she could smile and wave, but have a cast-iron excuse not to talk. That surprised me, because she was such a social person.'

'Do you know, that's sort of what I was thinking about? That word *gather*. To begin with I kept seeing an image of Kate Winslet at that Hollywood bash a few years ago – do you remember? She got a lot of stick in the press for saying "gather, gather" when she was trying to get her emotions under control when she won an Oscar. But then I started thinking that Anna had *gathered* us all here today. That's just what she was like. She gathered people around her.'

Theo smiled. 'You're absolutely right. She collected us. Waifs and strays. Me especially.'

'You a stray? I find that hard to believe.'

'Well, I was pretty lost when we met, you know. That's what I was thinking about.' And Theo found himself, hesitantly at first, telling Catherine an edited version of their meeting. The olive trees, and the wedding. The ex-boyfriend. How angry with life he had been at the time. How he'd dreamt for years of escaping

23

Farmleigh, and had finally done so at the age of twenty-four, only to be summoned home from Africa a fortnight later to take over the family farm when his father dropped dead from a heart attack.

'I still think he did it deliberately,' he told her. 'He couldn't bear the fact that I'd actually escaped his clutches. Inflicting the farm on me was his revenge from the grave.'

He remembered the terrible phone call from his mother down a crackly line to the office in the compound, as the tropical rain beat noisily on the corrugated roof. He'd gone to Africa with such high hopes. Hopes of forging a new life, away from the vice-like grip of his father. Dreams of making a lasting difference, working with a small agricultural charity in south-western Kenya, although he'd immediately realized how much he had to learn before he would make a useful contribution. For now, the three years he'd spent at agricultural college and a lifetime farming Hampshire chalk-land might as well have been spent at catering college for all the use his know-how appeared to be in Nyanza.

Coming home felt like a total anti-climax, and yet more evidence of his uselessness. *See? Couldn't hack it in Africa, could you?* whispered the voice of his dead father in his ear. It was as if he'd known how much Theo had struggled with the heat, the mosquitoes, the unfamiliar food. The whisper morphed into a sneer when, eighteen months later, Theo broke the news to his tearful mother that the farm must be sold. *I always knew you'd let me down. You're such a disappointment.* All these years later she still blamed him for the decision, referring always to 'losing' the farm, as if it had been idle carelessness on Theo's part, rather than an agonizing, gut-churning, desperate decision reached only after he'd exhausted every possible alternative.

It was Anna who turned the situation round. A few weeks into their relationship, just at the point of her moving in with him, torn between the need to expose the full ledger of his shortcomings to her and the certainty that once she learned the truth she would cast him aside, it all came pouring out. He catalogued his ineptitude, his guilt at forcing his mother to move away from the house she had called home for the past thirty years, his overwhelming sense of failure.

'I can see it's been hellish,' Anna said carefully, having listened in silence to the litany of his failings. 'Hell for your mother, but surely far worse for you. But have you ever thought that perhaps you did a brave and difficult thing, letting the farm go? Everyone knows what a tough gig farming is. Was calling time really so terrible? From where I'm standing, it looks as if you've got a job you love and are very good at. Why else has Mike made you his deputy manager? You're using your skills and you still get to work outdoors. You look forward to going to work every morning. How many people do you think have that privilege?'

He told Catherine now, 'Quite simply, Anna saved my life. I was the luckiest man alive, meeting her.'

'I'd say she was pretty lucky to have you. You were well suited. The perfect couple, eh?'

'No,' said Theo, abruptly. 'Never that. I let her down. Anna deserved better.'

13 miles
Beth

Beth woke early. The curtains in the hostel were thin, made from off-white cotton, and not quite wide enough to cover the window. All around her she could hear breathing. It was weird sharing a room with a load of other people. A *dormitory*, for God's sake, like boarding school or something.

The last time she'd shared a bedroom was . . . at a sleepover when she was still in Year Eight? Or perhaps it was on that family holiday in Wales when she had to share a bunk bed with Sam? God, that was stressful. She'd lain awake half the night, listening to his noisy breathing. Every now and again it seemed to stop altogether, and just as she started to panic, there'd be a sudden snort, and she'd hear herself let out her own breath, a breath she hadn't even realized she was holding. She'd relax for a moment, and then the exhausting cycle would start all over again. She could still conjure up the gritty-eyed tiredness of the days cooped up in the cottage, playing board games as the rain fell relentlessly outside. The first night home, she'd almost wept with relief to be back in her own bedroom.

The girls' dormitory was in two sections. At least she'd managed to manoeuvre herself into the smaller area, with Tamsin and the other women. On balance it was better to be in with the grown-ups. She'd really had enough of pretending to be interested in Chloe's cheerleading team (the girl was *obsessed*; it was tragic). As for Lucy and Ella – she'd admit they'd all been friends at primary school, but *puh-lease*. Their preppy-good-girl act made her want to scream. It was probably their inescapable *destiny*, having Mary Anne as a mother, but they were so pretty, so *perf*, so *vanilla* that she just

26

couldn't stand it. Both sisters would witter on at great length about anything and everything – none of it of even the *slightest* interest – and it was all *who* was wearing *what* to the Prom, what some boy at their stupid posh school had or hadn't said to someone else she didn't know . . . Bor*ing*. Then – worse still – one of them would suddenly remember about Anna and nudge the other and then they'd both put on their *concerned* voices and ask if she was OK, and remind her that as her *oldest friends* they were *there for her*.

She'd changed in one of the outdoor washrooms, flung a fleece on top of her PJs, padded upstairs in her socks and climbed quickly up into a top bunk without anyone batting an eyelid, let alone expecting a full-on pyjama party. Round the corner, Lucy and Ella and Chloe were gasping over non-existent spots, scooping up their hair into top-knots and sharing their armoury of cleansing products. They'd probably spend half the night whispering about how Beth was *coping*. Actually, now she thought about it, they had bossy-boots Mary Anne for company, so that would cramp their style a bit.

Beth rolled onto her back, and stretched out her legs under the covers. She could feel a slight ache in her calves from yesterday, and the beginnings of a blister on her left heel. Sliding her hands down her body, she found her pyjama trousers waistband comfortingly loose. Her hip-bones definitely jutted out a bit. One thing about all this walking: even at only two miles an hour, yesterday's walk had used up 828 calories. She'd downloaded a handy app on her phone that kept a running total.

It was actually quite tiring. She really had been exhausted when she sloped away from the supper table early and said she was heading to bed. As soon as they'd arrived at the hostel, Mary Anne had made four big pots of tea and a jug of squash and magicked up several packets of biscuits. Then she pulled on her Cath Kidston apron (honestly, who carried one of *those* in their backpacks? only a bloody food tech teacher) and marshalled everyone into chopping and stirring to produce a giant spaghetti bolognese. Spotting her chance with the salad, Beth had busied herself washing the lettuce and tomatoes and slicing the cucumber, putting as much distance as possible between herself and the gleaming mountain of pasta and grated cheese.

Now she reached down the bed, feeling for her phone, which appeared to be trapped between the mattress and the side of the bunk. All she needed to do was check Instagram and she'd know if the worst had happened last night. Or not. After a moment's indecision, she booted the phone awake and braced herself. Only to find that there was no update for the simple reason that there was no signal.

Bugger. She'd have to get up, then, and go in search of civilization. She reached to the end of the bed to the neat pile of clothes. Everyone else seemed to be safely asleep: Tamsin below her; Catherine in the single bed by the window; and Jackie and Celia, Mum's music therapist friends, in the other set of bunks. She would risk getting dressed where she was. She quickly stripped off her pyjamas, and pulled on the layers of clothing, ending with her *#walkforanna* T-shirt.

Beth slid quietly down the ladder to the floor, and tiptoed to the door in her bare feet. As she did so, she heard Tamsin stir, and held her breath, afraid she'd woken her. But Tamsin merely turned over, and laughed gently in her sleep. How could she *do* that? God, it must be nice to have no worries! What was she dreaming about? A beach in Australia?

She made her way down the steep stairs, towards the kitchen. The boys were out of reach, up another narrow flight. Sam was Dad's problem, for now. Let Dad worry about his breathing this time. She let herself into the kitchen and ran a long glass of water. Eight glasses a day, minimum, sometimes twelve. That was the regime. A nauseating smell of yesterday's breakfast bacon lingered in the room. She picked an apple from the fruit bag and washed it. If she ate that, no one could argue. Everyone knew fruit was a healthy breakfast.

Outside the air was still heavy with dew and the promise of summer. The grass was cool and wet underfoot, and a low mist hung around the trees. You could see for miles over the fields below. It was rather magical. It made the hostel seem more than ever like something out of a fairy tale, Hansel and Gretel, maybe, or Little Red Riding Hood. She'd honestly wondered *where* they were going when Father Stephen strode off so confidently down the track into the woods last night, just at the point when it had started drizzling and everyone was getting really tired and fed up. Sam, Milo and George had looked fit to drop. She really wondered if Dad had thought this through. What planet was he on, for fuck's sake?

But just when she thought they would never get there, they'd emerged through the woods into a clearing and discovered the hostel: a half-timbered green and white oldy-worldy house with low beamed ceilings and a big open fireplace. It was like an American tourist's dream of Little Ol' England. The boys had been captivated to the point that they suddenly seemed to forget their tiredness, and disappeared with Uncle Tom to collect sticks for firewood.

Beth sat on a garden bench. Still no signal. It was so *lame*. What next? She thought she'd head up the track, back up towards the road, try her luck there. She retraced the route to the car park (too early for the ice-cream van, thank God) and turned left along the common. Ahead she could see a church. Might there be a phone mast in the spire? She set out purposefully, and bingo – signal! But still nothing on Instagram. Or Snapchat. Was that a good sign? Was everyone who'd been at the party still asleep? It suddenly dawned on Beth that it was only seven o'clock and she was probably the only fifteen-year-old in Surrey awake and dressed and walking on a fucking hill. Deflated, she walked up the path and pushed open the church door.

Why was it so *massive*, for God's sake? What was a great cathedral of a church doing in the middle of absolutely flipping nowhere? She entered quietly, breathing in the familiar old church smell, and slipped into a pew. Closing her eyes, she sat in silence for a few moments.

'Hello, Mum. It's me,' she said aloud. 'I'm doing my best. I'm looking after Sam, and keeping an eye on Dad. But it's not much fun. I miss you! Wish you were here.'

'Bethany?'

She jumped. 'Sorry to startle you,' said Father Stephen gently. 'Are you OK?'

'I didn't think there was anyone here!' Beth could feel the blood flooding her cheeks.

29

'There isn't really. Only me. I'm sorry I disturbed you . . . Were you praying?'

'Talking to Mum. Keeping her posted.'

'Ah. I see . . . Shall I leave you to it?'

'Yes. I mean no. I don't know. What are you doing here, anyway? It's the crack of dawn.'

'Probably much the same as you,' he said. 'Woke up early, thought I'd seek out some peace and quiet before the day begins. It's a good time to pray, I find. It's really rather splendid in here, don't you think?'

'If you like that kind of thing,' said Beth. 'Why's it so flipping *big*? There are no, like, *houses* round here.'

'I think it was built by some Victorian grandee. Probably had over-inflated ideas about leaving a legacy extravagant enough to show he'd made it in life. You know what men are like – mine's bigger than yours, and all that.'

She smiled. 'D'you think that was it?'

'Well, a bit of that. To be fair, I imagine the population this place served probably moved away at some point. Happens a lot with country churches. Can be something as simple as a factory closing. Or a bit more dramatic, like the Black Death. Actually, now you're here, perhaps you can give me a hand. We're going to have a little service here today before we set off. I'm trying to choose between two hymns. You can tell me whether people will know them. I can't decide between "Guide me, O thou great Jehovah" and "He who would valiant be". What do you think?'

'Is that the hobgoblin one?' asked Beth.

'Yes! Do you know it?'

'It's seriously *weird*. Very *Lord of the Rings*, all that stuff about giants and fiends. "Guide me, O thou great Jehovah" would be much better. If anyone feels awkward singing, they can just pretend they're at the rugby or something.'

'Good point!' he smiled at her. 'Glad I checked.'

'Wish I had my sax here. I could give it some welly for you.'

'You mean you didn't fancy carrying it? Lightweight!'

She laughed. 'Father Stephen, can I ask you something . . .' she began, when suddenly there was a ping from her phone. A text!

From Matt! 'Um, excuse me, gotta go,' she said, and made a dash for the door.

Revision = boring. Party = boring. Missed u. You ok? M x

Oh my God: *M x*! Surely that was the first time he'd signed off with *M x*. But what did *x* mean? Was it just Matt-the-good-friend or could it be Matt-the-maybe-boyfriend? Given that it was still so early, did it mean he hadn't *gone* to Natasha's party? Or that he went and left early?

But the main thing was – unless he was a total liar and that she could not, *would* not believe, at least not yet – that he hadn't ended the evening hooking up with Molly O'Riordan. Because if there was one thing Beth knew, it was that Molly's sights were absolutely set on Matt. But he'd texted her – *Beth!* – at ridiculous-o'-clock in the morning and that surely, surely, *surely* meant something? It had to, didn't it? You *so* didn't text someone at the crack of dawn to tell them how boring a party had been *without them* if you didn't like them at least a *bit*. Unless – aargh! – he felt *sorry* for her and was trying to be nice because his mum had said he should be or something crap like that.

Though that was silly because there was no reason to suppose that Matt's mum knew anything about Beth. In fact one of the reasons she *liked* Matt was because she'd only got to know him quite recently, and she didn't have to talk about Mum unless she wanted to. Sometimes they just had a laugh together. To think she'd dismissed him as a geek! But Big Band had changed all that. She barely knew his name – didn't even know that he played the tenor sax, let alone had lessons with Mr Shepherd – until that rehearsal when he'd turned up for the first time. And he was bloody brilliant.

She loved band practice. That made Wednesday the best day of the week by far. There was something so wonderfully freeing about playing swing: the way everyone had a go, when Mr Shepherd gave them a new arrangement, and it was all a bit random to begin with – let's face it, it was a school band, not exactly Jools Holland – but once the players had the shape of the piece under their belts, and the rhythm section had worked out what needed doing – that was *crucial* – the whole thing could begin to fly.

And just when you thought it had settled and they were beginning to make *music*, Mr Shepherd would casually point at someone for a solo. The first time he'd done that to her had been the most terrifying, exhilarating experience of her life. She stood up with her knees knocking, thinking *OMG, this cannot be happening to me*. But by the time she wrapped up her improv and sat down again, she was pink with excitement, and aching for another go. Mr Shepherd grinned and nodded at her in approval, and turned his attention to Kyle Jones, who was a show-off on the trombone, and after Kyle, had called on Matt. Who'd been totally *awesome*.

That night, when they were stacking the chairs and clearing away the music stands, Matt had come over to congratulate her and she'd returned the compliment and they'd had their first ever proper conversation. He'd only been at Farmleigh High – or Farmleigh *Academy*, you were supposed to call it now – since Year Twelve because he'd moved house after taking his GCSEs somewhere in London. But that had meant she'd lingered, and totally missed Dad's text, so that the unexpected sight of his car at the school gate had taken her by surprise.

By the look on his face she assumed that she was in for a bollocking and racked her brains to think what she'd done. Or not done. But when she opened the car door and saw the tears streaming down his cheeks she found herself wishing and wishing that he *would* shout at her, ground her, dock her allowance. Any of that would have been better than hearing the news he had come specially to school to tell her.

Now Matt was in Farmleigh revising for A-levels while she was on this stupid walk. Her head spun suddenly: revision! *Oh God, oh God, oh God*. Her GCSEs were going to be a disaster. Ever since Mum died she'd found it impossible to concentrate. Couldn't see the point really. Without Mum to chivvy her, it was hard to summon the energy. When she sat down to study, the words on the page seemed to swim before her eyes. Dad appeared oblivious. True, he'd turned up to parents' evening, but he'd sat stiff and silent like a trapped animal while the teachers rabbited on, giving no sign that he had a clue about her coursework or mock results or the marks schemes for different subjects.

It had been so different when Mum was alive. She'd be gassing to the teachers – knew at least half of them by first names, probably through Mary Anne, really quite *embarrassing* – and asking really, like, *specific* questions about modules and stuff that meant Beth knew she was on her case, and the teachers did too. But since Mum had been sick it had all gone pear-shaped. It was going to be a train wreck.

For now, though, she had to reply to Matt. *Wish u were here. B xxxx* Even without the four kisses, was that too obvious? She tried again: *12 miles down, 92 to go. So far, so ok. Only one blister! Miss u 2. B x* That was better. She pressed 'send'.

Back at the hostel, people were beginning to emerge from their beds and search for breakfast. Beth could hear Dad persuading Sam in the direction of the shower. Oh *God*, she hoped he hadn't wet the bed. It was a new . . . *thing* since Mum died and it was horrible. He'd be mortified. Lucy and Ella were laying up the tables in the dining room with bowls and plates and cutlery while Mary Anne was unpacking big boxes of cereal, sliced loaves and jam. She pulled cartons of milk and juice and packs of butter from the fridge and passed them to the girls to carry through.

'Thank goodness for Ruth and her Volvo!' she was telling Catherine, who was counting out non-matching spoons and knives. 'It's made catering so much easier. Imagine if we had to carry this lot from place to place.'

'We'd be more like pilgrims, though,' said Catherine.

'What do you mean?'

'Well, you know . . . Carrying only what's sufficient unto the day. Anna said it was amazing how little you actually needed for the journey when she came back from Spain. When she started out, she said her bag was stuffed with a whole load of junk she'd brought along in case of emergency. But apparently you very quickly get rid of all the extras if you've actually got to carry them. She said a pilgrim spirit meant only thinking about a day at a time.'

'Anna was on her own,' said Mary Anne crisply. 'She didn't have a horde of hungry teenagers to feed. She only had herself to think about. If you ask me—'

She broke off as Beth came in. 'Beth! We were wondering where you'd got to. Are you OK?'

'Fine thanks. Just, like, been for a walk.'

'A *walk*? I'm impressed you've got the energy,' said Catherine. 'I ache all over! Don't know why, but even my shoulders hurt.'

'So it was more of a stroll, really?' Beth conceded. She liked Catherine. There was a deep-seated kindness about her. She didn't intrude. What could she possibly have said to Dad yesterday to upset him? Beth had been well out of earshot, but one moment the pair of them seemed to be chatting quite easily, and the next minute you could *see* from his body language that he'd gone all rigid. She'd watched Catherine hover uncertainly for a moment, and then move away to join Jackie and some of the others. She seemed cheerful enough this morning.

'Toast?' Catherine offered now. 'Cereal? Cup of tea?'

'No thanks,' said Beth, backing out of the kitchen. 'Need to sort out my bed, get my things together. Laters.'

The formal part of the day began, as Father Stephen had indicated, with a short service at St Barnabas. It suddenly occurred to Beth that it was Sunday morning. Glancing around, a quick tot-up suggested that no one – except for Smith, who was waiting outside – had swerved it. Sam sat on her left, swinging his feet annoyingly. Dad was on his other side.

Father Stephen caught her eye and winked when he announced the hymn. Beth rewarded him by singing enthusiastically, enjoying the astonishment of Lucy sitting next to her. For once, it seemed, she was in a situation that put Miss Perfect Lucy at a disadvantage because she, Beth, knew how to behave in church. She crossed herself with an unnecessary flourish; and then, noticing that William had caught her in the act, closed her eyes and dropped to her knees, her cheeks hot with embarrassment.

She felt comfortable here, she realized. For one thing, at least while they were in church she felt that God could keep an eye on Dad and Sam. That might not be entirely logical, if God was supposed to be everywhere, but surely this was *his* watch and she was allowed a bit of slack. For another, there was something about the rhythm of the words and the singing and the periods of quiet (*shit!* her phone! better put it on silent) that she found soothing, even if she didn't always get the point of the readings.

Some of the Bible was in her opinion both bloodthirsty and brutal. But if she allowed herself to tune in and out, and let it all wash over her, she enjoyed the poetry and found it restful. Being in church made her think of her mother. Then again, what didn't? *Please, God, look after my mum, whatever you've gone and done with her,* she prayed. *And keep an eye on Sam for me? And stop Dad being quite so miserable? And please, please, please don't let bloody Molly get her teeth into Matt while I'm away . . .*

Even in a different building, it all felt reassuringly familiar. She had gone to church with Anna and Sam throughout her childhood, and until a couple of years ago – when the onset of hormones had dealt a killer blow to the appeal of Sunday mornings – she sang in the choir. Who was taking the service at All Saints this morning, she wondered? Singing the hymn now – hearing her clear voice fly up to the rafters, high above her head – released a flood of nostalgia. It dawned on her that she hadn't been back to church since her mother's funeral. It just seemed . . . too difficult, somehow. But perhaps she should. If playing the sax was the most fun you could have with your clothes on, singing came a pretty close second. Should she rejoin the choir?

'Thank you for joining me this morning,' Father Stephen was saying, and Beth realized the service was almost over.

'I hope you're all rested and ready for a new day. I should warn you that we're facing some pretty steep climbs today. We'll be walking right up Box Hill, and you'll know how steep that is if you watched the Olympic cycling in 2012. It's not for the faint-hearted! But the views will be breathtaking. Quite magnificent. And we've got the stepping stones over the River Mole to look forward to this morning. Plus another reward at the end of the day, in the shape of the Millennium Standing Stones. I think they're rather special.

'And now, before our final blessing, there's another poem I'd like to share with you today. It's by the American poet Walt Whitman, and I'm just going to read you an extract. It's a poem that encourages us to press on with the journey:

'Away, O soul! hoist instantly the anchor!
Cut the hawsers – haul out – shake out every sail!
Have we not stood here like trees in the ground long
    enough?
Have we not grovell'd here long enough, eating and
    drinking like mere brutes?
Have we not darken'd and dazed ourselves with books
    long enough?

Sail forth! steer for the deep waters only!
Reckless, O soul, exploring, I with thee, and thou
    with me;
For we are bound where mariner has not yet dared
    to go,
And we will risk the ship, ourselves and all.

O my brave soul!
O farther, farther sail!
O daring joy, but safe! Are they not all the seas of God?
O farther, farther, farther sail!'

The church was quite literally on the path, so the group was soon on its way. Theo came over to find her. 'Sleep all right?' he asked.

''Kay,' she said. 'Did Sam ... *you know* ... ?'

'No. All well there ... Ah, now that's what I wanted to show you.'

'What?'

'Over there. Can you see the vines?'

'So are we in flipping France or something?'

Theo laughed. 'Looks a bit like it, doesn't it?' he said. 'It's Denbies. The biggest vineyard in England. Something like three hundred thousand vines, covering an area of several hundred acres.'

'So how did you end up a, like, world authority, Dad?'

'Looked at a job there, once upon a time.'

'Yeah?' Beth couldn't imagine her father job-hunting somehow. Greene Fingers had always been part of their life. Mum used to say that he was so entrenched in his work that taking even a week's holiday meant digging his roots out of the soil.

36

'Yes. After we sold the farm. I rather fancied winemaking. Thought it was rather romantic. Mind you, back then English wine had a fairly terrible reputation. It's different now. Denbies pick up international awards, these days.'

'So why didn't you go for it?'

'The garden centre seemed a safer bet, somehow,' said Theo. 'I could hear your grandfather's voice telling me that there was no future in English wine. Shame, really.'

'Well, you get to be your own boss, now Mike's gone,' said Beth, with a sudden surge of sympathy for her father. 'Your name on the shop front. That's pretty cool.'

At that moment a railway bridge came into sight. 'That's my cue to round up the boys,' said Theo. 'There's a nasty bit of main road coming up. Better make sure everyone knows. But thank you.' With the ghost of a smile, he took off, leaving Beth the choice between talking to Mary Anne (no thanks, who wanted to spend half-term with a teacher, for fuck's sake?) and catching up with Lucy, Ella and Chloe. Oh well. Perhaps it was time to play happy teenagers for a bit. She'd probably outpace them on the steep hill anyway.

The sight of the stepping stones had her anxiously checking around for Sam. Where was he? Would he keep his balance if the stones were slippery? In the event, though, she saw him pick his way across carefully enough, safely sandwiched between Uncle Tom and Catherine. Perhaps he was beginning to learn his limits.

Milo, on the other hand, had no such brake on his exuberance and decided to jump from stone to stone. He was clearly showing off, trying to impress Sam and his friend George. Milo's arms and legs were flying, windmill-like – he was shrieking with excitement – and then, almost in slow motion, it seemed, he overreached himself, misjudged the gap and slipped backwards into the river with a great splash. Luckily, Uncle Tom was just behind him and swiftly fished him out of the water, slung him over his shoulder, and fireman-style carried him over to the other side of the river.

'Milo,' said Tamsin, exasperated, when she caught up with him. 'Why is it always you? Now you'll have wet feet for the rest of the day.'

37

Milo, tipping the water out of his boots and tugging off two wet socks, was chuckling, lapping up the attention. Then Smith emerged from the river and shook himself over Milo, setting him off into new peals of laughter.

'Piggyback needed?' asked Theo, who had turned back to see what the commotion was all about.

'No, really ...' said Tamsin. 'It's his own fault entirely. He'll have to put up with squelching for a bit.'

'I've got spare socks,' said Mary Anne. 'Why not let Theo carry him for a bit while his boots dry out?'

'Well ... if you really don't mind,' said Tamsin. 'Thank you. Don't suppose you've got a carrier bag for the wet pair, Mary Anne?'

'Of course.'

'And I'll take over when you need a break, Theo,' added Uncle Tom, smiling at Tamsin.

'We'll manage,' said Theo firmly.

Beth could feel Tamsin's discomfort as Theo began the steep climb with Milo on his back. 'I don't think Dad, like, *minds*,' she told her.

'He's being very kind,' said Tamsin with an effort. *Why do* you *mind?* wondered Beth, watching Tamsin stealing anxious glances in Milo's direction. Fortunately, the novelty of carrying – and being carried – soon wore off and before very long Milo had wriggled down off Theo's back, put on the dry socks and reclaimed his soggy boots from Uncle Tom.

'Silly joey,' said Tamsin, and hugged him. 'He's always been a ding-bat,' she told Beth, as Milo went to reclaim charge of Smith from George. 'I lost him once in Melbourne when he was little. It was the worst half-hour of my life.'

'What happened?'

'We were in the Botanic Gardens. We used to go there a lot. It's a wonderful place – full of trees and plants, a beautiful lake and great bird life. There's always something new to see. And it's cool in the heat because of all the vegetation. One really hot day, I was buying icy-poles at the little café, and when I turned round he'd vanished. Of course I was frantic – he was only four – and I ran around like a mad woman. I thought maybe he'd gone after the flying-foxes.'

'What's that?'

'A kind of fruit bat. They hang upside down out of trees. They were Milo's favourite thing in the gardens. But in the end we found him inside one of the glasshouses. He said it was a scientific experiment. He wanted to know how long he could stay inside on a forty-degree day without passing out.'

'God, I'd have melted,' said Beth. 'I can't do heat!'

'That's because you've got your Mum's lovely colouring. You're even worse than I am in the sun,' said Tamsin, who was a Nordic blonde. 'At least Milo's olive-skinned. But he still looked like boiled beetroot by the time I found him. I forced him under a sprinkler till he'd cooled down. We were both crying our eyes out by that stage.'

'D'you *miss* Australia, Tamsin? Doesn't Milo, like, miss his dad?'

'Well . . . it's complicated. Yes, there are things I miss . . . and people, I guess . . . but this is home. I was born here, you know.'

'I didn't know that.'

'Yeah. My parents emigrated when I was a baby. So I'm a British citizen, even if I don't sound like one. Reckon this is where I belong. Where we both belong now.'

They were nearing the top of the hill. Beth was pleased to see that she and Tamsin had outpaced most of the others. She could feel her heart racing against her ribcage and forced herself onwards, upwards, faster until she was quite light-headed with the effort. And then – right on cue as she made it to the viewing platform, the perfect prize for effort – ping! A text! *Blister? Need air ambulance? M x*

Beth grinned from ear to ear. *Keep u posted. Emma x*

Seconds later, ping! *Emma? wtf??? Someone kidnapped Beth?*

Hmm. She replied: *'Emma'. At Box Hill, btw*

A pause, when she could practically *hear* the cogs in Matt's brain turning, all those miles away in Farmleigh. Then, a minute or two later, ping! *Miss Wodehouse, I presume? x*

Oh my *God*, he'd got her reference to Jane Austen! How cool was that? Cultured as well as hot! He was doing English A-level, after all. *Think its Woodhouse but clever boy ;) 2 early 4 picnic x*

Thank God. It wasn't long since breakfast, so most people were content with their water bottles, for now at any rate.

My mum helped . . . Don't spose other Emma walkd up, tho! Matt x came the reply. OMG! So Matt's mum *did* know about Beth. Was that *good* – that he cared enough to mention her to his mum? Or *bad* – that she wasn't important enough to be kept a secret? Mind you, if Anna had been alive, Beth would have been telling *her* all about Matt, she was pretty sure. So perhaps it was OK.

At that moment Milo arrived and threw himself down on the ground in a dramatic flourish. Sam appeared just behind him, out of breath but cheerful. Beth turned to her phone: *Gotta go. Keep in touch. 'E' x* She pressed 'send', and slipped her phone into her pocket. Mustn't seem too keen. A bit of self-discipline (and let's face it, she had plenty of *that*) only added to the anticipation.

After the dramatic climb of the morning, the group settled into a more even rhythm again. The sun was bright, now, and most of group – apart from Beth who was *always* cold these days – had stripped down to T-shirts. Having made sure that Sam had a good drink of water at the viewing platform, Beth left him to it, and edged her way to the front of the line of walkers where her grandfather was leading the way.

It really was amazing: he had to be the oldest here by some distance but there was no question that Grandpa William was one of the fittest walkers. While other people were quite honestly huffing and puffing (you'd have thought all that bloody cheerleading would have kept Chloe fit, for one, and Jackie looked as if she might have a heart attack at any moment), Grandpa William was striding ahead, clearly wanting to go rather faster than the group pace allowed. He was deep in discussion with Uncle Tom, quizzing him about his latest work project. Dull as *ditch*. But with a bit of luck she could hover alongside them, and anyone who happened to be looking in her direction would assume she was part of their conversation and leave her alone.

Because she needed some headspace, she really did. For a start she wanted to take her encounters with Matt out of their special place in her mental library, examine them one by one, polish as needed, and stow them carefully back again for future reference.

And then she had to think about what she was going to do when her GCSEs went pear-shaped, which they sure as shit were going to. Back in the old days, she'd had a plan. How naive that seemed now! She was going to do her A-levels and then go to uni to study Physiotherapy. She wasn't sure where yet, but Cardiff was supposed to be really good for Physio, although she'd wondered if London would be a better bet because then she could still live at home. But now – since she was *bound* to have to do retakes – she needed to be absolutely certain that she could face all those science A-levels.

Added to which, ever since she'd joined Big Band she'd started thinking more and more about pursuing her music. Which was ironic, when you came to think about it, because she knew, she just *knew*, that that was what Mum would have wanted her to do, though she would never have tried to push her in that direction, and Beth had always resisted any such suggestion. But what were the options anyway? Could you go to college to play swing band music and jazz or did you have to start with all that hyper-formal classical stuff (like Mum, of course) before you were allowed to have fun? She supposed she could ask Mr Shepherd, but otherwise she didn't really know where to start.

Father Stephen had asked the front walkers to stop for lunch at Colley Hill, where another lookout point offered open views of the landscape after a morning largely spent in woodland. Spotting what looked like a temple ahead, Beth went in search of a bench to sit on while she checked on her blister. As she unlaced her boots she was joined by William.

'Legs surviving?' he asked.

'Fine, thanks, Grandpa. Just one little blister on my heel. You OK?'

'Tickety-boo, thank you very much. There's life in these old bones yet.'

'I've noticed. You want to push us on a bit, don't you?'

William grunted. 'Having to exercise patience, yes. This group pace. Doesn't sit naturally, I'm afraid. But *pro bono publico*, and all that. Doing my best, for the common good. But while we're here, have you looked overhead?'

Beth leaned backwards, and tipped her head. The ceiling of the folly was painted cobalt blue, spangled with gold stars. 'Oh my God, what's that about?' she said.

'Rather lovely, isn't it? It's an astronomer's view of the heavens.'

'Stars always make me feel so, like, *insignificant*,' she said.

'Like the psalmist?' said William. ' "When I consider thy heavens, the work of thy fingers, the moon and the stars, which thou hast ordained; what is man, that thou art mindful of him? and the son of man, that thou visitest him?" '

'How do you *know* this stuff, Grandpa?'

'Misspent youth. Your great-grandfather prescribed a Bible verse a day and a psalm a week. This one's Psalm 8. It goes on: "For thou hast made him a little lower than the angels, and hast crowned him with glory and honour. Thou madest him to have dominion over the works of thy hands; thou hast put all things under his feet: all sheep and oxen, yea, and the beasts of the field; the fowl of the air, and the fish of the sea, and whatsoever passeth through the paths of the seas. O LORD our Lord, how excellent is thy name in all the earth!" '

'I can't even!'

'Can't even what?'

She laughed. 'No, it's an *expression*. I'm, like, not sure there's anything to say to that.'

'Ah, but there is,' came Father Stephen's voice. 'How about Psalm 147? There's another lovely bit about the stars: "He telleth the number of the stars; he calleth them all by their names." Now I come to think about it, the verse before is lovely, too: "He healeth the broken in heart, and bindeth up their wounds." '

Beth stared at them both in disbelief. 'This is so random! If you're on about wounds, I'm off to find a plaster before this blister gets any worse.'

Not eating took concentration. As long as Beth was prepared, and nothing unexpected came at her sideways, it was fine. The trouble was that other people seemed to eat *constantly* – honestly, even the *thought* of the amount most people ate made her feel quite sick – and appeared to think that you should, too. The plus of being part of a crowd was that with a bit of skill and a bottle of water in your hand, you could flit from group to group and give the impression that you were grazing as you went.

On this occasion Beth had a rock-solid excuse to wander, as William had asked her to look out for her grandmother, who had the tricky task of joining the walkers wherever they fetched up at break times. This sounded simple enough in theory – Father Stephen had the whole thing planned out on a series of Ordnance Survey maps – but it was proving harder in practice. It only took someone to fall in a river (mentioning no names, Milo Carter) or for the road Granny was supposed to take to turn out to be impassable to motor vehicles (yesterday, for example) and it could all go majorly wrong. It was *just* possible that Granny Ruth might miss a turning, but if so Beth didn't think she'd ever admit to it, any more than Father Stephen would admit to having given her crap directions in the first place.

On this occasion, since they were ten minutes ahead of the agreed meeting time, Beth thought she'd better walk down the path in the direction of the appointed car park. She saw her grandmother coming slowly up the steps, leaning heavily on the wooden handrail as she walked, unaware that she was being watched. As soon as she saw Beth, she straightened up, smiled and waved cheerfully.

'Am I in time for lunch?' she called up.

'Yeah, you're fine. We've only just arrived. You're in time for silence, too!'

'I suppose there's no avoiding that,' said Ruth, smiling conspiratorially. 'How are you getting on with it?'

'So … actually … I kind of liked it?' said Beth. 'It's like … restful. Walking and not having to talk. You get into a *swing*, if that makes sense.'

Ruth appeared to consider for a moment. 'Well. Let's see what he's got in store for us this afternoon, shall we?'

'I was reminded of one of my favourite psalms at lunchtime,' said Father Stephen as the group gathered round. Beth rolled her eyes in William's direction.

43

'Psalm 147 has some lovely lines about God wanting to bind our wounds, and healing the heartbroken. It's such a vivid metaphor, the idea of a broken heart. I know that everyone here is experiencing different degrees of heartbreak. But even broken hearts mend, over time, however impossible that seems right now.

'Now. About our period of silence this afternoon. Let's see if we can extend it a bit – let's try and manage forty-five minutes today. It's going to be different from yesterday, because even if we're quiet, there's going to be a certain amount of background noise, I'm afraid.' He gesticulated in the direction of the motorway, audible though screened behind the trees.

'But we'll just have to live with that. There's something very *real* about life carrying on all around us, even when we're in the middle of personal tragedy. Maybe we'll even be able to incorporate the noise into our reflections. Because today's word is "remembering". I want us to try dwelling in our memories – the precious memories, the painful ones. Memories of Anna, of course, but other memories that are important to us. How have they formed us? Do they need laying down? Can we offer them up to God?'

Remembering was exactly what she'd been so desperate to do this morning, thought Beth. Now she wasn't quite sure. At one level, it was ridiculous. She never *stopped* remembering her mum, and missing her. She thought about her *constantly*. But just occasionally, recently, she found the hours between her morning glass of water and, say, lunchtime had passed without thinking of Anna, and then she'd feel simultaneously relieved and hideously guilty. Panicked, even, that if she didn't think about her enough, the memories would fade altogether and she'd one day stop being *able* to conjure her to her side.

Thank God she had lots and lots of pictures – Anna had loved taking photos of them all, to the point that it was really embarrassing – and the day before the funeral Beth had put a whole load onto a memory stick and taken them down to Boots so that she could make a giant collage, because the electronic versions suddenly seemed too insubstantial.

44

She had her voice, too, safely stored in her phone, because she was dead lazy about deleting voicemails, and even if it was just Mum sounding rather cross ('Where *are* you, Beth, we said quarter past and it's after half past already and you know I've got to get Sam'), or just plain ordinary ('Mum here, lovey, you forgot your music case, I'll drop it off at Reception on my way past'), well, that was better than nothing.

The smell of Mum – that was still in her clothes, especially her chunky South American cardigan (which was a fashion *mare*, but still), because it was difficult to wash. Beth had raided it from Mum's wardrobe the day she had died and had slept with it until Sam's sobbing one night had worn her down and she'd passed it on in desperation.

The *feel* of Mum ... well, that was harder. Could she summon up the memory of a hug? She thought she could just about remember how it felt in those last few days, when she lay on the bed next to Anna after school and moaned about her GCSE Physics mock which had been unutterably *crap* and told her about horrible Mrs Jones who had threatened her with detention which was *seriously* harsh, when it had quite obviously *not* been her fault that some stupid Year Sevens had been pushed out of the practice rooms because she and Charlotte had to record their GCSE compositions.

By then Mum hadn't wanted to be hugged, or touched at all really, although she'd *tolerated* Sam wiping her forehead with a flannel while Beth painted her nails, because she obviously didn't want him feeling left out. But Beth could tell she was making a major effort. And actually the smell of the sickroom permeated everything. Not that she would ever admit it, but that was one reason she'd done Mum's nails, because the pear-drop smell of nail varnish remover was sufficiently powerful to cover up all the other smells. Beth shuddered. Even now if she went into her parents' bedroom she had to fight between sadness that her mother was no longer lying there and relief that at least the room felt like a *bedroom* again, not a bloody hospital ward.

Shit. She could feel her guts twisting. She needed to remember other, better times. Before Mum was sick, when things were just

45

boringly *normal*. With a massive act of will, she summoned a memory of Mum cooking tea. Mum's macaroni cheese with the crispy top that she loved. Peas (her favourite, Sam's *worst*). She could practically taste it. But no; not *food*, for fuck's sake! That didn't help at all. What else? Mum playing the cello. That was safer. Going over and over and *over* a single bar of Bach to make sure it was *exactly* right, not just technically but musically, too. How she'd explained this to Beth, shushing Sam when he tried to interrupt, showing her the different ways you could play the bar, and why it mattered. Her patience when they were practising their scales, however hideous the noise they produced. Her impatience – to the point of fury – with technology, with their broadband when it crashed (which was all the fucking time).

The way she made birthdays so special. Oh God, how was she going to cope when Anna wasn't there for her sixteenth next month? Would it be like that other awful birthday, her seventh? When Mum wasn't even *there* because she'd been delayed by heavy rain in Spain and Dad forgot until the absolutely last possible moment and only got his act together then because Granny Ruth had phoned? And Dad had given her a gross Barbie – which to be fair she would probably have *loved* even the Christmas before but by then what she really wanted more than anything was a Bratz doll. Which Mum would have known if she'd only been around, instead of in stupid Spain. Tamsin was staying with them then, of course, but she was away that week, something to do with work. And Beth had waited and *waited* for Mum to phone – and ended up being late for school, so terrified was she that Anna would get the time difference wrong and call when Beth was out, which made Dad cross with her because he had to take Sam to the hospital for a check-up.

After school, it was almost all right, because Grandpa William and Granny Ruth collected her as a surprise, but when they said they were taking her home to their house for tea she burst into tears. So Grandpa William dropped them at home, after all, and drove to Aston to collect her cake and present. And she'd been right: almost the moment she walked in the door, the phone rang and it was *Mum*. Mum saying how sorry she was not to be there for her birthday and asking all about her day and telling her that her present was hidden under their bed. And the present was a set of multicoloured fairy lights to hang round her bedroom and was so *exactly* what Beth didn't know she wanted that she couldn't stop herself sobbing down the phone.

'Cheer up, chicken!' said Mum. 'If Dad's still out, why not ask Granny or Grandpa to rig them up for you? And then, can you draw me a lovely picture to show me how they look and email it to me? Make sure Granny takes lots of photos of you blowing out your candles, and you can send them over too. And I'll see you very, very soon.'

Even then, through her distress and inarticulate longing for her mother, Beth could remember thinking there was *something*, something different about Anna, that she sounded more like the old Mum, the pre-hospital Mum. She barely asked after Sam, so that in the end it was Beth who found herself telling her, unprompted, that he was *fine* and running about and hardly cried at all now when Dad dropped him off at nursery.

And Mum said that was good news, and asked her what sort of cake she had. Which was perfect timing as Grandpa William arrived at that moment and carried it in, in a big white cardboard box, and it was *beautiful*, a mermaid cake, made and iced by Granny Ruth especially for her. Beth started crying all over again and handed the phone wordlessly to Grandpa, before seeking comfort from her Granny.

'Beth? You OK?' Tamsin was all concern. Beth hadn't realized she was crying. *Shit*, she thought, bet everyone's watching. She diverted off the route, down a small footpath to her left, heading blindly for the cover of the wood. Tamsin followed her, took her in her arms and rocked her like a baby. They stood there, swaying together for a moment, until Beth had her emotions in check. She threw herself down under a tree.

'It just hurts so much!' The words came out in a tangle. 'It's so *unfair*. Why the *fuck* did she have to die? I don't even know who I *am* yet.'

'I know, I know,' said Tamsin, sitting down beside her. 'Let it out. Just let it out. I'm here.'

'Where *were* you? When Mum was in Spain and it was my birthday? You were away all week.'

'God, Beth-ster, that's a few years ago, now.'

'It was always so much better when you were there. When Mum wasn't, I mean.'

'It was a course,' said Tamsin. 'Yeah. Definitely. Manchester. But she came back just after your birthday, didn't she?'

'Yes. On the Sunday. But she won't be here for my sixteenth. Or seventeenth. Or eighteenth. How am I going to *bear* it, Tamsin?'

'I don't know, doll. But I think we just have to take it a day at a time, put one foot in front of the other. Remember the good times, and be thankful for them. But can we spend your birthday together? Or is it a school day?'

'It's a Tuesday.'

'OK, well, how about I park Milo with George, and we have a day out shopping the weekend before? In London? Unless you've got other plans?'

'No plans. That would be ... great.'

'Look, I know it won't be the same, doll. But we'll have some fun. Max out my credit card? Take stupid selfies? Now look, are you OK to catch up with the others now?'

Beth got to her feet, brushed a few twigs from her trousers, and offered her hand to Tamsin. 'Think so. Let's pretend it was a pee break.'

By the time they caught up with the others, the walkers had reached a field of granite standing stones.

'Take your time,' Father Stephen was saying. 'These standing stones have been erected here especially for people like us.'

'How do you mean?' asked Theo.

'Well, they were created to commemorate the Millennium, by demonstrating the spiritual power of words through the centuries. You'll see there are ten of them, each one representing two hundred years of history. On each stone you'll find a quotation appropriate to the period. Look, here's a handout that explains. To start with, this was a travelling exhibition, hard though that might be to believe of something that looks so permanent. But now they're here for ever. The site was chosen because it lies on the Pilgrims' Way. The idea is that this is a place for people to rest and reflect. Have a wander and read the inscriptions.'

Intrigued, Beth moved in for a closer look. Each was a different shape, and the quotations were carved in a range of calligraphic styles. *In the beginning the word was. And the Word was with God.* That was familiar from carol services at Christmas, even if she didn't entirely understand it. St Augustine she'd heard of. But Boethius? John Scotus Erigena, however you pronounced that?

She liked *The soul is known by its acts*, carved in a tall, thin font. St Thomas Aquinas was onto something there. You could say all the right things and *pretend* to be squeaky clean but in the end what mattered was how you actually behaved. St Anselm was interesting, too: *For I do not seek to understand in order to believe, but I believe in order to understand. For I believe this; unless I believe, I will not understand.* The quotation was carved in a spiral, onto a stone with a hammer-like head. God, you always assumed the saints had life sorted, didn't you? But perhaps faith was as hard for them as it was for normal people?

And here was *There is a tide in the affairs of men* . . . in sort of flowing italics. Shakespeare, of course; that was probably, like, *compulsory* or something if you were a sculptor and British. And T. S. Eliot was here. From *Four Quartets.* The words *still point* appeared twice, carved extra big, drawing your eyes to them. Matt would like this. He loved poetry. He'd be able to explain the text to her. She took a picture of the Shakespeare stone on her phone, and messaged it over to him. *Guess where now? 'E' x*

'Beth – over here!' said Tamsin. 'Here's one for you, I reckon. *Do not wish to be anything but what you are, and try and be that perfectly.* St Francis of Sales, whoever he was, according to Father Steve's sheet. Spot on, I'd say.'

'I like that,' she said, suddenly cheered. Ping! *Standing Stones. Been there, done that! Mr K xx* Beth smiled. *Two* kisses! But *Mr K*? Matt's surname was Walker. Oh. My. God! Did he mean . . .

49

Mr *Knightley*? Was he saying what she thought he was? She couldn't keep the grin off her face.

'Everything all right, Beth?' asked Theo, coming up to her, Sam in tow.

'Yeah, Dad. Like, cool.'

8 miles
Stephen

When the alarm went off, Stephen stretched out luxuriously in the double bed, enjoying the unfamiliar sensation of professionally laundered sheets. The hotel – part of a budget chain – was cheap-ish and cheerful-ish, and while the decor left a lot to be desired, at least it was a step up from the dormitory in the hostel. Which had been very basic. Here, there was even a gym in the basement, something that normally would have pleased him immeasurably, but Stephen felt he could grant himself a rare day's grace in the circumstances.

Today's walk was shorter than the previous two. Some of the group would no doubt be mightily relieved that the target was a mere eight miles. Parts of yesterday really had been very steep. Jackie was struggling, certainly. Celia was on the slow side, too, but whether that was down to solidarity with her friend rather than physical fitness it was hard to gauge. As it was, the pair of them constantly stopped for quite unnecessary drinks and snacks from their rucksacks. They had an unerring eye for coffee and cake opportunities along the route.

'You go on – we'll catch you up!' they insisted, waving the group onwards. Stephen found it intensely irritating – he was responsible for keeping the group together, after all – but he supposed that they were simply two middle-aged women doing their level best. They were clearly out of their comfort zones. They were both overweight, Jackie in particular. And if walking was a foray into alien territory, pilgrimage was an entirely foreign language. They'd bailed out at lunchtime yesterday, and bagged a lift with Ruth. Rather easier to manage, actually.

Otherwise, everyone seemed to be coping. Age was no barrier for William, who looked so at ease striding over the hills that it was tempting to conjure up a parallel life for him as a herdsman in place of the years spent respectably commuting into the City. In contrast, Anna's brother Tom was puffing a little on the uphill stretches, something Stephen ascribed – cattily, perhaps – to too many business lunches in five-star hotels.

Mary Anne was treating the walk with customary briskness. Stephen was sure her spare time (never *leisure*, surely, for that implied time-wasting) included regular aerobics and Pilates classes. Catherine and Tamsin were complaining of stiffness, but cheerfully so. Stephen had no fears about their ability to complete the week. The same went for the teenagers. Good bunch. Nice kids. Even the blessed dog was more or less behaving.

As for Theo and the children ... it was hard to tell. Theo appeared to be managing fine physically – no surprises there, of course, he was Mr Outdoors – but Stephen wasn't at all sure that the same could be said for his emotional state. What was it – four, nearly five months now? Early days, of course. Bereavement took the time it took. Theo had never been the type of man to wear his heart on his sleeve, but he'd most definitely adored Anna. He was the sort of man, Stephen suspected, whose life only came properly into focus when he found love. The trouble was that if someone held you at arm's length – and Theo's arms in this instance appeared to be longer than most – there wasn't much you could do, pastorally speaking. You couldn't *make* someone open up if they didn't want to. But Stephen was concerned that Theo's unhappiness was eating him up. He seemed so hostile, so angry. Stephen feared he was stuck in that destructive phase of grief that could all too easily become a way of life if nothing happened to break the cycle. *Lord, help him*, he prayed.

Bethany was a worry, too; her face was unhealthily pinched and pale, though Stephen was heartened to observe her apparently at ease with Tamsin. Last night he'd even overheard her giggling like the schoolgirl she too rarely allowed herself to be. Samuel seemed to be managing surprisingly well with the walk – Stephen had been worried about how he would find the steep ascents, in particular –

but so far, so good. There was always the option of a lift with his grandmother if he ran out of steam. Ruth was keeping a watchful eye on them all, he could tell. He could feel her checking her grandchildren and son-in-law for signs of strain each lunchtime, and he'd overheard her reminding Samuel to soak his feet in a bowl of warm water before she left for the evening.

He ran through his mental checklist for the day. First off was a service at the parish church. He was rather looking forward to seeing it; he'd read that it had a rather splendid whitewashed interior and some interesting wall hangings. It was dedicated to St Katharine of Alexandria, a fourth-century martyr once the object of an astonishing medieval cult, but now somewhat neglected. Shame, really; she was a notable scholar (unusual for a woman in her era) and no slouch when it came to arguing the Christian cause. According to tradition, hearing of her Christian convictions, the Roman Emperor Maxentius had pitted her against fifty of his most learned philosophers and she'd out-argued the lot of them in her defence of her faith, making the Emperor so cross in the process that he'd condemned the so-called wise men to death and thrown her in prison. Feisty, in other words.

When incarceration failed to dampen her ardour – she set about converting her fellow inmates – she was condemned to die in agony on the eponymous Catherine Wheel. There was something rather distasteful in the thought that her name lived on only through a firework. But no less peculiar, perhaps, than the annual burning of the effigy of the Catholic plotter Guido Fawkes. What inexplicable habits we fall into, he thought.

As usual, Stephen had prepared all his homilies before setting out. But was he judging the tone right? A sudden dart of anxiety shot through his soul. Anna had been so specific, so *clear* about the pilgrimage element of the walk. She wanted her friends and family to have a taste of her own experience on the *Camino*. He feared his concern not to frighten the horses might mean he was leaning too far in the other direction. Had he compromised by trying not to be over-churchy, and serving up poetry instead of the Gospel?

Where were the group, when it came to faith? William, if he remembered correctly, was a churchwarden at St Mary's, Aston, five miles down the road from Farmleigh. Bethany and Samuel had come to All Saints with Anna, of course, but even so a little sporadically, as was the reality for all families these days. The old pattern of boiled eggs, church and Sunday roast was no more, a long-gone era swept away by rugby practice and Sunday trading.

He knew a great many Farmleigh families through All Saints Primary; assemblies on Wednesdays, class visits to church, Harvest Festival, carols at Christmas, Mothering Sunday and Easter all punctuating the school calendar as surely as the liturgical seasons. You saw the children in between times through Brownies and Cubs when they carried their banners at parade services. The more musical ones were scooped up into the church choir by Jenny, who as well as teaching Year One at All Saints, served as his highly talented choir director.

What a godsend she was, quite literally! When he'd arrived at Farmleigh twelve years ago, music at All Saints was definitely in the doldrums, with a stubbornly deaf organist and a handful of obdurate, elderly choristers who weren't prepared to sing in parts. One or two even believed that reading music was beneath their dignity. Changing that – the sense of defeat had been *palpable* – had been like turning round a tanker, but he'd managed it somehow. Force of character and a great deal of heartfelt prayer. Now All Saints had a choir it could be proud of – not quite cathedral standard, of course, but really not all that far off in his humble opinion. Or possibly, *not* very humble. Certainly good enough to enhance worship and inspire the spirit and, he admitted with an unworthy thrill, a source of some envy among the neighbouring clergy. But it was a bit of a revolving door. Secondary school meant more homework, new interests and activities, and it was all too easy for churchgoing to slip off the radar.

As far as the belief or otherwise of the other pilgrims, he couldn't, and probably shouldn't, make any assumptions. They were here, after all; they had made the choice to take part in the journey. Interesting how there'd been an exponential surge of interest in recent years – to the point where some would argue that the *Camino*, the famous route to Santiago de Compostela, part of which Anna had walked, was now hideously overrun. He'd read somewhere that annual figures had reached the hundred thousand mark, which seemed extraordinarily at odds with an age of increasing secularism. Other new routes were springing up or being resurrected all over the place, around some frankly questionable saints.

The point was that a remarkably small percentage of pilgrims set out for straightforward reasons of faith. Many claimed to be motivated by the desire to mark a special birthday, the physical challenge, or because they were at a personal crossroads and wanted some space to consider their next steps in life. Not *religious* reasons, exactly, but quite possibly *spiritual* ones. Then, maybe pilgrimage had always been like that. Take Chaucer's pilgrims – hardly model Christians! And did it really matter, what motivated people, as long as they approached the journey with an open mind?

Stephen let out a long sigh. Time to get up, to shower, and to offer up the day in prayer. He would pray for each pilgrim by name, entrusting them into God's good hands. There was absolutely nothing wrong with using poetry to comfort or inspire, he reminded himself sternly. For some, it might open the door to deeper spiritual exploration. He had spent considerable time on preparation, both logistical and liturgical. While he must, of *course*, be open to the prompting of the Holy Spirit, he should also trust his training, his experience, and above all his instincts, which he knew to be sound.

Breakfast was in full swing by the time Stephen had said Morning Prayer and packed his bag. Most of the party were in the dining room, lingering over coffee. The tables were littered with the detritus of the breakfast buffet, croissant crumbs and butter wrappers, half-empty sachets of jam and marmalade, spatters of concentrated orange juice staining the white cloths. The odour of fried eggs lingered in the room. Such a *messy* meal, Stephen reflected, experiencing a brief pang of longing for his customary platter of fresh fruit in his own immaculate kitchen. It was his luxury of the day: prepared the night before, refrigerated overnight and then left on the kitchen side to await his return from the gym. He'd treated himself to a juicer in the January sales, and was currently experimenting with a whole series of energy-boosting concoctions: kiwi and lime, carrot and ginger.

'G'day, Father Steve! Come and have a look at this! We've raised almost a thousand bucks online and I've got whole bunch of new followers on Twitter,' called Tamsin as he approached. He bit back his annoyance: he hated anyone abbreviating his name, and there was something about the upward lift of Tamsin's antipodean twang that always made him suspect she was poking fun at him. Now she waved her laptop in his direction, smiling broadly, leaving him no alternative but to take the empty seat next to her.

He hadn't seen the website before: it had a gaudy purple *#walk-foranna* logo along the top, with a picture of Anna and the family below. It must have been taken two or three years ago, he thought; Samuel had gaps where his adult teeth had now grown, and Bethany's face was more babyish, rounder certainly. The children and their parents were sitting on a bench somewhere by the sea, without a care in the world, it seemed with the benefit of hindsight. Theo – tall, dark and ruggedly handsome – was smiling broadly. Anna was laughing, her head thrown back in amusement, and pointing at something just out of the shot.

She looked so alive! Even as the sentence formed in his head, he realized what a cliché it was. *So-and-so was so full of life* was a phrase he'd heard any number of times at pre-funeral visits, especially when the end was untimely, as Anna's had been. Death these days was bewildering, incomprehensible in a society that preferred to hide it away in hospital. So that when it arrived it was an unfamiliar stranger, embarrassing as it was unwelcome.

Next to the photo there was a red fundraising thermometer and the words, *You have exceeded your target of £500.* The current total stood at £983. 'Impressive!' he said. 'Where's it all come from?'

'A whole mix of people,' said Tamsin, beaming. 'Friends, family, strangers . . . plenty of anonymous donors, too. I'm doing a daily audio diary for the radio and tweeting as we go, and it's picking up. We could do with a bit more drama, but it's a beaut start.'

Stephen was reluctantly impressed. 'Good for you,' he said. 'What's the charity?'

'We thought fifty–fifty between Cancer Research and Hope House.'

'Excellent idea. Was that Ruth's suggestion?' Anna's mother was a founder – and remained a trustee – of the hospice that had helped with her daughter's care.

'Just seemed to make sense,' said Tamsin.

'I checked with Theo, and he was happy,' added Mary Anne, bringing over a jug of coffee and a fresh tray of cups and saucers. 'Now, what have you got in store for us today?'

'A less arduous day,' he said. 'It's only eight miles to Oxted. There's a leisure centre there, so I thought if any of the young had spare energy to burn at the end of the day they might enjoy a swim. Or there's a vineyard we could stop at and visit en route, if that would appeal.'

He accepted the proffered cup. 'But the main thing about today is that we're forsaking the Pilgrims' Way – or rather, it's forsaking us. Sadly for the modern-day pilgrim, this section's been entirely swallowed up by the M25, so we have to divert onto the North Downs Way. There's quite a lot of overlap between the two routes anyway.' He paused to take a sip of coffee. Remarkably good. 'We have to cross two dual carriageways and a motorway today, so we're rather surrounded by traffic.'

'I guess it just goes to show that the pilgrims had the right idea,' said Catherine.

'How do you mean?'

'Well, they chose the best route – and the road builders followed in their wake.'

'That's certainly one way of looking at it,' said Stephen.

'What's the weather forecast?' asked Mary Anne.

Stephen pulled a face. 'Sunny this morning, but there's rain on the way later. Tomorrow looks a bit hit and miss, too, I'm afraid.'

'Typical bloody British public holiday,' said Tamsin.

'In that case, let's make the most of the sunshine while we've got it,' said Mary Anne.

Stephen was the first to arrive at the church, which was perched on a hill on the edge of an A-road. Meticulous in his habits, he liked to walk through even the shortest act of worship ahead of time. It was all the more essential in a space he didn't know. What he knew his unkinder colleagues described as control freakery he preferred to think of as thorough preparation.

To his irritation, he found the door locked, and there was no sign of the man who had promised to open up. He took off his backpack and rummaged for his phone and his folder of notes for the week. He was further annoyed to find that he couldn't make out the phone number without his reading glasses, which meant another scrabble in a side pocket. Just as he'd finally punched the numbers into the phone, the key-holder arrived, out of breath but entirely unapologetic.

Worse still, he wanted to chat. Wheezing chestily, and lurching from side to side on a hip that was obviously overdue for replacement, he wittered on about the history of St Katharine's (long) and his own family's service (considerable) to the church.

'If you don't mind, I really must get on,' said Stephen shortly.

'Don't let me stop you,' said the key-holder, whose name was Fred. 'I'll just sit here, quiet as a mouse. You won't know I'm here!'

'Really – don't feel you have to stay!'

'Oh, but I couldn't desert you. It's my responsibility,' said Fred.

'But you'll give me a moment, I'm sure,' said Stephen, sinking to his knees theatrically in the priest's stall.

'You go ahead, Father,' said Fred. 'I'll be right here at your side if you need anything. You only have to ask.'

Lord, bless your faithful servant Fred, prayed Stephen silently through gritted teeth. *And forgive me for failing to love him as you do.* Surely his body language was sufficiently unambiguous to avoid further interruption? He needed to prepare for the act of worship, and indeed for the day ahead. He steadied himself with a few deep breaths and, with great difficulty, hauled his fragmented attention back towards the demanding business of prayer.

'Friends, I've been doing a little homework about this church, and I came across an interesting fact,' Stephen told his congregation. 'Like many of our churches, this is an ancient building, much of it built during the thirteenth century, and the foundations are older still. If you look *very* carefully, you can find odd fragments of Romanesque stone carving built into the flint walls. Now, in medieval times, this part of the world was famous for its sandstone quarries. The stone was of such high quality that King Henry III sent for supplies to build his Palace at Westminster. A hundred years later it was used in the building of Windsor Castle, and then in due course for St Paul's Cathedral and London Bridge. And what do we know about London Bridge?'

'It's falling down!' said Milo.

'Precisely! What we call London Bridge today has had several incarnations. When the bridge that was built from the local sandstone was dismantled, the stone – or some of it, at any rate – came back here again, and was built into the church walls. And we think we invented recycling!

'That reminded me of another of the Psalms. Psalm 118 says, "The stone the builders rejected has become the cornerstone." Jesus quotes that verse in the New Testament. He often spoke in practical building terms. His listeners would have appreciated the importance of getting that vital cornerstone in place if your house isn't going to fall down.

'This image throws up a couple of thoughts for me. First, how sound are our foundations? What are the cornerstones in our life? For me, Jesus Christ is the true cornerstone of the household of God. Second, sometimes in spite of all our plans, our hopes, a terrible blow can bring our world crashing down about our ears. We find ourselves sitting in a pile of rubble and dust. We're bloodied and bruised, and feeling pretty hopeless. At that point we need to pick up the pieces of our life and rebuild. That's never easy, though it is a little easier if we have firm foundations in the first place. Foundations built on love, or faith, or friendship. Sound values, at the very least.

'What we have in the way of material to rebuild with may look pretty unpromising to start with. But if we go back to this verse, we find that even something that the builders rejected can end up being the key stone. In Jesus' day, many people failed to recognize that he was the Messiah, the very person that they had been waiting for. For the builders of the new London Bridge, they rejected this very fine stone that had served them so well in the past. Sometimes we can overlook the very thing – or person – that is right under our nose, which could turn a situation round for us if we'd only allow it. That might be something for us to think about today.'

'You know I'm not a believer, but thank you for your words,' said Ruth as she opened her car boot for Stephen. He looked up, surprised.

'Thank you for acknowledging our pain. For recognizing that our world has collapsed. For trying to help.'

'That's what I'm here for,' said Stephen. 'If ever you want to talk . . .'

'I'm not at all sure that I do,' she said. 'Death is hardly a stranger, you know. It's been my life's work, probably just as much as yours.'

'I know that. But it's not the same, is it?'

'What are you driving at?'

'Just that it's entirely different when it's personal. You could have cared for a thousand patients and written the definitive book on bereavement and still be knocked sideways by your own loss.'

'That old chestnut about *who cares for the carers*?' she said with ironic emphasis.

'If you like. I was thinking about my father, actually. My family couldn't understand why I was unwilling to take his funeral.'

'What happened?'

'I caved in, in the end. Couldn't bear their disappointment. It was as if at long last they'd stumbled across a practical use for my vocation. They thought I was being bloody-minded, refusing to do my duty. This was eighteen years ago, and I'm still not sure my brother's totally forgiven me. But all I wanted to do was grieve as a son. To have a little cry in the service, if I needed one. Not to have to be the one who held it all together for everyone else.'

He could feel Ruth's eyes on him. 'Point taken,' she said. 'See you at lunchtime?'

The map suggested it might not be the most scenic day on the route. Stephen suspected it would be dominated by the noise from the motorway half a mile away, and for beauty, the landscape certainly didn't compare to Box Hill or Newlands Corner. Once out of the village, the walkers faced a steady climb up the ridge, and then it flattened out to pretty easy, level terrain. Yesterday the boys had enjoyed a run around Reigate Fort. He thought there were a couple more Victorian hill forts on today's route, but it wasn't entirely clear from the map whether these were accessible.

'William, you'll know,' he said, catching up with him. 'Pilgrim Fort. It's clearly marked on the map. I'm intrigued by the name. Can we visit, do you know?'

'Afraid not,' said William. 'It's hidden in the depths of the wood. Private property, these days anyway. Used to be owned by the local authority. Field study centre, I think. Sort of place city kids were sent to, to discover the great outdoors.'

'That sounds rather glorious,' said Stephen. 'I trust that wasn't the end of that. I do hope they opened up somewhere else instead.'

'I'm surprised,' said Theo, joining them. 'I wouldn't have thought the whole *Dangerous Book for Boys* was exactly your cup of tea, Father Stephen.'

'Really? Why on earth not?'

'Well, I'd have thought you might be rather too fond of your creature comforts.'

Stephen laughed. Theo and William clearly had no idea. His reinvention of himself appeared to have exceeded even his own high standards. If only they knew!

'Have I never told you about Lough Derg and St Patrick's Purgatory?' Both men looked blank. 'No? It's what you might describe as the Ironman of pilgrimages.'

'Go on,' said William.

'Well, Lough Derg is in County Donegal in Ireland. It's home to the sacred Sanctuary of St Patrick. There's a cave which is supposedly the entrance to Purgatory. Anyhow, it's a really significant part of Irish Christian heritage, somewhere pilgrims have been going for over a thousand years. It's a remarkable place – hard to describe if you haven't been there. The very air feels steeped in prayer. The cave's on an island in the middle of lake. So not the slightest hope of mobile signal or Wi-Fi, and they don't let you bring phones or laptops. I don't know what it is exactly, but there's a tangible sense of peace.

'It's closed all winter, but in the summer – the season runs from May to September – you can go there either for a one-day retreat, or if you're really hard-core, on a three-day pilgrimage. If you do that, you have to fast for three days and undertake a twenty-four-hour vigil. You take off your shoes when you arrive, and walk round the island barefoot, praying in a number of sacred places, inside the monastery church and outside on the rocks.'

'And you've done that?' said Theo.

'Yup. Four times.'

'What's the hardest thing about it?' asked William.

'For me, staying awake. Sleep seems so seductive, especially when it's cold and wet, which it can be. And if it's not raining, the midges can be pretty horrible, too.'

'So why? Why on earth put yourself through that?' asked Theo.

Stephen thought for a moment. 'I suppose it's a chance to step back from everyday life. For me, it's a time to come closer to God through prayer and reflection. But that would be the same for any pilgrimage. I guess what's different there is the element of testing yourself. Seeing if you really do trust God when you're pushed to the limit.'

'Bit of a niche sport, surely?' said Theo.

'You'd be surprised,' said Stephen. 'All sorts of people turn up. Mary McAleese, the former Irish president, was there one year, and the poet Seamus Heaney another time. The island gets about fifteen thousand visitors a year, just in those few summer months. Not all of them do the full caboodle, of course, but numbers are pretty steady. And a lot of the pilgrims are repeat visitors, so that tells you there's something about it that seems to touch a deep spot in the soul. There's a bit in Mark's Gospel where Jesus tells his disciples, "Come away to a quiet place and rest awhile." That's what it's all about for me.'

'Doesn't sound like my idea of a rest,' said Theo. 'But fair play to you.' Stephen thought he could detect the faintest glimmer of respect in his voice.

'Does it get any easier?' added William.

'Not really. Each time it's been different. I go thinking I know what's going to happen, but somehow God always takes me by surprise.'

'So you're saying that Santiago de Compostela is for softies?' said Theo.

'Hardly! For most people on the *Camino*, they're in it for the long haul. St Patrick's is intense, certainly. I guess you could think of it as a sprint, of sorts, as opposed to a marathon.'

'So why send Anna to Spain?'

'I beg your pardon?'

'She was away *weeks*. Was that *really* necessary?'

'I didn't send her anywhere!' retorted Stephen, before he could stop himself. 'I think that was what she felt she needed,' he added more gently.

'She said it was your idea.'

'Really? Well, we certainly talked a lot about pilgrimage. That I remember. She was fascinated … kept asking me questions, wanted to know more. But we also talked about retreats. I remember lending her a directory of retreat houses in the UK. There are a lot, you know, many in the most stunning locations. I think she wanted to get right away from Farmleigh for a bit. She thought a change of scene might help.'

'It did,' said William. 'Don't you think?'

'It's a long time ago,' said Theo. 'I don't really want to think about it.'

Ruth was waiting for the walkers at the viewpoint. She'd set out picnic rugs on a wide grassy strip. Stephen watched William's face light up when he saw her, sitting on a bench, and Ruth smile in return. Theirs was a good relationship, he thought. They were as solid as could be. Anna had inarguably had a good start in life. Who could put a price on growing up in a happy family?

Of course, it wasn't a given that the children of happy marriages would be equally lucky in love – but there was something about passing on the torch of mutual respect, of good communication, of not allowing small problems to escalate, that gave the next generation a head start. He wondered about Theo's parents. His father, he was pretty certain, was dead, but he thought he remembered the mother – thin, worn out, weeping quietly into her hanky – from Anna's funeral. Was she much involved in the life of her son and grandchildren, he wondered? Was she a support to Theo or just one more worry on his list?

Checking his watch, he realized that it was nearly time for the silence again. He thought it was proving effective, but it was hard to tell. There was so little quiet in today's world that it was doubtless a novel experience for many in the group. On balance, he thought the children and young people were managing slightly better than he had anticipated, but he was less sure about the adults. Certainly in a world of portable media, quiet was a worryingly unfamiliar experience. Was it a misjudgement? He had to remind himself that while in his case silence was an old friend, for others it was a new acquaintance, and one they were not altogether sure they wanted to get to know.

On balance, though, after only two days he thought he could detect an element of thoughtfulness, a different rhythm in the group, when they walked without talking. After the initial oddness – the mimed *After you*'s and self-conscious *Thank you*'s as the pilgrims passed each other on the path – it seemed to settle, somehow. The quality of conversation that followed felt richer for the time apart.

'Friends!' he called. 'Just before we set off again, can I nudge you into silence? I thought we'd try an hour. Today's theme is all about "wilderness". What does that word conjure up, I wonder? The dictionary definition is something about those parts of the natural environment that have escaped human intervention. That handful of truly wild places that are still untouched by roads or other infrastructure. I was telling Theo and William about a wild place in Ireland I've visited a number of times. It's pretty remote but I love it. You may be able to summon up your own images. For some of us, wilderness sounds very attractive, romantic even. But for others, wilderness is a place of isolation, of abandonment, of fear. It's somewhere we feel, quite literally, *bewildered*.

'One of the things about pilgrimage is that it gives us the opportunity to explore our inner landscape, to reflect on our own lives a little. That may be frightening or painful. Perhaps you're living in a spiritual wilderness at the moment. Grief can leave us feeling as if we are groping around in the darkness.'

He hesitated. 'There are no easy answers, I'm afraid. I wish there were. Sometimes it's a matter of just pressing on, looking for the light of Christ in the distance, even if for now it's just out of sight. We just have to wait for the way ahead to become easier. There's a prayer, written by a Jewish prisoner in the Second World War, that says:

> 'I believe in the sun, even when it's not shining.
> I believe in love, even when I don't feel it.
> I believe in God, even when there is silence.

'Can I invite everyone to take that prayer into the silence this afternoon? Try and remember that God walks with you, even in the wilderness. Perhaps especially in the wilderness.'

He hoped that he hadn't pushed them too hard. He'd deliberately stopped short of describing the transformative moments Jesus had experienced in the wilderness. Or talking about wilderness as liminal space, where identity shifts and new possibilities emerge. He wanted to avoid any suggestion that suffering was good for the soul. Pain was pain, even if at some point in the future people looked back at a dark time and felt that they had learned something important along the way.

He thought of Anna, a decade ago, brutally felled by loss, like a tree cut down at its roots. Poor Anna. And Theo, of course. But it was Anna who had made the deepest impression on him. The flood of tears that coursed down her dazed face. Her utterly heart-breaking rendition of 'The Swan' from Saint-Saens' *Carnival of the Animals* at the funeral, as she poured heart and soul into every single note. And then the inexorable slide into that alarming black depression. She had spiralled lower and lower, barely able to function, until the combined offices of an understanding GP and the right medication lifted her onto a plateau just high enough that she found the resource to seek out bereavement counselling from the surgery and pastoral care from the vicarage.

Experience – and faith – taught him that it was possible to walk through the wilderness and emerge transformed. Anna had done so. *Yea, though I walk through the valley of the shadow of death, I will fear no evil: for thou art with me; thy rod and thy staff they comfort me*, as the psalmist put it so beautifully. *Surely goodness and mercy shall follow me all the days of my life: and I will dwell in the house of the* LORD *for ever.* How he loved the poetry of the King James Bible! So much more evocative than those worthy but pedestrian modern translations. Useful they might be on occasion, but they left his soul untouched.

He wrestled his way through a stretch of the path overgrown by brambles and nettles, and then paused as he crossed the noisy dual carriageway. From his vantage point on the bridge, he watched the traffic hurtling onwards, to London one way and the south coast the other, the drivers heedless of the ant-like specks of the walkers overhead. Was that an image for his own barren spiritual landscape, he wondered? Plenty of activity, but very little thought to what was going on around him? Was he stuck on a relentless treadmill? A one-way journey that allowed for no diversions, no turning off the course he'd started?

Maybe. He certainly believed that he knew where he was going, until he'd met David. The carefully constructed carapace of his character had served him well for the best part of thirty years. He inhabited the suave personality – the opera-loving Anglo-Catholic priest, devoted to his parishioners, serving his Lord in London, Bristol and, for the last twelve years, Farmleigh – with such determination that he'd almost forgotten that life had ever been different.

David had changed all that. Falling in love – at the utterly *absurd* age of fifty-five – threatened to bring his flimsy house of cards crashing down in one fell swoop. And what would that collapse leave in its wake? He pictured a handful of playing cards scattered on green baize. What was face up on the table? The measly two of clubs? The ace of spades? Was David the joker in the pack?

David! He'd be seeing him in just a couple of hours. Given the knots the dear old C of E had tied itself into, Stephen had reconciled himself to a lifetime on his own. However unsatisfactory the Church's stance – that while it was acceptable for the laity to enter into a monogamous same-sex partnership, celibacy was required of the clergy – and however widely the rules were flouted by others, Stephen had always felt that this was a matter of discipline under God and a duty of obedience he owed to his bishop.

There was another, more pragmatic reason: though renouncing the possibility of intimacy was a deprivation, Stephen was convinced that for him, at least, celibacy presented the lesser of two evils. He knew himself too well: once the genie was out of the bottle, as it were, he knew that he would find it almost impossible not to behave very badly indeed.

He had form, after all. He'd got himself unforgivably entangled in an impossible relationship while still at school, and somehow found himself engaged to be married at the tender age of nineteen. Linda was pretty, kind and a sympathetic listener, but with the benefit of hindsight he could see that her mother, Elaine, had been the driving force behind the wedding plans. It was as if she saw Stevie (he wasn't yet Stephen) with his good grades and plans for university as her daughter's ticket out of the depressed north-east. Linda's burly father, Brian, was unemployed after decades down the pits, while her mother scraped a living as an office cleaner.

Stephen knew the pitch first-hand: his own father had sunk into sullen alcoholism after he was laid off by the shipyard that had employed him for twenty-three years as a welder. But beyond their shared fury at losing their livelihoods while the economy that had sustained their families for generations disappeared down the pan, the two households had nothing in common. When Stephen's evident reluctance to set a date for the wedding reached an impasse, Elaine sent Brian round to find out what exactly he thought he was playing at. The results had not been pretty.

Hearing the row, his father roused himself from stupor just long enough to throw Stephen out of the house in disgust. As a result, he found himself moving to Manchester in pursuit of university and a new life several weeks ahead of schedule. His one regret – the loss of Linda's undemanding friendship – soon melted away when his older brother turned up on the doorstep in early October with the startling news that he was to be a father and he'd better come home and face the music.

At which point Stephen finally dug in his heels: he knew, absolutely *knew*, that Linda's pregnancy (if indeed it existed) was nothing to do with him for the simple reason that they had never slept together, though not for want of trying on her part. Nobody would believe him; he recognized at once that the cost of *not* returning to Tyneside and marrying Linda would be the permanent loss of his family and his home, along with the last few shreds of his reputation. But equally he knew that this was his Rubicon moment, and that if he didn't draw a line in the sand now, he never would.

Perhaps it was no great surprise, then, that his early twenties – when he finally acknowledged his sexuality, but thankfully well before he was ordained – were spent in a mindless quest for anonymous sexual encounters that he soon knew to be thrillingly addictive and destructive to his soul in equal measure. By the time he started theological college he'd begun the wholesale reconstruction of his persona, which included a well-polished patina of amused detachment on the subject of love and sex, and a lightly ironic, throwaway remark about *saving himself for the Lord's work*. Alongside his studies, he devoted significant attention to observing the traits and tics of his fellow ordinands (especially those who hailed from public school and Oxbridge) and adopting those mannerisms that appealed to him. He was a swift learner, and soon sloughed off the skin of his old life along with his Geordie accent. (His life-long passion for the Magpies he refused to abandon, on the grounds that every parish priest worth his salt needed a football team to follow.) By the time he started his curacy, the transformation was complete.

But the way he felt about David was so totally different from anything he had experienced before that he was in turmoil. Cupid's arrow had well and truly pierced his heart, and all the old clichés turned out to be true. It was like seeing the world in colour for the first time after decades of black and white. Birdsong seemed louder and sweeter. Heavens – he even caught himself humming snatches of Frank Sinatra!

What, if anything, to do with that love was the question. David was deliciously unbothered by the age gap – he was a mere thirty-two – but was it fair on him, to form a permanent relation-ship? Could Stephen really cast aside so lightly the principles he'd clung to for the past thirty years? And if he *did*, how would he explain David's presence in his life to his parishioners, let alone to his bishop? On the other hand, having tasted such wholly unexpected joy, could he really let that slip away from him? Wouldn't he be consigning himself to the very worst sort of wilderness imaginable? And quite unnecessarily?

Out of the corner of his eye, he caught sight of Bethany in the distance, gesticulating in his direction. Glancing at his watch, he was startled to find that an hour had slipped by without his noticing. He smiled and waved back, about to tell the pilgrims that they could begin conversation again, when William appeared at his side.

'Think we've gone wrong somewhere, Father,' he said.

Stephen looked around. Where were they? A railway station? That wasn't on the route, surely? Disconcerted, he reached into his backpack for the file of maps. *Bugger, bugger, bugger.* They had strayed badly off course. So absorbed had he been in his own inner landscape that he'd taken his eye off the all-important terrain around him. And he'd led the party well and truly up the garden path as a result. How humiliating! He could already hear the grumbles, the questions, the inevitable complaints.

'Friends!' he called, putting as brave a face on it as he could muster. 'I'm *so* sorry. I have to confess I've made a major cock-up. I'm not quite sure how it happened but we've taken a wrong turning. I was miles away. And now we're *all* miles away. *All we like sheep have gone astray*, you might even say . . .' He laughed awkwardly.

'Sorry, troops. We need to retrace our steps, get back to the main path.' Just then, as if to rub in his foolishness, it started spitting with rain. There were groans as people fished in their bags for cagoules. Oh *Lord*, he was going to have a mutiny on his hands if he wasn't careful. He pulled on his own waterproof, and made to zip it up, only to find that in his haste the fabric jammed in its teeth. He tugged at it furiously before abandoning the attempt with a curse. 'This way!' he called angrily.

In the end it rained, albeit lightly, for the rest of the afternoon. The day that had started so promisingly deteriorated rapidly, along with Stephen's spirits. The promised couple of hours of sunny leisure melted away like a mirage.

'I just hope there's going to be lots of hot water when we get to this convent, because we're going to need it,' said Mary Anne grimly. 'Do you know it well, Father Stephen?'

'I have every confidence in the good sisters,' he said, hoping against hope that the guest wing was as comfortable as the convent website suggested. 'I haven't been there personally, but it comes highly recommended.'

He racked his brains. Who *had* recommended it? Someone in his clergy chapter, he was pretty sure. But if it had been Colin, for example – and he was apt to disappear off on retreat at the drop of a hat so was the most likely suspect – they could be in for an unpleasant surprise because Colin was oblivious to his surroundings. He was the sort of priest who, offered instant coffee in a chipped mug, said 'Lovely!' and actually meant it.

'We'll find out soon enough,' said Catherine. 'How much longer now, do you think?'

'Yeah, the kids are beginning to wilt,' Tamsin lobbed in.

'There's a steep bit down at least a hundred steps, and then it can't be more than a mile after that,' he said. 'Ruth should be waiting, along with my good friend David who's bringing his school minibus so that we can shuttle down to the convent.' Good Lord, was he *blushing*? 'So the end is in sight! Meanwhile, do take care on those steps, one and all – they could be slippery in the wet.' He bustled up and down the line of walkers, spreading the word about the forthcoming descent and its hazards. The very last thing the pilgrimage needed was an accident.

And then, and then . . . just as he was allowing himself to imagine that they were on the home strait, Stephen saw a familiar frame at the viewing platform halfway down the steps. A tall, stooping figure of a man, coatless and dressed in an incongruous bubble-gum pink *Hello Kitty* T-shirt over the sort of long-sleeved, finely striped shirt more commonly worn by office workers. Below, he sported a baggy pair of grey tracksuit trousers that – judging by the expanse of grubby underwear on display – had long since parted company with their elastic. His feet were shod in bright yellow rubber boots more suited to a yachting weekend than a walk in the countryside. He was carrying two tatty supermarket carrier bags, each bulging with heaven-knew-what. And to cap it all – quite literally – he sported what must once have been a plain white safari hat, but today was liberally decorated with pink, purple and yellow flowers. Snapdragons, thought Stephen. There was a rather lovely display of them in a glazed green container in the front garden of the vicarage. Or at least there had been when Stephen had left home on Saturday. Oh *fuck*.

'Adam!' he said. 'Goodness. What a surprise!'

At the sound of his name, the man flinched, and bobbed his head up and down in a characteristic nod. 'Hello, Father,' he mumbled, grinning vaguely and looking into the middle distance.

'Where are you headed?' asked Stephen. Adam's head dipped again, and he half turned away, so that Stephen missed his muttered reply. 'Dorking or Oxted?' Even as he posed the question, Stephen realized it was almost certainly meaningless. He tried again. 'Up or down the steps?'

'Following you, Father,' nodded Adam.

'Me?'

'Everyone,' he mumbled. 'For the music lady.'

'Anna?'

'Yes,' said Adam, more distinctly. The snapdragons wobbled alarmingly as he nodded. 'Walking for Anna. The music lady.'

'Ah. I see,' said Stephen, thinking quite the opposite.

'On the radio,' added Adam, in a burst of loquacity. 'At the hostel. Walking for Anna today.'

By now the whole party had made it to the place Stephen had stopped, by the platform. They were stacking up behind him. Bethany looked miserable and bedraggled, and Samuel was pale with exhaustion. Even Smith seemed to have lost some of his exuberance.

Theo pushed his way down and came over. 'Everything OK, Stephen?'

71

At the sound of his sharp tone, Adam skittered away like a foal, bobbing furiously. Stephen could feel him trying to melt into the background, but he was hemmed in by the wooden railings.

'All well, thank you, Theo. Would you mind taking the lead for now? Keep straight ahead till you reach the road, and then turn left towards the quarry. Do make sure everyone looks out for lorries, though. You'll come to a car park a few hundred metres beyond, where Ruth and David should both be waiting to ferry us onwards. I'll catch up with you all later.'

By the time Stephen finally made it to the convent, most of the walkers were clean, dry and considerably more cheerful. The guesthouse was simple but clean, warm and welcoming. David was holding court in the large guest kitchen. Tamsin, Catherine and William were sitting on benches at a long scrubbed pine table, and Theo stood leaning against a cast iron range, nursing a mug. David was wearing Mary Anne's flowery apron and pouring tea from a vast enamel tea pot.

'At *last* – the wanderer returns!' he cried, as Stephen walked into the kitchen. 'Earl Grey or Lapsang? And *do* try one of my flapjacks. I've chucked in some cranberries for a change and I must confess I'm rather thrilled with the result. Just sharp enough. Practically a health food! Or are you heading straight for the shower?'

Stephen felt his heart turn a somersault. He was torn between fury that he couldn't throw himself into David's arms and sheer joy at seeing him. His initial disappointment that their reunion was so public gave way to delight in the way that he was evidently bewitching the assembled company with the full force of his considerable charm.

'Good man! Earl Grey would hit the spot, I think,' he said lightly, hoping the inane smile on his face would be interpreted as simple pleasure at the prospect of refreshment at the end of a long day.

'You're too kind,' he said, as David presented him with a mug.

'Now tell *all*,' said David. 'Who was your mysterious stranger? Did you bring him with you?'

'Oh, just Adam,' he said. 'No great mystery. A gentleman of the road. Turns up every now and again on my doorstep in need of a little TLC. He caught you on the radio, Tamsin. Heard about the walk and thought he'd come along for the ride.'

'So what have you done with him? You didn't bring him here, did you?' said Mary Anne, walking into the kitchen. 'I'm not sure that would be exactly appropriate.'

'Well, there we differ,' said Stephen cheerfully. 'I can't think of anything more appropriate than a convent offering the blessing of hospitality to someone in need. It's up to us to look after the needy where we can.'

He took a slug of tea – nectar! 'But Adam does his own thing, by and large. I bought him a sandwich and a drink, and he's gone on his way. For now, at any rate. He'll probably pop up again somewhere along the journey.'

He drained his mug and put it down on the table. 'That was just what I needed,' he said.

'Time for that shower. Can anyone point me in the right direction?'

'Let me,' said David, taking off the apron and flinging it over the back of a chair. 'This way.'

12 miles
Tamsin

Tamsin drew the curtain in her room in the convent and sighed. Bloody Poms and their rain! It was nearly the end of May and supposed to be half-term, for heaven's sake. Why was the weather so unreliable? Having said that, her home city of Melbourne – wide open to all the elements the Southern Ocean was capable of throwing at it – was famous for producing four seasons in a day. Still, you knew where you were with Aussie weather. It was the endless grey of the British climate that got her down.

Mustn't grumble. Milo was having a ball, and broadly speaking if he was happy, she was happy. While she loved the little scrap to pieces, it was no picnic being a single mother of an eight-year-old boy. He was a tornado of energy. As far as she was concerned, any activity that kept him entertained and wore him out at the same time was a gift. The fact that she found herself in sole charge of two small boys (well, three if you counted Sam, since Theo wasn't exactly on the case) and a mongrel to boot was easily outweighed by the fact that he was happily occupied.

Thanks, Anna, she thought. *Just wish you were here to share it with us.* Which she kind of was, she supposed. She was there in spirit, in the conversation, in the air about them. But it was poignant that she wasn't there in person. It was a bit like going to a party where the host nips out to the bottle shop to top up supplies. Trouble was, they could all wait till they were blue in the face but Anna wasn't ever going to come back. It was hard to get your head around that. It was bloody sad. *Miss you, mate*, she thought. *Life's just not the same.*

She checked her watch. Just time to edit the latest instalment of her audio diary and send it over to Ian in the studio for the breakfast show. She should still be able to grab a shower, provided Milo stayed asleep. She fired up her laptop, pulled on her earphones and opened up yesterday's sound files. There was a good bit of singing from the service on Sunday which she could use as an intro – that church had a great acoustic – but on the other hand they hadn't sung at all yesterday, so maybe it wouldn't work. Hymn-singing took her right back to childhood. A quick canter through that old pilgrim hymn gave a sense of coherence to the walk. Something that bound them all together. A unity of purpose, perhaps? Once a Catholic, always a Catholic, she thought; you could take the girl out of the convent, but you never took the convent out of the girl. *See, Sister Bridget? Something rubbed off.* She'd ask Father Stephen if there was going to be any singing today.

She scanned quickly through the files. There was an earnest bit of conversation where a dog-walker had asked Catherine what they were all doing, and why no one was speaking to anyone else, and she'd done her best to explain in a whisper so as not to disturb the others. With the result that the bloke hadn't heard a word, and Catherine had to repeat herself, twice over, until her stage whisper was at least as loud as normal speech would have been in the first place. Poor woman! She'd looked mortified to be breaking the silence. But fair dos, she was doing her best.

Personally Tamsin thought Catherine was a bit of a goody-two-shoes. But if Anna loved her, that was good enough for her. Catherine had been Beth and Sam's childminder when Anna went back to uni on her return from Spain. It had been gutsy, retraining like that, when you'd have thought her hands were pretty full already, what with Beth and Sam to look after. And the rest. Tamsin, meanwhile, had been on a plane to Oz within days of Anna's homecoming. A move that made her about as popular as a rattlesnake in a lucky dip. Still. At the time there seemed no alternative.

Now here was Father Stephen going on about wilderness. He'd warmed to his theme, all right. She liked the image of the inner landscape. In her mind's eye she saw the Australian bush, the red dusty soil, the burning sun, the snakes, and miles and miles and *miles* of bloody nowhere. It was inspiring, awesome landscape, to be treated with fear and respect. She wondered if he'd ever been down under, seen the outback. Talk about isolation! Most Brits had absolutely no clue. Another question for him.

Then there was that bit where she'd caught up with Celia and Jackie just as they were heading off for the station at the end of the afternoon. She hadn't appreciated they were leaving yesterday, and it had all been a bit last minute. They'd been quite choked up, Jackie in particular. 'I've never done anything like this, and it's been a real challenge,' she'd said. 'Just look at me! Not exactly built for walking! But I've loved every moment. With so many of her friends and family here, it's been the next best thing to having Anna walk with us. I'm just so sad we've got to go back to work and can't finish the course. But we'll be with you all in spirit.'

And here was a funny part, but maybe not one for broadcast, given the fruitiness of his language: Theo going troppo when that bloke with the flowers in his hat turned up at the end of the day. Where in hell's name had he sprung from? You could hear the rain in this clip, too, splashing down onto windcheaters as they flapped in the wind. She'd need to clean that up a tad. Which reminded her: the weather outlook. Did she really want to know?

Tamsin finished her edit, added an intro and a wrap-up, and delivered a perfect two minutes and thirty seconds' worth of audio into the station Dropbox for Ian to pick up the other end. She texted him to expect it, tweeted a picture from yesterday with a link to the fundraising site, and then logged on to see how they were doing. Eleven hundred bucks! Not at all bad. Although come to think of it, she'd probably hoped for a bit more than that, after yesterday's spectacular leap. She needed to try and get something on the afternoon show, she reckoned, give it a bit of a boost.

She wondered what they were going to see on the route today. If there was anything quirky along the way, that would help to build a story. And who would make a good interviewee? Tom perhaps? He had presence. She quite liked him, although she was beginning to find him a touch over-attentive. Or Ruth, maybe? Yes; Ruth sounded authoritative and calm, and she'd done a great job a year or two back when Tamsin had inveigled her into being an on-air expert for a phone-in during Hospice Week. The fact that this was such a personal story would add poignancy. Tamsin would try and sweet-talk her into it later.

By now, most of the walkers were in a routine. The end of breakfast saw sandwiches made and bags packed. Ruth and William arrived in time for a leisurely cup of coffee so that the walkers could stow any heavier items in the boot of the old Volvo. They also – bless them – brought along Smith; he was billeted out with them overnight on the grounds that not all the accommodation was dog-friendly. As always, Smith greeted her with lavish delight, out of all proportion to a twelve-hour separation. Milo, at eight, was almost as demonstrative in his affections, even in front of his friends. Tamsin was realistic enough to know that this couldn't last, but surrendered to the present with joy. At least she had one bloke in her life who was reliably loving.

Because of the location of the convent, the minibus was in service again today to shuttle the walkers back to the day's starting point. Which meant another glimpse of the delectable David. Blond and finely chiselled, and clearly a man who knew how to look after himself, he'd arrived that morning with a box of home-made *macarons*. A bit of a turn-up for the books! Mary Anne was practically salivating. Good for Father Steve, the old dog.

'We're a smaller party today,' Father Stephen announced in his morning briefing. 'It was sad waving farewell to Celia and Jackie last night. But duty calls. And Tom – I think you're leaving us tonight? We'll miss you. As far as the route goes, it's a twelve-miler today. There are a couple of quite steep climbs in store. The first goes up Botley Hill and takes us to the highest point on the entire route. Then there's one more steep ascent at Westerham, but otherwise it's a reasonably gentle day.'

There were groans from the group. 'If you say so!' said Catherine.

'We'll take your word for it, Father Steve,' added Tamsin, winking at Beth.

The priest smiled serenely. 'My suggestion is that we stop off for a short reflection at a little church later in the day. I'll tell you more later, but for now, St Botolph's is a significant site along the Pilgrims' Way. Then there's another noisy section where we'll have to endure the din of traffic. But all being well, we'll end the day walking through lavender fields. Too early in the season for olfactory pleasure, I'm afraid, so we'll have to use our imaginations. But it'll make a pleasant diversion from the blight of the blessed motorway. And I know this rain's a bit tiresome, but the outlook's better for the afternoon. So bring your coats, and here's to another good day!'

'Milo!' called Tamsin. 'You all sorted, doll? Good to go?'

'*Mum*,' said Milo, rolling his eyes. 'Course I'm ready. Me and Sam and George have been ready for *hours*.'

'So how come I just found your toothbrush – which I might add is completely *dry* – on the basin next to your washbag, huh?' She chased him in the direction of the bathroom. 'George? Sam? Do I need to do a teeth inspection for you guys, too? Go on! Get your skates on. Everyone else is pretty much good to go.' Presumably there would come a time when Milo would remember to clean his teeth without a reminder and maybe even change his socks once in a while, but so far there wasn't much sign.

She had a sudden vision of a thirty-year-old Milo, still living at home in her tiny cottage, with her doing his laundry and making him a brown-bag lunch every day. She absolutely mustn't let that happen. It was too easy to do everything for him – far quicker, for one thing, and they always seemed to be running late – but she knew that wouldn't be doing either of them any favours. She only had to think of Frankie – her ex – so comprehensively mollycoddled by his Italian–Australian mother that he was entirely incapable of taking adult responsibility. It was practically a disability. When they'd first met – he'd been section editor of *The Age* when she first returned to Melbourne – he'd still been living with his parents, although he was thirty-four, for heaven's sake.

'It's an Italian thing,' he'd assured her with a complacent smile. 'My mamma needs to spoil me. It'd break her heart if I left. She'd worry I wasn't eating properly.'

I should have seen the writing on the bloody wall, she thought now. But Frankie had been such a godsend as she established her freelance career that she allowed herself to be swayed by his lazy charm and handsome Mediterranean looks until she fancied herself in love with him. She'd arrived back in her home city on the very slenderest wing and a prayer. A desperate, late-night phone call to her cousin Tegan had resulted in an offer of a bed for six weeks while Tegan's flatmate was overseas, and the promise of an introduction to a journo she'd been at college with, who might be able to put some work her way. Who turned out to be Francesco Rossi.

God, *Frankie*! It had all been OK to begin with. Well, more than OK, if she was honest. She couldn't believe her luck and clung to him as if to a life-raft after a shipwreck. After an email exchange, they met in his third-floor office in the Fairfax building on Collins Street. He looked her up and down, for rather longer than he looked at her CV, in truth, and smiled appreciatively.

'Tell you what, it's almost lunchtime,' he said, never taking his eyes off her. 'There's a bar on the corner called O'Connell's. Meet me there in ten and pitch me three decent ideas for features. If they're any good, you get an assignment and I stand you lunch. If not, you're on your own. Right?'

When Frankie showed up half an hour later, Tamsin had three ideas ready and waiting: a run-down of the ten hottest nightclubs in London (how would Francesco know, anyway?); an investigation into the alarming rise of elective C-sections in Australia, based on a brief conversation over breakfast with Tegan, who was a midwife ('Melbourne Mums: too posh to push?'); and an exclusive interview with an up-and-coming Aussie comedian, just back on home turf after a sell-out tour of Europe, who'd sat next to Tamsin on the plane over and whose card she later found tucked into her handbag (bit of a sleazebag, but hey). Frankie had been impressed. He also turned out to be good company, sexy as hell, and expansive with the compliments and his wallet. Lunch turned into a long afternoon at the bar, and the start of a highly productive partnership. One that quickly moved from the office to the bedroom.

By the time Tegan's flatmate returned, Tamsin was sufficiently solvent to put down a deposit on a one-bed rental unit in Hawthorn. Frankie all but moved in when she did. Thanks to the steady stream of commissions he put her way, within three months of her arrival she was offered a rare staff post on the paper. The knowledge that she was pregnant led to a brief crisis of conscience, but she accepted the offer anyway on the assumption that it would all come good in the end. By the time her bump was impossible to conceal she intended to be indispensable.

Frankie, to his credit, proved a devoted father. Which was good of him, since fatherhood had not exactly been on his game-plan when they met, and an unplanned sprog swiftly turned their care-free life together upside down. He took enormous paternal pride in the infant Milo, and insisted on having a vast Italian family christening at St Patrick's Cathedral followed by a lunch party for fifty of his nearest and dearest. Tamsin herself was pitifully short on family. A late child of elderly parents, she had been orphaned in her early twenties while she was still a student, living in London. At which point, Frankie's mother Teresa, appalled that Tamsin could muster only Tegan and her boyfriend to represent the distaff side, finally let down her defences and embraced Tamsin to her capacious bosom as the mother of her newest grandson.

It seemed exactly the new beginning Tamsin had yearned for when she fled England the year before. With remarkably little effort on her part, a ready-made life beckoned. It was as if she'd landed in a parallel universe. So complete was the package the large and noisy Rossi family offered that she sometimes felt like an amnesiac who'd awoken to find her past obliterated. She perpetuated this herself, in part, by losing contact with her friends in the UK. She persuaded herself that this was because she'd been waiting till she was fixed up before sending out change of address cards, and had then been too busy working her socks off and setting up home with Frankie. In the end, in a fit of hormone-induced contrition after Milo's birth, she dropped cards to a handful of friends, including Anna and Theo, announcing the news. 'Sorry I've been so *crap* at keeping in touch,' she scribbled inadequately on the back. 'Bit of a whirlwind this end! One day you guys must meet my new family ...'

Anna, characteristically, responded with flowers rather than recriminations, and soon they were in touch again by email, exchanging pictures of the children, and cheerful news about their respective lives. By then Anna was halfway through her two-year postgrad training as a music therapist and loving every moment. Tamsin didn't allow herself to probe either Anna's feelings or her own. She was just relieved to hear her sounding so cheerful. *Feel I've finally found my true calling*, wrote Anna. *Somehow everything that's happened seems to have been leading up to this.*

Only wish I could say the same about motherhood! replied Tamsin. *Am all at sea. Wish you were here, mate!* Well, whose fault was that, you silly moo? Tegan had recently moved to Sydney, and no amount of well-meaning advice from the Rossi womenfolk made up for the absence of her own mother and her best friend. But she'd made her bed and she was bloody well going to have to lie in it.

And the first year or two with Frankie were good. They had fun together, plenty of laughter as well as the occasional blazing row. It all started to go belly-up when Tamsin decided it was time to go back to work, and Frankie did everything he could to prevent her. He pointed out that Milo was teething and fretful, waking up several times a night. She'd never survive the office if she was dog-tired, and besides, who was going to look after Milo if she went out to work? Her suggestion that she would look into day-care or maybe ask Frankie's mother or sister for help met a brick wall of silence. When she suggested that she'd be a lot less tired if they shared the load a bit, that he might just occasionally take a shift on night duty, he swore and threw a plate at her. She was so shocked that she laughed out loud, further infuriating him. He slapped her then, and hard.

And so it went on. She abandoned the idea of a return to work (she was knackered, he was right about that) and threw herself into caring for Milo and running the home, telling herself she was lucky to have a man who could provide for them both. She found that she could keep things on a more or less even keel, by cooking and cleaning and ensuring Frankie had ironed shirts for the office, until something – often quite a tiny thing, such as running out of his favourite *formaggio Parmigiano* – went wrong and he lost his temper again. In between times, they were happy. Well, as happy as permanently walking on eggshells allowed her to be. At his best, he was romantic and loving. It was as if he needed to let off steam from time to time and home was the safest place to do so. Afterwards, he was always contrite. He hadn't meant to hurt her; it was just that she pushed him to the limit.

Tamsin became adept at tiptoeing around Frankie's temper. She became a past master at reading his mood by the sound of his key in the lock and bracing herself accordingly. She took to wearing long sleeves to cover her bruises, and large dark glasses when necessary. Her acute shame was harder to conceal, so she increasingly avoided company and kept herself to herself. It was easier that way.

Her main concern was Milo: keeping him safe and out of harm's reach. Once he was at kindergarten, she started writing for women's magazines, which she could do almost entirely from home, without Frankie's knowledge. She even became an agony aunt, a commission that brought with it a certain black humour.

It was easy work, and bored her to tears. But it was sufficiently well paid for her to start building a nest egg. A chunk of the money she used to enrol in a distance learning course so that she could update her skills. Otherwise her training in broadcast journalism was beginning to feel frighteningly rusty in the light of the exponential speed of developments in digital and social media in the years since she'd graduated. The very act of signing up for the course made her feel more in control. The rest of her earnings went straight into an account she opened in Milo's name for which she was the sole signatory. She never actually referred to it as her running away fund, even to herself, but she took to keeping the pass-book in her handbag, along with her and Milo's passports.

The point of no return finally came when Milo was almost six, and a colleague of Frankie's let slip an idle remark about a magazine article she'd read in the dentist's waiting room, in which Tamsin expounded the virtues of the latest spa treatments available on the Mornington Peninsula. Frankie drove straight home from the office, found Tamsin at work, and went mad as a meat-axe.

Fortunately Milo was on a playdate with a friend and witnessed nothing. Bloodied and bruised, Tamsin walked out of the house in the clothes she was wearing, stopping only to pick up her laptop and bag. She collected Milo from his friend's house and drove straight to a women's refuge in Port Melbourne; ironically, in one of her first ever assignments for Frankie she'd interviewed the founder and a handful of grateful clients for a full-page feature. A week later, the swelling around her broken nose and black eye had receded sufficiently for the doctor to declare her fit to board a plane to London on a one-way ticket.

'Hey, Beth-ster, any news from Mr K?' Tamsin asked. They'd been on the move for half an hour or so and were skirting the edge of a wood on a chalky white footpath. She'd seen an opportunity to hand over the care of Smith into the willing hands of Lucy, Ella and Chloe, which gave her the perfect excuse for a quiet word with her goddaughter.

'So, he keeps texting? And sending me these silly songs to keep my spirits up,' said Beth, blushing and quite unable to keep the smile off her pinched face. 'He's, like, supposed to be revising, but I don't think he's getting all that much work done. I've been telling him to knuckle down.'

'Good on-ya!' said Tamsin. 'Keep cracking the whip, girl!' It was good to see Beth smiling. She'd looked like a bag of bones yesterday after the long afternoon in the rain. Poor kid, losing her Mum at fifteen. It had been bad enough for Tamsin and she'd been twenty-three when her mum died, just six months after her dad. That had been grim, especially at a distance. To be honest (and she did her best not to think about it), she still felt guilty for being the other side of the world and having such a ball in London while her parents were in their last days.

Beth looked so bloody vulnerable. She found herself hoping fiercely that this Matt was going to step up to the plate. If he let her down, he was going to have to answer to Tamsin. She toyed with the idea of sounding out Mary Anne, who probably knew him from school, but there was no way of doing so without arousing her curiosity. And Beth would *kill* her if she found out that Tamsin was poking her nose in. Quite right, too. It was none of Tamsin's business, except to be there to pick up the pieces with godmotherly tea and sympathy if it all went wrong.

'Tell me all about him, Beth. What's he like?'

'Oh . . . he's sweet. And funny. Really brainy too. And, like, totally *awesome* on the sax. Listen to this.' She pulled out her phone, and held it up so that Tamsin could hear. *O when the saints go marching in* . . . 'That's him playing. Yesterday it was "Is this the road to Amarillo?"'

'Sounds like a good bloke. Did Anna get to meet him?'

'No,' sighed Beth. 'I wish she had. But I only got to know him quite recently.'

'Well, I bet she would have loved him, doll. Do I get an intro? I need to make sure he's up to scratch.'

'Um . . . We'll see. I mean, I'm not actually sure we're, like, together.'

'Well, he sounds keen to me. Keep me posted, huh?'

'So . . . about Mum . . .' said Beth.

'Uh-huh?' Tamsin wondered what was coming.

'What was she . . . *like*? When you first knew her?'

'Why?'

'Sometimes I just need reminding,' mumbled Beth. 'I keep worrying I'll forget her. The more I know, the better.'

'Well . . .' said Tamsin. She thought back to their student days sharing a flat in London. Anna had been at the Guildhall while Tamsin was at City studying journalism. At the time Tamsin had a job in a bar where the music students drank from time to time. Anna and her then boyfriend Laurence (what a dickhead) came in one evening after a session busking on the underground. It was in the days before buskers were licensed and everyone had to take their chances. Laurence was furious that they'd been moved on by a not particularly talented black soul singer. The singer had appeared when they were halfway through a Vivaldi concerto, parking himself uncomfortably close by on a fold-up camping chair. He switched on his boom box, blasted out his backing track, and helped himself to two hours' worth of their takings, on the grounds that they were on his pitch. When Laurence began to argue, the singer – who was a good six inches taller and several pounds heavier – loomed over him menacingly. Anna, meanwhile, quietly packed up her cello, and left them to it on the grounds that life was too short.

'How the hell can you just walk away?' Laurence demanded, following her into the bar.

'We got to play for a couple of hours in the most amazing acoustic, and our audience loved us,' she said with a shrug. 'Let's not sweat the small stuff.'

Laurence angrily abandoned Anna, taking his sense of grievance off to the pool table. Anna apologized to Tamsin for his rudeness, and stayed at the bar to chat. And that was the start of their friendship. Most Friday nights Anna would try her luck somewhere on the underground, and afterwards she slaked her thirst with Tamsin. Sometimes Laurence joined her, sometimes not. After a week or two, Tamsin managed to persuade Anna to play the piano in the corner; a month later she had a regular gig, which livened the place up no end. And when Tamsin mentioned she was looking for a new place to live – she'd had more than enough of her rugby-playing Aussie flatmates in Earls Court – Anna mentioned the box room in her own flat, recently vacated by a violinist called Sophie who'd unexpectedly thrown in the towel and gone home to Hong Kong. She and Neil, a student pianist, would be delighted to have her.

'She was always generous,' Tamsin told Beth now. 'Saw the best in people. A glass half-full person. And great fun – I remember lots of laughter. Bit of a cliché, but she had a smile that lit up a room. You must remember that.'

'Yeah . . .' said Beth in a small voice. 'Except . . . *then*.'

'Fair dos. Except then. People often get sick when sad things happen, you know. But back then in London . . . well, she was a blithe spirit in those days. And it was music, music, music, always her music. She even used to sing in the shower. Drove me nuts!'

'Why?' asked Beth.

'Not a morning person. At least not then,' said Tamsin. 'Too busy burning the midnight oil, I guess, what with the bar, and clubbing when I had a night off, and the occasional lecture. But you could set your clock by Anna and her bloody practice timetable.'

'So . . . how long were you flatmates?'

'Couple of years? Then she went on the road with the quartet and I started work. And then she met your dad and . . . the rest is history, I guess.'

Beth plodded on, at her side, saying nothing. 'That any good?' asked Tamsin. 'Help at all?'

'Yeah. I guess. Thanks . . . Lucy's waving at me. Think I'd better, like, catch up? Laters.'

At least she was talking about her mum, thought Tamsin. She wondered about Theo. Did he have any idea how Beth was doing? Or Sam for that matter? She looked around, and located Theo at the front of the line of walkers, head down, his long-legged frame set against the rain. He wore no hood, and his dark hair was slick against his head. He was striding ahead purposefully, apparently blind to the fact that he was setting a pace just too fast for the rest of the group. An increasingly lonely gap was opening up between him and the other walkers. Even from behind she could tell that he was he was lost in his own world, unaware of his surroundings. It was as if he was punishing himself by the exertion. Well, if it helped him to walk out some of the grief, that was up to him.

The rain persisted all morning, just as forecast. Glancing around the group, Tamsin thought everyone looked pretty fed up. The boys were dragging their heels and grumbling. Ella, Lucy and Chloe had the sleeves of their waterproofs pulled right down over their hands. Were they really going to be able to keep this up for the next six days? It was only Tuesday, for heaven's sake – and they weren't scheduled to arrive in Canterbury until Sunday.

'How're we doing as far as the route goes?' she asked Tom, who she found at her side. 'I'm beginning to lose the plot here.'

'It's the rain. It makes you so cold.'

'Too right. It's dreary as hell. How much further today, do you think?'

'Did you see the milestone earlier? Dad pointed it out. We're in Kent now, at least. Sixty-five miles to Canterbury, it said. By tonight that should be down to under sixty.'

'And that's meant to make me feel better?' said Tamsin. 'Mind you, if Anna could walk three hundred miles, I guess we can manage sixty. But what's all this about you bunking off?'

Tom grimaced. 'I know. I feel bad. But I'm in the middle of trying to tie up an important contract. I'll only be gone a couple of days. Back on Friday. Saturday at the very latest.'

Tamsin looked at Tom appraisingly. He took after William, whereas Anna most definitely favoured Ruth. But he had his sister's blue eyes. There was an older brother too, James, but he and his family lived in the US. 'What was it like, having Anna as a sister?' she asked. 'When you were growing up, I mean?'

'Infuriating, wonderful, annoying . . . Everything you'd expect from a big sister,' he said. 'She was bossy and liked to keep me in order. But of course I couldn't imagine it any other way. You know how it is.'

'No, I don't,' she said seriously. 'I'm an only. Like Milo. Sad, maybe.'

'Well, I guess the grass is always greener. It was certainly busy – noisy and chaotic – with three of us. There was always someone having a drama. When she was a teenager she spent hours on the phone to her friends, which used to drive the rest of us mad because she tied up the line. Mum used to nag about the cost. It's so different now everyone's got their own mobile. But the main thing I remember is the music. The hours and *hours* she spent playing the piano and the cello.'

'You played, too, didn't you, Uncle Tom?' Tamsin hadn't noticed Beth walking alongside them. She now had charge of Smith, who was trotting surprisingly obediently beside her.

'Yeah. The trumpet. And James apparently played the cello at one stage, too, but he gave up when Anna overtook him. It made him furious.'

'Why?' asked Beth.

'Well, it was before I was born. But the story your granny tells is that James started learning when Anna was really quite little. She begged to be allowed lessons, but Mum said she was too small and her hands weren't big enough. So she sat in a corner and listened to him practise. One day when he was out in the garden, she picked up his cello and started playing. She could read music almost before she could read words.'

'So what did Uncle James do?'

'Oh, he sulked,' said Tom. 'Stuck it out for a couple more terms, then got so fed up with being outclassed by his little sister that he thought he'd stick to football.'

'But he still loved her, didn't he?' asked Beth anxiously.

'Too right he did,' said Tamsin. 'We all did, doll.'

'You know what we need, Father Steve?' said Tamsin. 'A break from the rain for our lunch.'

'I've been thinking about that,' said Stephen. 'There's a church just a few hundred metres off the path. If it's open we could shelter in there for a bit.'

'I was thinking more in terms of a boozer. Not suggesting that we go on a bender, mind. But it would be good to dry off a bit, don't you think? Maybe get some hot chocolate or chips for the kids?'

'What's this?' said Tom. 'Is the lovely Tamsin leading you into temptation, Father?'

'Just a suggestion, mate. No biggie.'

'No, I think it's a good idea,' said Father Stephen, getting out his map. 'Looks like there's a village in another half-hour or so, with a couple of pubs. Now Tom, just an idea. How about you go on ahead with Theo, and look at the options?'

The pub turned out to be an excellent plan. The landlord – glad to see a sizeable party on a wet weekday – fell upon them, and ushered everyone into a bar where there was an open fire and even a rack for damp coats. Seeing the purple T-shirts, he asked what the walk was about, and promptly insisted on a whip-round.

'Milo – you and Sam go,' urged Tamsin. 'They'll be eating out of their hands,' she explained to Beth. 'And actually it's a good chance for me to get some audio.'

She ordered a beer, and then did the rounds. It was amazing, the sound quality you could get with a smartphone; it was broadcast standard. With practised charm, Tamsin worked the room, explaining about Anna and telling the story behind the pilgrimage.

She gave anyone who'd take one a purple *#walkforanna* card. Aside from grunts from a couple of old-timers, her powers of persuasion appeared to do the trick. When Ruth arrived, Tamsin grabbed the moment to talk her into doing a phone interview for the afternoon show.

'Result!' she told the clutch of walkers at the bar as she returned to claim her beer. 'Some quality audio and a good few quid in the box, I'd say.'

'Don't you ever stop?' asked Theo, half smiling. It was almost the first time since setting out that he'd spoken directly to her.

'Not when I'm on a mission, no,' she replied, meeting his glance and holding it till he looked away. She lifted her beer glass and smiled. 'Here's to Anna!'

'To Anna, God rest her,' echoed Father Stephen.

'Anna!' the others joined in.

'Now, boys,' said Tamsin. 'Who's for a bowl of hot chips?'

After that, the day improved. Having dried off and warmed up with hot food and drink, they emerged out of the pub to find that the rain had stopped and there were signs of watery sunshine. Father Stephen steered them down the lane, out of the village, but then shepherded them away from the Pilgrims' Way, down a steep track through the woods in the direction of the ancient church he had earmarked for the day's reflection. They emerged out of the trees into a vast, green valley. First Milo, then Sam and George spread out their arms and hurled themselves down the grassy slope, aeroplane style.

It was an elaborate building, for a country church. An information board inside told Tamsin that Jane Austen's uncle had once been Rector of the parish, a fact that she took delight in sharing with Beth. Awaiting the others, Tamsin wandered up to a side chapel. Peering through the glass she could make out a series of grand tombs. Her eye was drawn to a life-sized white marble effigy of a mother tenderly cradling a child. She tried the door, and was disappointed to find it locked.

'Ah, you've found Lady Frederica,' said Father Stephen beside her.

'Who is she?'

'A Stanhope. She lived in the big house, up the lane. Chevening. These days it's the official residence of the Foreign Secretary. Lady Frederica died in childbirth, aged just twenty-one.'

'How tragic! What about the baby?'

'Not sure. But from the effigy I assume the baby died too. Death in childbirth was much more common in the nineteenth century, of course, but it doesn't make it any less sad, does it?'

'I guess at least Sam and Beth knew their mum,' said Tamsin.

When everyone had gathered, Father Stephen invited them to sit in the choir stalls, and drew their attention to the window above the altar.

'You'll notice it's modern. Like much of the glass in this church, it was put in to replace the Victorian stained glass that was destroyed by enemy bombing during the Second World War. Can you see what the picture shows?'

'It's a Christmas card,' said Sam.

'Spot on,' said Father Stephen. 'It's a nativity scene, created by Moira Forsyth, the same artist who designed some of the windows in Guildford Cathedral. Look at the very top of the arch and there are some rather splendid angels, playing various musical instruments. I rather like the two at the top with those long trumpets.'

'I like the cymbals!' said Milo.

'Yeah, because they're noisy, like you, mate,' said Tamsin.

'Now, earlier today I mentioned St Botolph, the saint whose church this is. Botolph was a Saxon abbot from the seventh century, and from our point of view he matters because he's the patron saint of pilgrims and travellers. Because of this, four churches at the gates of the old City of London were dedicated to St Botolph. On their way to and from the City, people would stop and pray, and give thanks for safe travel.

'That leads me into our theme for today's silent hour,' he continued. 'Here we are on day four of this journey. I wonder how it feels, to be a pilgrim? And how many of you are still carrying the same things in your rucksacks as when you set out on Saturday? Of course, we've got a back-up car, so unlike most pilgrims we don't have to carry our overnight things with us. Most people who go on pilgrimage don't have that luxury and end up cutting down their baggage to the bare minimum as the days progress. It's astonishing how little you actually need.

'I wonder, though, if we might think what else we're carrying with us? My hunch is that we're all carrying burdens of one sort or another. Is there anything that feels heavy, that's weighing you down? One of my favourite verses in the Bible is one where Jesus says, "Come to me, all you that are weary and are carrying heavy burdens, and I will give you rest."

'Perhaps you might like to bring the hard things you're carrying to God. I know that's not easy. Some luggage just has to be carried for a while. But there might be ways of lightening the load, perhaps by sharing what we're carrying with others. Anyway, I leave that thought with you: what are we carrying, and is there anything we can put down? Can we allow ourselves to rest in God's love?'

The huge plus of the silence was the lack of distraction, thought Tamsin. That meant the boys – and Smith – could concentrate on the hazards around them, which in this case included the cars and lorries hurtling past. Father Stephen had warned them about the short but tedious stretch of the route that ran alongside the main road beyond the church.

What was she carrying? While she refused to give house room to the thought that he was a burden, Milo was surely the greatest load that Tamsin carried. Literally in the early days, of course: first in the womb, and then in her arms. Mind you, he still needed carrying today, occasionally; think what happened on Sunday. And that responsibility rested fairly and squarely in her court. Ever since she'd left Frankie she'd been driven by the compelling need to provide for the pair of them. She would do whatever it took to create a stable and loving home for him.

What a drongo she'd been! She couldn't understand why she'd stayed with Frankie so long. While she now understood far more about domestic abuse – and her research showed that her own case was just one statistic in a depressing trend – she still berated herself for being a doormat, and far worse, for putting Milo at risk. She didn't think Frankie would ever have turned on him, but you never knew. And no one wanted a child to witness such behaviour. But they'd survived. Frankie made a half-hearted attempt to win her back, but soon backed off in response to a stern letter from her solicitor. She was pretty confident he was out of their life for good. Thank goodness she'd never given in to the Rossi pressure to marry him. That would have been far more complex to unravel.

But it hadn't been easy, starting again. While she knew beyond doubt that she had done the right thing, she had to admit that Milo had struggled with the move halfway around the world and so had she. Along with her face, her self-esteem had taken a severe battering. Rebuilding her confidence required a massive act of will. The week she spent in the shelter was the game-changer, she saw now. The counselling provided by Shelley, her case-worker with an abuse story all of her own, had been spot on. Thanks to her wise counsel, even in those early days Tamsin was able to see that she had a choice over whether she became a victim or a survivor. Shelley also gave her the details of a helpline in the UK, which she called within twenty-four hours of touching down in London before she lost her nerve.

For a couple of months they camped in a flat in London, sublet from a friend of a friend. She called in favours from everyone she'd ever worked with, and got enough shift work to put food on the table and pay for some counselling. (She even kept on the agony aunt column, until the editor fired her when she wrote an unguardedly robust response to a reader wondering whether to leave her husband.)

Then, just as she was beginning to feel strong enough to contemplate getting in touch with old friends, the offer of a job as a producer at BBC Radio Hampshire came up. She almost bit the station manager's hand off, so deep was her desire to get out of London and find a more permanent home for Milo. Anna had been surprised but thrilled by her phone call and insisted that she caught the first train down to Farmleigh.

Milo had taken a while to adjust to their new life. For the first year or so he was extremely tearful and clingy. He had found

London alarming. School was not a particularly happy experience; it was huge, with three parallel classes of children in each year group, housed in a vast dark brick building that resembled a Victorian workhouse and was surrounded by high security fences. The other children were streetwise and tough, and playtime was noticeably rougher than it had been in Melbourne.

Life at All Saints Primary in Farmleigh was an altogether calmer experience. The school building was bright and cheerful, and the imaginative head teacher had signed up to an eco-scheme that gave the children a vegetable plot and a pond in the playground. Beyond the school gates you could see green fields, and in the middle distance, cows.

Best of all was Mrs Lewis, Milo's class teacher, a forbidding-looking woman with grey hair pulled into a bun and thick glasses, who stood no nonsense and had a heart of gold. On day one, she'd swept up Milo, informing him that he was the very person she needed, because they were making a giant collage of Noah's Ark and no one had remembered the kangaroos and koalas. Milo let go of Tamsin's hand and followed Mrs Lewis into class without a backward glance. That, and the knowledge that Sam had promised to look out for him at playtime, meant that Tamsin had walked away from the school gates without knots in her stomach for the first time since their arrival in the UK.

Two years on, and Tamsin felt they had settled. Until Anna's illness, life was rosier than she ever dared hope. Were they still carrying the Frankie years around with them? Despite the counselling, she was not given to introspection; she found it altogether safer to pull up the drawbridge on the past. But now she thought about it, Milo rarely mentioned Frankie these days. It appeared she had succeeded in overlaying the memories of his early life in Melbourne with new, happier ones. He had plenty of friends at school, and though he still hero-worshipped Sam she was confident that Milo would survive Sam's move up to secondary school in September.

Thank *God* she'd been back in touch with Anna before she died. She couldn't bear to think how she would have felt otherwise. If Tamsin had been anxious about re-establishing their friendship, she needn't have worried. Through a combination of generosity on Anna's part and wilful amnesia on her own, they'd easily fallen into their old, relaxed intimacy. She'd adored catching up with Beth and Sam – *great* kids, those two, Beth such a mother hen and Sam so sweetly determined – and they'd both been brilliant with Milo. Theo she'd seen less of, largely because he worked such long hours, and, as she explained to Milo, it was important not to encroach on the Greenes' rare time together as a family.

By the time Anna's diagnosis came, it seemed the most natural thing in the world to pop in and out of the Brew House with fresh flowers or home-made cordial or anything else she thought might give Anna a lift. (Anna gave her the very same key on the Lego keyring she'd had all those years ago.) Hell, it was unfair, though. Anna's death was a bloody tragedy. No wonder Theo looked as though he was carrying the weight of the world on his shoulders.

'Any thoughts on carrying?' asked Tom, as the silence ended. The sun was properly out now, and the coats had gone away. George and Milo had stripped to their T-shirts. Theo was holding Sam's backpack while he peeled off his sweatshirt. William was pouring tea from his flask.

'Plenty!' said Tamsin. *Back off, chum.* 'You?'

'Oh, a bucket of guilt, mainly.'

'Guilt?' asked Theo, strolling over. 'You?'

'Why, what have you done, mate?' said Tamsin.

'Oh, I guess it's more the things that I didn't do,' replied Tom. 'I wish I'd given Anna more time. Visited you all more. All the time, really, but especially at the end. I can't believe I thought work was more important than family.'

'There is no health in us,' said William.

'Sorry?' asked Theo.

'Bit from the old Prayer Book. Where we ask forgiveness, not just for the things we've done which we ought *not* to have done, but also for the things we've left undone. Often think that's the harder bit, our sins of omission.'

'And does God forgive us, do you think?' asked Theo, handing the bag back to Sam.

'That's the promise,' said William. 'Forgiveness freely given.' Theo opened his mouth as if to say more. Then he abruptly turned his back, and walked away.

'Brave of you to admit that,' Tamsin told Tom. 'I don't think any of us realized how little time she had. But I bet you did your best. I guess we all fell short, one way or another.' *Me certainly. Though I tried to make it up to her.*

'Well, if this has taught me anything at all, it's not to put things off,' said Tom, looking down at his feet. 'You don't always get a second go.'

'True enough,' said William.

'Are we nearly there yet, Mum?' asked Milo in his whiniest voice. 'I'm tired. So's Smith. Look at him. He needs a *drink.*'

'Well, that we can manage, doll,' said Tamsin. 'Fish out his bowl from my rucksack and there's a bottle of water in there too. Talking of carrying . . . funny how I ended up carrying the Smith kit, huh?'

'He couldn't carry it himself, Mum. Dogs don't wear rucksacks.' Milo snorted with amusement at the thought.

'No, but *you* could have done, you cheeky monkey!'

'I'm not a monkey, I'm a *boy,*' he insisted. 'And I'm *tired.*'

Tamsin looked around for Father Stephen, to get a steer on the route. It did seem to have been a long day. She wouldn't mind a breather herself. Where was he? It took a moment to locate him, standing to one side of the path. He was talking to someone. Goodness – it was that crazy bloke with the flowers in his hat again. Had he been tailing them all day? She'd leave them be, for now.

'William? Any idea how much further? Think the kids are getting pretty weary.'

'Nearly there,' he said. 'See those houses? That's the edge of the village. Can't be more than a mile to the centre. Then it's only a mile on to the place we're staying. Don't suppose you chaps could manage an ice cream when we get to the village?'

WEDNESDAY

15 miles
Ruth

Ruth scarcely needed an alarm these days, although she tended to set it anyway. She and William needed to join the walkers wherever they were – and the distance from home was growing by the day – by no later than nine o'clock and there was much to be done before setting out.

Awoken as usual by the dawn light, she eased her stiff legs out of bed to the floor and went downstairs to make a pot of tea. Over her nightdress she pulled on an old fleece as a concession to the neighbours she judged rather too conventional for their own good, and while the kettle was boiling opened the back door so that Smith could run into the garden to relieve himself. He scampered around the lawn, wagging his tail delightedly. How wonderful to wake each morning with such energy and optimism! She poured the boiling water into the old brown teapot and put it on one side to brew while she retrieved a couple of her favourite mugs from the dresser.

In the old days, this had been William's domain. For almost forty-seven years he had brought her tea in bed, always served in a proper cup and saucer. Only since Anna's death – when sleep had become as elusive as a unicorn – had their roles been reversed. Secretly Ruth had always longed for a big mug of tea without the fuss of a saucer, especially in bed, but she had never told him so, instead gratefully accepting his daily gesture for the act of love it was. Now, though, if he noticed the change in routine or the lowering of his long-dead mother's standards, he never drew attention to it. It was just one of all manner of tiny ways in which they had both numbly accepted that life would never be quite the same again.

After a moment's thought, she decided that she would leave William to sleep for another half-hour while she made a start on her morning chores. Much as the dear man loved walking – and goodness me, he was sprightly for his age – she could tell that the cumulative mileage was beginning to take its toll. Or perhaps it was the day-long company of the other pilgrims. William had always needed his space, at least in part because as the youngest of six children he had spent much of his childhood seeking refuge from his noisy siblings. The periods of silence imposed by Father *Friends* (as she couldn't help calling him, to herself anyway) were an unexpected blessing, balm for his soul. Without that, she feared he might come home rather frazzled around the edges.

Today, if she remembered rightly from the briefing sheet Father F had emailed over, was another long walk, with lots of ascents and descents. But it looked as if the route travelled through some lovely countryside, and should be less overshadowed by the motorway than the last couple of days. In the old days, she would happily have walked with William. Although, if she was honest, it was probably decades rather than years since they'd been out walking together. One got so busy with work, with the children. With her committees. The garden.

The garden! She mustn't linger a moment longer. Ruth put down her mug and went to the back door in search of her wellies. Stiffness again as she leaned down to put them on! Were her hips going to be next on the list for treatment, once her knees were sorted? She'd ignored the symptoms for long enough as it was, largely through stubbornness: it didn't *do* to give in to pain too easily. She finally agreed to go on the list for a knee replacement when the grating sound as she climbed the stairs betrayed the extent of her condition to William. She knew in her heart of hearts that surgery on her right knee would swiftly follow the operation on her left. It was a confounded nuisance getting old. *Although how I dare complain when my daughter will never see her children grow up, let alone meet her grandchildren, I simply don't know.* What was putting up with a bit of osteoarthritis in comparison?

Ruth began her rounds, pausing only to admire the wisteria around the back door, which was at its glorious best. It was all very well trying to follow Chaucer's dictum – that in spring folk *longen to goon on pilgrimages* – but there really was rather a lot to do in the garden at this time of year. If she'd had any control over the timing she wouldn't have chosen the last week of May. Still, she had to agree with Theo and Father F that this was probably as good a time as any, psychologically speaking. These early stages of grief were so terribly hard. Having something to look forward to, to plan, had been good for everyone. Herself and William included. And there'd been an interesting article in the *British Medical Journal* recently, providing solid scientific research to prove what everyone had already suspected: that walking was as good for mental health as it was for physical well-being.

At least it wasn't hot this May; watering once a day was easily enough in the cool weather, and last night she'd avoided that job altogether because of the rain. Instead, she'd shoved a casserole to warm in the Aga and just found time to tie in the sweet peas (Anna's absolute favourite) while William took his bath. The lad next door was more than happy to mow the lawn in exchange for a little pocket money, so that was one less worry. But there was planting to do – the brassicas, for instance, not to mention the runner beans and the sweetcorn – all of which she would normally do this week. They would just have to wait. First things first. She simply must check on the asparagus – *such* a treat, the first real sign of summer, and she hoped there'd be enough for tonight's supper – and put straw around the strawberries.

Almost inevitably, Ruth got sidetracked. She suddenly remembered the fuchsia cuttings Theo had given her; she wanted to see if they had taken root and were ready for potting on. She only realized the time when William appeared in the garden, fully dressed, and summoned her to breakfast.

'Cutting it fine, dear heart,' he said, handing her a mug of coffee. 'Need to be on the road in under half an hour.'

'I'll be there,' said Ruth. 'You couldn't just . . .'

'Lunches made. Flask filled. Up you go!'

Ruth went upstairs to shower and dress, and sent up her daily prayer of gratitude to the universe for the blessings of marriage to

William. He was endlessly thoughtful and constantly picked up the pieces; she knew she was prone to losing track of time when absorbed in the garden. It was the same for Anna, when she played; Ruth could remember her daughter's astonishment at the way whole mornings disappeared when she was practising. *We do miss you, my darling*, she told Anna's picture in her bedroom. *I'm trying to believe it's getting easier, but it still hurts like hell.* A sudden dart of grief pierced her heart, almost taking her breath away with its sting. She sank heavily onto the bed, put her head in her hands and wept.

They weren't quite late, thanks to William's instinct that something was wrong. He appeared at her side, took her in his arms, and rocked her wordlessly until the crying fit had passed. She went without a shower and breakfast, stopping only to brush her teeth, and promised him she would have a bite to eat later if she felt hungry. By the time they reached the retreat house where the pilgrims were staying she was composed and ready to face the day.

It helped that as soon as she arrived her son-in-law asked her to take a look at Sam's foot. 'He's limping,' said Theo, who had clearly been loitering in the car park for their arrival. 'I'm really not at all sure he's going to last the day. Today's a long haul again. But of course he won't even admit it hurts.'

'Where is he?' asked Ruth.

'Outside somewhere with Milo. I think he's avoiding me.'

Ruth, glad to be needed, left William to gather the group's belongings into the car and took Smith with her into the garden as bait.

'Milo!' she called. 'Delivery for you!'

She watched as the boys hurtled up the lawn towards her. Both were dark-haired and long-limbed, lanky as anything, in the way prepubescent boys so often were. Two of a kind. But whereas Milo was grinning as he ran, Sam was biting his lip. And most definitely hobbling.

'Milo, would you take Smith, please? Tell your mum he's here? I need to borrow Sam for a minute. Now, young man,' she said firmly as she steered Sam inside and sat him down. 'Doctor Granny at your service. May I have a look, please?'

Sam undid his left trainer and reluctantly peeled off his sock. As Ruth took his misshapen foot in her hand he winced. 'Sorry,' she said. 'But I need to see what's going on.' She felt gently and looked at the skin. The outside of his foot, where the little toe had once been, looked OK. The problem appeared to be on the knobbly gap left by his missing big toe. There was a blister about the size of a five-pence piece on the scar tissue around the metatarsal stump. His skin was red and warm to the touch.

'Hmm,' she said. 'Looks a bit sore. How long's that been bothering you?'

'Only since yesterday.'

'You've been soaking your feet in the evenings?'

'Well . . .'

'Sam-I-Am?' At the sound of his pet name, Sam looked up sheepishly. Had he guessed that the nightly soak in warm water was partly a ruse to ensure that either she or Theo caught a regular glimpse of his feet?

'I might not have done last night. There's table tennis here, and table football, and a really cool ropes course. We all stayed out quite late.'

'I thought perhaps you'd missed your shower.' She wrinkled her nose in mock disgust.

'But I think it started hurting yesterday morning.'

'In the rain? Do your boots leak?'

'Don't think so.'

'And you went to the clinic last week?' Sam nodded. 'OK, here's what we'll do. You go and wash your stinky feet and find some clean socks. I can dress that blister, but we do need to keep an eye on it so that it doesn't get infected. So you've got a choice. Take a break and keep me company for a bit. Or press on and see how you go. What do you think?'

'Don't know. I . . . um . . . I . . .'

Ruth waited. Sam was chewing his lip again. 'You what?'

'I don't want to let Mum down.'

'Oh, Sam!' Ruth reached out and hugged him. 'Do you have any idea how well you've done? Do you know how many miles you've walked?'

'Not really . . .'

'Forty-five! Over four days on the trot. That's pretty impressive for any eleven-year-old, let alone one without quite the full complement of toes. Don't you dare imagine for a single second you're letting Mum down, even if you don't walk another step. I'm extremely proud of you – we all are – for what you've achieved already.'

Sam gave a diffident smile. 'Look,' said Ruth, 'go and have that wash, and think about it. I'll fetch my first-aid kit for the dressing and I'll let Dad know you're in one piece.'

'Right, everyone,' said Father Stephen as the group assembled outside the retreat house. 'Today's a long day, but at least the terrain isn't too challenging. We'll be back on the Pilgrims' Way proper for quite a bit, and the route is going to be very scenic. Lots of woodland and then some rather lovely open countryside through two beautiful valleys this afternoon. There should be some wonderful wildflowers. And the good news is that the forecast looks fine today. Questions, anyone?'

'What about lunch? Could we just have another look at the map?' Ruth asked Stephen. She wanted to be clear on the options if Sam chose to take some time out. 'And does anyone need any shopping done? I've got Mary Anne's grocery list, but if you're running out of toothpaste, now's the time to let me know.'

Lucy or Ella – Ruth could never remember which was which – came over and asked Ruth if she wouldn't mind buying some shampoo, and Milo put in his usual request for chocolate. Father F showed her the lunch stop on the map: a country park with an award-winning eco-friendly visitor centre.

'Any idea which will be the easier leg?' she asked. 'Morning or afternoon?'

'Is there a problem?'

'I'm a bit worried about Sam. He's hobbling, but reluctant to dip out.'

'Poor chap. I'm sorry to hear that. He's been doing so well,' said Father Stephen. He turned back to the map. 'Looking at the contours, I'd say it was six of one and half a dozen of the other. But it's a long day, all right. Fifteen miles at least. What do you want to do?'

'I'm not sure. I don't think it's anything to worry about. But his dignity is at stake.' She thought for a moment, and then called him over. 'Sam? Any thoughts on what you'd like to do today? Because it might be worth my mentioning that I could do with a hand, if you find yourself at leisure.'

'A hand with what?'

'Don't look so worried! It's just that according to my guidebook we're very near a couple of extremely interesting nature reserves. I'm on the lookout for orchids, and I could really do with a pair of young eyes.'

'Orchids?'

'Orchids. Not to mention cowslips, fairy flax and squinancywort. Though it's probably too early in the year for that.'

'Granny, you sound like a *witch*. Professor Sprout out of *Harry Potter*! What do you want all that lot for?'

'Come to think of it, people used to use squinancywort for treating quinsy, which is a nasty sort of abscess on the tonsils. Not to be recommended.'

'Would it work on my foot?'

Ruth laughed. 'I'm rather hoping we'll manage to sort that out with some good old-fashioned TLC,' she said. 'And if not, there are always antibiotics. But I'm taking photos today, not harvesting plants or boiling up potions in my cauldron. Broomstick and black cat safely left at home. Anyway. How about it?'

'Can Milo come?'

Ruth hesitated. She might be being selfish, but she felt a fierce need to have her youngest grandson all to herself. It was for his own good, too; unwatched by his peers, Sam would allow himself to take it easy. She could – if not *baby* him, exactly – perhaps spoil him a little. 'Well . . . I'm not sure it would be quite fair on George if we took Milo. And it probably isn't really an outing for Smith, either. Bear in mind how slowly I walk with my stick. How about we give your foot a bit of a rest this morning, and then meet the others at the picnic spot? My guidebook tells me there's a really good café there. If we get there early, perhaps you could escort your old granny out to lunch.'

'Cool. I'll go and tell the others you need me,' said Sam. 'You're not *that* old, Granny,' he added as an afterthought over his shoulder. 'After all, Grandpa's a whole year older.'

'Impressive work,' said Father Stephen, once Sam was out of earshot.

'I'm an old hand,' said Ruth, absurdly pleased by his compliment. 'Not *that* old, remember.'

Ruth laughed. 'I like your young man, by the way. Very charming. And he makes a marvellous *macaron*.'

'Oh! He's not . . . I mean, well, ahem . . . Gosh!' stammered Father Stephen.

'Ah,' said Ruth, raising her eyebrows. 'It's like that, is it? Sorry if I've spoken out of turn. Better let you get on. Have a good morning.'

The nature reserve was just a short walk away from the retreat house. Straddling the ridge, it was divided in two by the footpath: a backdrop of ancient woodland on one side, a sloping grassy meadow on the other. Ruth walked slowly, leaning on her walking stick, in the knowledge that it would do no harm to her knees or Sam's blister to take it gently. In normal circumstances she was as stubborn as a mule about the stick. She preferred to grit her teeth – quite unnecessarily, she would have told any patient seeking her advice – and push on through the pain, making little or no allowance for her condition. Old habits die hard, she thought. One of hers was impatience. So compelling was her need to get things done that she generally overcame obstacles by simply refusing to admit to their existence.

She paused, in part to take a breath, but also to admire the panoramic view before them. The weather was clear and you could see for miles – twenty? thirty? – in each direction over magnificent landscape. The downs unfolded below, unscarred here by the motorway, though she was sure she could just hear the thrum of traffic in the distance. The colours were those of early summer: that dazzling fresh green of May in the grass and the leaves, peppered with snowy pink and white blossom. A carpet of wild-flowers. A kestrel hovered above on the gentlest of breezes.

The skyline might be short on white-capped mountains, but otherwise it could have been the opening scene from *The Sound of Music*. Anna had played the lead role in a school production. Closing her eyes, Ruth could picture her entry on stage, hear her voice in the opening number. 'The Hills Are Alive with the Sound of Music.' The memory was so close she could almost reach out and touch it.

She drew in a deep breath. At this precise moment, for even just a few seconds, it was good to be alive. She and William had married on just such a day as this, the church filled with cow parsley gathered from the hedgerows. Oh, *gracious*! Had she forgotten their wedding anniversary? Had he? She thought for a moment, and realized with a pang that it would be on Sunday, the day the pilgrimage was due to finish. Would they mark it, and if so how? Neither was given to grand gestures; they shared a healthy scepticism about the manufactured commercialism of occasions such as Valentine's Day. As war babies, even all these years later they found it next to impossible to splash out on family birthdays. But William had always treated their wedding anniversaries with a special reverence. He took great care and imagination to seek out small but thoughtful gifts for her: an early Elizabeth David cookery book, long before the author was famous, the year after their first ever holiday in France; a beautiful eternity ring, discovered in an antique shop, for their ruby anniversary; and last year, a particularly luxurious hand-cream for gardeners, made from almond oil and shea butter that he'd tracked down in a little shop in Winchester.

The other thing she discovered, quite by accident, was that William always slipped into church on their wedding anniversary to give thanks for their marriage. She found this out when he mentioned, very much in passing, that he'd bumped into his older brother Richard at a lunchtime service in one of the City churches. Surprised, she remarked that he'd never mentioned going to church during the working day before. It was part of their weekend routine; he was as regular as clockwork in his Sunday churchgoing. In fact they all went in those days. One did. But the working day was usually so demanding that he barely stopped for lunch.

'Don't often manage it,' he replied. They were eating Dover sole and drinking cold white burgundy at the kitchen table, a rare extravagance to mark the anniversary without the need for a babysitter. (Their eleventh? Of course it was; that was the night that Thomas was conceived.)

'So what was special about today?'

'Need you ask?' he said, giving her a look of such intensity that she went quite weak at the knees. 'I give thanks for your love every day of the year. But today of all days, it's only fitting that I do that in the house of God.'

And all over again, she'd been bowled over with love for this quiet but passionate man, whose faith and integrity ran through him like writing in a stick of rock, who had somehow managed to fall in love with her, of all people, with all her imperfections. Now, she thought, we must celebrate on Sunday, somehow, even in our sadness. We simply have to find a way to keep living. And much as I loathe ascribing thoughts to the dead, I really do believe that Anna would have wanted us to try to be happy.

Sam and Ruth spent a quiet morning pottering in the sunshine. In the grassland they found the fairy flax with its wiry stems and small white flowers. The warmer weather had brought out a cloud of butterflies: she soon spotted a flutter of Common Blues (absurd that something so beautiful was termed 'common'), and a Brown Argus. She pointed out to Sam a good patch of early purple orchids, resplendent with their dense, cone-shaped cluster of flowers. Nestling in the grass she discovered what she thought was a green-winged orchid, but she'd really need to double-check Keble Martin when she got home. And to her great delight, Sam himself identified a tiny patch of what must be one of the first pale pink common spotted orchids.

'Well done, Sam! Why don't you take a picture, and then perhaps you could make a note in my flower journal for me,' she said.

'What's so special about orchids, Granny?'

'Good question. I suppose it's a mix of their exoticism and their perfection. Some of the species you find in tropical countries are quite outlandish – huge great blooms, extraordinary, spectacular colours. Everything from tangerine and puce to scarlet and snow white. They're a bit more *restrained* in Britain but still rather special. Look how absolutely perfect each flower is. They're also quite rare, these days, so that makes them extra precious. Though this part of the country is a particularly good area for them.'

'What's your very best orchid?'

'Ah, that's easy enough,' she said with a smile. 'My absolute favourite is the bee orchid. It's tiny and velvety and really very clever. I must show you a picture when we get home. It's actually evolved to look like a bee. That means that bees fly in, and try to mate with the flower. Which of course they can't, but when the bee touches down, it picks up the pollen. Which it spreads around when it flies off again.'

'Are there any here?'

'I don't think so,' said Ruth. 'Though you do find them in Kent. But it's a bit early in the season. They're more of a high summer flower.'

'Well, I think that's a bit unfair,' said Sam.

'Unfair?'

'The flowers are playing a rotten trick on the bees, pretending to be something they're not. Poor old bees.'

Ruth chuckled. 'You've got a point,' she said. 'But that's the birds and the bees for you.'

The morning soon slipped away. Ruth had rather hoped to go in search of any last lingering bluebells, but looking at her watch (and she really was trying to be conscientious about her time-keeping) she realized that the minutes were ticking by and they still had to retrieve the car and drive several miles through the lanes to the meeting place. The Pilgrims' Way was much more direct. The woods really were at their best at this time of year. Yesterday the smell of wild garlic had been quite overwhelming. The lunch spot itself was a site of special scientific interest and on her list for further exploration. And if she could manage it, the afternoon stretch was supposed to be another hotspot for orchids.

She and Sam made their way slowly back to the car. Out of the corner of her eye, Ruth watched him walk, and decided he looked more comfortable. Certainly he had regained his colour and was chatting happily, recounting for the *n*th time the story of Milo falling in the water on Sunday.

'You should have seen him, Granny. He was absolutely *sopping*,' said Sam. 'Uncle Tom had to pull him out like a great big fish and he was squealing. Then Dad ended up giving him a piggyback but he was so *wriggly* he kept sliding off. It was so cool it was *sick*.'

'Was he by any chance showing off?' asked Ruth, doing up her seat belt.

'Oh, I suppose so,' said Sam airily. 'But you have to remember, he is only eight.'

'Ah, that explains it,' said Ruth as she started the car. 'But what about you? How's that poorly foot feeling now?'

'Better, I think. I can't really feel it. Specially now I'm sitting down.'

'Well, that's a relief,' she said as lightly as she could. She reminded herself, as she had done so often over the years, that the lasting damage the meningitis had inflicted on Sam could so easily have been far worse. To lose two toes to septicaemia was cruel, but other children lost entire limbs. At least he had all his fingers; missing toes were a nuisance, but nothing like so obvious. Her unvoiced fears about brain damage, deafness and tinnitus had all proven unfounded. Sam had, it was true, regressed from walking to crawling for several weeks, but as Ruth told Anna at the time, that was entirely understandable. His foot was badly wounded and extremely sore. He would learn to walk again; and indeed he did. One day he simply pulled himself upright and took a few steps, tentatively at first until he got the hang of it. In fact his balance was overall surprisingly good – he learned to ride a bike with very little fuss, for instance – and he only really wobbled when very tired.

Her further anxiety that the septicaemia might turn out to have damaged his growth plates, stopping his limbs from developing properly and resulting in a whole series of wretched operations, was also in due course allayed. Honestly, sometimes she wondered if her medical knowledge was a burden in the circumstances. It required iron self-discipline not to assume the worst, simply because one knew all the possible implications of a condition. And then, when the worst *did* happen—

'Granny! You've missed the turning!' Sam's urgent voice next to her interrupted her train of thought. *Bother.* She signalled and pulled into a layby. Time to turn round. She needed to get a grip.

The walkers appeared to have had a good morning, too. Everyone was appreciating the better weather. The path had taken them along the ridge, down to a pretty village sandwiched between two motorways and a bypass. Then they had climbed uphill again into the woods.

'It was *really* steep!' Milo told Sam. 'Can I come with you and your grandma this afternoon?'

'Better not,' said Sam. 'Orchid-hunting is delicate work.'

'But—'

'Hey, Milo, want some lunch?' said Tamsin. 'And you know what, I really think Sam needs a little space this afternoon. You and George and I have got Smith to look after, anyway. We can all have lunch together, though. Come over and sit on the rug, both of you. Sandwiches? Crisps?'

Good, thought Ruth. *One battle I don't need to fight.* She wandered over to find William, who was talking to Theo.

'Good morning, dear heart?' he asked, kissing her cheek.

'Bliss!' she replied with a smile. 'And Theo, I think Sam's on the mend. We've been enjoying a little meander.'

'What about this afternoon?'

'See how he feels after lunch. But my hunch is he'll stick with me.'

'What are your plans?'

'More of the same. There's another reserve I want to visit, at the other end of today's route. We've been filling in my journal, and I'd say we're on a roll.'

'I'm so grateful,' said Theo. He looked relieved.

'Don't be daft. You know I love having him. It's a great treat for me.' Perhaps, she reflected, Theo didn't quite appreciate the joy Sam brought her. She was fairly certain that none of the family suspected that Sam was her favourite grandchild. Of course, it wasn't really *on* to have a favourite, but somehow one couldn't help it, just as she'd always had an extra soft spot for Thomas – darling Tom, the sunny, happy accident of a late baby. She concealed this secret knowledge through scrupulous even-handedness in her interactions with both children and grandchildren. If anything, she overcompensated the less favoured children to be sure they didn't miss out.

With Tom, it had been his easy-going nature, a breeze compared with James's earnest desire to please and Anna's fierce determination, both of which proved exhausting in different ways. And Tom had been her baby, when the others were both at school. He turned out to be sweet-tempered and utterly portable, simply gurgling with pleasure wherever you took him. It helped, no doubt, that his brother and sister provided constant entertainment; there was always something to watch, someone to amuse him. Probably she was also a more relaxed mother, third time around. Even today he had the same sunny optimism, the same expectation that life was good. Or he had, until the sudden death of his sister. She wished he had a partner. She and William had always assumed that he would marry Mel, his college sweetheart, a wholesome and capable primary school teacher, but eventually they had gone their separate ways. Ruth couldn't decide whether Tom's unpredictable working life was to blame, or if the relationship had simply expired from natural causes. She didn't ask. But something she had noticed over the last few days was the magnetic pull Tamsin seemed to hold for him. He constantly seemed to be seeking out her company. Did that mean anything?

As for Sam ... well, it was hardly surprising that she had a special bond with him. Not that she didn't adore Beth, or James and Kelly's three almost-grown children, thousands of miles away in Washington. But Sam had been such a *trooper*, so dogged in his fight for survival as he lay there in his hospital cot, covered in tubes, that he'd totally won her heart. She directed the full force of her character into willing him to pull through. Theo and Anna had been so utterly unable to take care of him at the time that she naturally assumed the task herself, taking a sliver of comfort in the fact that, here at least, she could be of some practical help, by fighting the good fight with him.

109

'Ruth. *Ruth!*' She looked up.

'William?'

'Father Stephen was just telling us about the afternoon.'

'Of course. Sorry. What's the plan? What do I need to know?'

The priest was consulting his map. 'There's a church I had my eye on for our lunchtime reflection,' he said. 'But the weather's so glorious, and this place is so lovely, that I thought we might hold it out of doors instead. What do you think?'

'What – in among the standing stones?' said Ruth. 'Isn't that a little pagan?'

'Well, why on earth not?' he said, looking up the hill in the direction of the Neolithic long barrow. 'The views from the top are utterly splendid. But it's a fair old climb up there, and off our route. On a long day like today I don't think we want any detours. Besides . . .'

'You don't think I'll make it. Probably right. Is there another quiet corner that's more easily in reach?'

'I'm sure we can find one,' said Father Stephen. 'And are you OK for the rest of the day?'

'I think so, thank you. I have plans. A few errands to run before we all meet again. I'd better go and find out what Sam's thinking.'

There was indeed a quiet corner, in the shape of a little amphi-theatre. Unlike Ruth, Father Stephen had no concerns about intruding on the privacy of others, and steered the party through a knot of walkers and a family picnic.

'This way, friends,' he called, waving at the strangers. 'Come through. I'm sure there's room for us all.'

'What are you doing?' asked one of the walkers, a man in his sixties, in a none-too-friendly tone.

'We're pilgrims, walking to Canterbury,' he replied. 'We pause for reflection each day. It's very short; just a chance to gather our thoughts, offer some short prayers. Would you care to join us?'

Ruth felt her toes curl with embarrassment. She could see Beth staring at her feet in a futile attempt at invisibility. Was he totally oblivious? 'Are you that group walking for the mother?' asked the man, in a softer tone. 'Anna someone? Saw something on Twitter.'

'We are indeed!' Father Stephen beamed. 'These are Anna's friends and family. You are welcome to join us.'

'Sheila, over here!' The man summoned his wife and their friends into the circle. Ruth stood back, and watched as introductions were made, and hands were shaken. Father F drew them into the group with outstretched arms.

'Everyone, I'm sure you'd like to welcome Bob and Sheila, and John and Elizabeth. They've heard about our journey and are going to join us, albeit briefly. It's always good to meet fellow travellers. You're most welcome,' he told them again.

He passed round orders of service, and led them through the liturgy. It was interesting, Ruth noted, how natural it now felt to lose oneself in the rhythm, to repeat the words, to enjoy the poetry. 'Oh God, make speed to save us. *O Lord, make haste to help us.* Make me to know your ways, O Lord, *And teach me your paths.*' Four days ago – was it really only four days? – it had felt forced and unnatural. With the exception of William, the group had stumbled through the words, embarrassed and awkward. Now it was as if they had been carrying out this small act of worship all their lives. She gave herself over to the simple aesthetic pleasure.

'Now, friends,' Father Stephen said at the conclusion of the prayers. 'Today's silence. For the benefit of our visitors, we spend an hour after lunch in silence, and we always have something to think about. Pilgrims, I don't know if you realize this but today is the fifth day. So we're at the midpoint of the middle day of our journey. That feels significant to me. There are many miles behind us, and many miles ahead. It's a stage of any journey when some of us may be feeling a bit fed up. We thought yesterday about the load we're carrying with us. Life is sometimes just plain sad. Does anyone know the shortest verse in the Bible?'

'Jesus wept,' said Theo.

'Thank you, Theo,' said Stephen, almost managing to conceal his surprise. 'Jesus wept. He wept because he'd just heard that his oldest friend, Lazarus, had died. Now if you know your Bible, you'll know that this wasn't the end of the story for Lazarus. But that very short verse reminds us that even Jesus wept. It's the most natural response in the world, to shed tears in the face of

111

grief. But we need to remember that when we weep, God weeps with us.

'Forgive me if this is painful. But I'm going to suggest that we think about weeping this afternoon. Can we allow ourselves to be held in the arms of Jesus as the tears fall? If that seems too much, can we instead try to remember that when there are no words to be said, God is there, at our side?'

Ruth and Sam lay on the picnic rug. Ruth felt it was important that Sam felt he was a full participant in the day's task, even if he wasn't actually walking the path. 'We'll have our own silence,' she told him as they packed up their picnics. 'Then we'll see what we feel like doing with the rest of the day. Sound OK?'

Sam nodded gratefully. 'I really think we ought to go to Ranscombe Farm, Granny. According to your guidebook, there should be poppies as well as orchids. And they've got something called the pink corncockle. Actually that sounds more like a *fish* than a flower. Anyway, it's so rare it's practically *extinct*. I can't see that anywhere in your journal. And something called a fumitory?'

'You've done your homework! Now you see why I needed your help. That sounds like a fine plan.'

Now they lay side by side on their backs in the soft sunshine. Ruth had pulled her old straw hat over her face. Sam had opted for sun cream and the iridescent blue surfer sunglasses he assured her were the height of cool. They must look a pretty bizarre sight to anyone passing, she thought. How much odder if that passer-by knew that they were meditating on the subject of weeping ...

Weeping. It was almost as if Father F had witnessed her collapse that morning. If it had been anyone else but William who'd seen her tears, one might have suspected that the priest had been given a tip-off. But that was absurd. He'd hit on tears quite naturally, in the context of the grief they shared. At least she *could* cry; it some-times felt to Ruth as if she'd done little else since January. Never in public, of course, but in the garden, in the car, in the privacy of her own home. She wasn't at all sure that William shed tears. It had probably been beaten out of him at that barbaric school, she thought savagely. They were of a generation that didn't – what was the phrase? – *let it all hang out*. Good thing too. She couldn't abide all that ghastly public *emoting* that people went in for these days. She dated that precisely back to the death of Diana, Princess of Wales. That was when the rot set in. None the less, she would admit there was a time and a place for grieving; she'd seen enough bereaved families through her hospice work to know that those who held it all in suffered the consequences later. Much later sometimes.

Just thinking about the hospice twisted the knife in her heart again. She would never in a hundred years have anticipated that one of her own children would be cared for by the very hospice she'd fought so hard to establish. There was a terrible irony in the fact that her life's work – the very enterprise that had taken her away from Anna at the time Anna needed her most – had proved its purpose in such a personal way. Was irony too mild a description? At her lowest moments her daughter's death felt more like divine retribution for Ruth's lack of attention to the home front. She tortured herself with the possibility that she could have spotted Anna's symptoms and thrown her a lifeline in the form of an early diagnosis. It seemed as if her life's work – all those patients tended, all those illnesses treated – had been worth not an iota when she'd failed to save her beloved daughter's life. No wonder she wept.

And yet, and yet . . . Anna had received the best of care from Hope House. She and Theo had been enormously grateful for the skill and understanding of the staff, as had scores of families ever since its opening almost a decade ago. The fact that Farmleigh finally had its own hospice was a huge achievement by anyone's standards. It was the professional success she was most proud of. She had stumbled into palliative care almost by accident. She'd always intended to stay in general practice, following in the footsteps of her father, a pioneer of Aneurin Bevan's NHS in the brave new post-war world. And she'd loved it: the sheer variety of the job, the fact that one got to know whole families in a community. Of course, it had its frustrations – though she had little sympathy with some of the complaints she heard from today's young doctors, which seemed quite honestly absurd – but it was a very fulfilling career choice.

The difficulty emerged as she tried to find a way of combining work with marriage and motherhood. William's hours in the City were long, and frankly in their day one simply didn't expect fathers to share the childcare. Neither of them could bear the thought of a live-in nanny or au pair. So, in common with countless highly educated women before and since, Ruth took a break, and poured her energies into motherhood until they were all at primary school. What she failed to anticipate was the response of her male colleagues when she tried to find her way back into the workplace. There was an assumption – occasionally hidden but frequently articulated – that as a married woman and a mother she was now an unreliable prospect as a partner in a practice. Fury was futile. The new Sex Discrimination Act might not have existed for all the good it did one, when time after time the male candidates emerged victorious at interview.

In the end, she cut her losses and resigned herself to what her American daughter-in-law called the 'mommy track' (ghastly phrase!), accepting the offer of a couple of sessions a week at a practice that found itself in need of what the senior partner until his dying day termed a 'lady doctor'. The surgery was the other side of Farmleigh, but entirely commutable from Aston. It was good to be back in harness, and the hours fitted in conveniently with the school day. She carried on, more or less content, for seven years, gradually adding in another two sessions to meet the demands of the patients who increasingly requested appointments with her. And then, just a month after Tom started secondary school, she was asked by an old friend from medical school if she had any hours to spare.

'Come and have a look round,' said Michael, who was the director of a hospice in Norton Chalvey, twenty miles away. 'We're doing something important here in our care of the dying. I think you'll be impressed. But demand is outstripping what I can provide, what with running the practice as well. I need some help.'

And Ruth had been impressed; very impressed, from the greeting she received from the receptionist to the calm professionalism of the Matron who showed her round. As she told William that night, she hadn't really understood how quite unlike a hospital a hospice would feel. Even in those early days, the care was much more holistic than anything she could offer as a GP, let alone in hospital. And, most encouragingly, it was an environment that allowed its staff to respond to the needs of patients, rather than being driven by the demands of time.

'I'm a convert,' she told Michael over a cup of tea in his office. 'I'll need some training in palliative care, but I assume we can arrange that. Count me in. If you're sure you want me.'

That visit had sown the seeds of what soon became an all-absorbing passion to provide the best possible end-of-life care to all patients. She worked at Norton Chalvey for the next few years, before turning her formidable attention to spearheading the campaign to open a hospice in Farmleigh. The work itself was immensely satisfying, though the constant battles with the local health authority and the endless fundraising had required tunnel vision and unsparing dedication. By the time the builders handed over the keys, Ruth was riding the crest of the wave. Three months later – on the very day the Princess Royal was due to visit for the formal opening of Hope House – disaster struck, and that changed everything.

Ruth was woken by the sound of sobbing. She shook herself out of sleep, disorientated by the bright sunshine.

'Sam-I-Am!' she said, sitting up. 'What is it, sweetheart?'

Sam was sitting up, hugging his knees, his head buried in his lap. 'Weeping,' he gulped. 'I'm . . . *weeping*.'

'Well, I'd more or less worked that out,' said Ruth. Sam gave a shaky snort, half sob, half laugh. 'Come here!' She put her arms round him until the sobbing had eased. As the final spasm passed, he extricated himself awkwardly from her embrace.

'Um . . . sorry,' he said, sniffing thickly. Ruth reached into her pocket for the large white handkerchief embroidered with a blue W that she knew would be there, and handed it to her grandson.

'There you are,' she said. 'Have a good nose-blow. It's man-sized. It can take it.'

'Thanks, Granny.'

'Now then. Do you want to talk about it?'

Sam sighed, a great shudder of a sigh. 'Um ... it's just ...'

'Just ...?'

'Granny ... what do you think heaven's like?'

Ah. Heaven. At least he hadn't asked her what she thought God was like. That would have been more challenging to answer with integrity.

'That's a tricky one, Sam,' she said slowly. 'Like you, I find it very hard indeed to believe that Mum's ... disappeared. It's lovely to picture her surrounded by all the good and beautiful and happy things we can think of. She hasn't gone. Besides, I can *feel* her.'

'Can you? How?'

Ruth considered – and rejected – the idea of trying to articulate her Maria moment on the hillside earlier that morning. 'I can feel her in the air,' she said instead. 'Very nearby. I talk to her. And I see her – in you and Beth, especially. In the way you look, but also in the way you speak, the things you do, in your habits and abilities and gifts. She lives on in you.'

'But that doesn't help *me*,' he said. 'I need to be able to *picture* her. Wherever she is.'

'Do you remember the poem I chose for her funeral? The one about the ship? Look. I've got a copy with me.' Ruth fished in her handbag and pulled out a creased sheet of paper. It was dog-eared and grubby with use. She put on her glasses and began to read aloud.

'A ship sails and I stand watching till she fades on the horizon
and someone at my side says, "She is gone!"
Gone where?
Gone from my sight, that is all.
She is just as large now as when I last saw her.
Her diminished size and total loss from my sight is in me, not in her.
And just at the moment when someone at my side says, "She is gone", there are others who are watching her coming over their horizon,
and other voices take up a glad shout,

116

"There she comes!"

That is what dying is.

An horizon and just the limit of our sight.

Lift us up, Oh Lord, that we may see further.'

They sat in silence for a few minutes. 'That . . . well, that helps me,' said Ruth eventually. 'A bit. It puts into words some of what I feel.'

Sam thought for a moment, then shook his head. 'I still need to *know* . . . about *heaven* . . .'

'Well, I think we all have our own particular ways of describing what happens when someone dies. We can only use the images and pictures we have. And that's bound to be limiting. It's a bit like . . . well, I suppose it's a bit like a piece of music. You and I could both go to a concert and listen to the same piece of music. Suppose Grandpa said, "Tell me about that symphony you heard tonight." You might say one thing, and I'd say something else. And whatever words we used, even if we'd remembered it all perfectly in our heads, he'd still only have an *impression*.'

'There's another problem, Granny.'

'Oh?'

'You'd probably *miss* half of the symphony by dozing off . . .'

'Oy! Enough of that, cheeky boy! That was once. *Once*. When I was *very* tired, mind you.' She elbowed him playfully. 'But what about you?'

'Me?'

'How do *you* picture heaven?'

'Well, it's sunny. There's lots of music. There's obviously a whole orchestra on call so that Mum can play concertos, if she wants to. And she's wearing her special green dress and everyone's clapping and cheering, because she's so brilliant. And there are bright colours . . . and flowers. People laughing. And cupcakes. But I honestly can't see how she can be *happy* there because even if she's got Josh to play with, I know she must be *missing* us all.'

'That's a hard one, isn't it? You do know . . . you do realize, Sam, she wouldn't have left us, if she'd had any choice in the matter. She couldn't help getting sick. It was just the horrible cancer.'

117

'But *why*? *Why* did it have to happen? Why couldn't you make her *better*, Granny?' He started crying again, huge racking sobs that shook his small frame. Ruth hugged him, and felt the silent tears course down her own face. *If only. If only.*

'I get so ... *upset*,' said Sam eventually. 'And *angry*. Sometimes I just want to *hit* someone. Everyone. And then I can't stop crying and it's totally *rubbish* ...'

'Sam-I-Am, it *is* rubbish. But it's also totally normal. Everyone feels like that when someone they love dies. I feel like that all the time.'

'Do you?'

'Of course I do.'

'But ...'

'What?'

'At least you don't cry in *public*. It *sucks*. What am I going to do when I go up to the Academy? It's bad enough with my stupid foot.'

Ruth thought for a moment. He was right, of course. Tears in the playground at primary school were one thing; secondary school would be much tougher. 'Well, I think you need to bear in mind that September is still quite a long way off. I'm not suggesting you'll suddenly stop missing Mum. Of course you won't. But it's not going to be quite so ... *raw* by then. You need to take it from me that it won't always feel this horrible. We'll make sure that your form tutor knows the score, so that you can take time out when you need to. Have you talked to Beth about this?'

'No! Why?' Sam looked alarmed.

'Why is that such a terrible idea?'

'She might laugh at me. Or get upset.'

'Sweetheart, she wouldn't laugh, I'm sure about that. And if she gets upset ... well, that's a risk you have to take. We're all going through this, and we need to keep talking to each other. Sharing the journey. I just thought she might have some ideas. She must be facing the same thing. You know, getting tearful at school. As for your foot ...' She pretended to look stern. 'I'd ask you to be a *bit* more respectful. I've put a lot of hard work into looking after that foot of yours over the years, and I'd say it's serving you pretty well.'

'Will it really ... get easier?'

'Yes. It will. Over time. It's not that the hurt disappears, exactly. More that we'll get used to living with it. Eventually. It's a bit like ... well, like your toes, I suppose.'

'What do you mean?'

'Well, they're missing and they'll always be missing. We both know they're not going to grow back. And that's a real shame. You could spend your life being cross about it. But actually, apart from the occasional blister – and *lots* of people who do long walks get blisters – everything's all healed up beautifully. There's scar tissue, for sure. But most of the time, you manage really well. You can ride your bike and play football. I bet there are times when you almost forget about it altogether. The human body is amazing at adapting. And so's the human spirit.'

Ruth took Sam to the café and ordered two large hot chocolates with marshmallows on top. In spite of the sunshine she was shivering, and judged they both needed a sugar boost. She steered Sam towards a table in the corner, got out the guidebook, her journal and the map, and asked Sam for his opinion on the most likely places to find wildflowers. Whether or not he spotted her distraction tactic, he obliged by searching out likely areas in easy reach. Ruth suggested they made a list of the flowers they might spot, with a points system for particular species according to rarity. Together they worked out a route that would enable them to visit the nature reserve and fulfil their shopping duties before meeting the rest of the party at the end point. Twenty minutes later, when they finally drained their mugs, the crisis appeared to have passed.

By the time they made it home that evening, both William and Ruth were exhausted. Ruth found that she ached to her bones. Thank heavens they weren't sleeping with the rest of the party on the floor of a church hall. She was almost – *almost* – too tired to pick the asparagus. The watering would certainly have to wait until the morning. After the quickest of suppers, Ruth let Smith out for a last run round the garden while William washed up. From the look of the sky, tomorrow would be fine as well.

As she climbed the stairs, leaning heavily on the handrail, it occurred to Ruth with a stab of guilt that she'd been so caught up with Sam that day that she'd given Beth only the scarcest attention. And from what she'd seen over the last few days, she was very much afraid that Beth was hovering around the edges of an eating disorder. She must alert Theo. There was something else, too, she thought, in the moments before she surrendered to sleep. Something from today that was snagging in her memory, something that needed her attention. Well, if it was that important, she'd remember in the morning.

12½ miles
William

William was rootling in the cupboard under the stairs. He was certain that the walking poles were in here somewhere, probably behind the suitcases. James had given the sticks to Ruth as a retirement present, in some fond vision of the two of them striding off into the sunset like a smiling couple in a Saga advert. Knowing James, he would have diligently researched the different brands, read all the reviews, and picked them out with care before having them gift-wrapped and shipped over the pond to Aston.

Dear boy! He meant so well, but had a habit of just slightly misjudging things. The distance probably didn't help, though William sensed he was probably making excuses for his first-born. In this instance, he feared that he and Ruth had let him down by failing to conform to James's hopes. For one thing, Ruth's retirement had come about so abruptly. She'd resigned without warning, and the Board had been very understanding, in the circumstances, and hadn't insisted on her working out her notice. Perhaps if the two of them had had a little more time to adjust, to plan for retirement, there would have been more chance of booking in some walking expeditions. As it was, Ruth had been so caught up in looking after Sam – not to mention propping up Anna and Theo, and seeing to poor confused little Beth – that the idea that they might take themselves off walking seemed utterly ludicrous. By the time William retired four years later, Ruth's knees were beginning to trouble her, and the moment passed.

At his insistence, Anna took the walking poles to Spain and wore them in on the *Camino*. She'd pronounced herself extremely grateful, too: not just for the much-needed cushioning the poles offered the joints, but equally as handy defence against the wild dogs that occasionally plagued the route. Dogs were something William hadn't anticipated; he'd been more fearful about . . . well, unsavoury characters. Ruffians. It didn't seem right, a woman walking alone. Still. She'd had a life-changing experience, and came home safely. In much better shape than when she'd left a month earlier. Almost the old Anna again. Sam was still several inches shorter than his mother, obviously, but William was reasonably confident he could adjust them to fit.

'Ah-hah!' he said with satisfaction, emerging from the cupboard. 'Got them! I'll take these fellows out to the workshop and see what I can do. Might need the vice. You all set, dear heart?'

'How long do you need?'

'Five minutes? Ten max. Just thought these might help the little chap . . .'

'Yes. Good idea. And he'll enjoy . . . the connection. Have you noticed what Beth's wearing on her feet?'

'Yup. Sensible man, Theo. Always thought so. Back in a mo.'

William and Ruth arrived at the church hall where the group had spent the night to find everyone somewhat subdued. Ella and Lucy were huddled in a corner, their backs firmly turned on the rest of the party. Beth leaned against a tired noticeboard, one knee bent, the flat of her foot on the wall behind. She was biting her nails and scowling. Mary Anne was organizing the clear-up in a bright, brittle voice. Chloe, George and Milo were wiping down tables in uncharacteristic silence. Of Sam there was no sign at all.

'What on earth's up?' Ruth asked Theo.

'Ah,' said Theo. 'Morning. I don't think spending the night here was such a good idea. Thank God we'll be in a proper guesthouse tonight.'

'What went wrong?' she pressed him.

'What *didn't* go wrong, more to the point.' Theo looked around, frowning. 'To start with, it took ages to get everyone off to bed because there's only one shower and it's not exactly powerful. The hot water ran out and half of us had cold showers. Then there were complaints that the floor was hard and uncomfortable. Which I have to agree, it was. So no one got much sleep. Then this morning there's been a huge row because one of the girls – Chloe, I think – blew the electricity by overloading the system with her hair tongs. Just when everyone was desperate for a cup of tea and a piece of toast. Tears and recriminations all round. We finally worked out that the trip-switch is in a locked cupboard, and we had to call the caretaker out. Who wasn't best pleased.'

'Hair tongs?' asked William blankly.

'Straighteners,' said Theo, leaving him none the wiser. 'And Sam . . . well, Sam wet the bed,' he added quietly. 'So all in all, not our finest hour.'

'Give me his sleeping bag, and I'll find a laundrette,' said Ruth. 'How long's this been going on?'

'Only since . . . well, Anna. And to be fair, it's the first time for weeks. I thought he was over it. He's probably just tired. He's desperate that no one finds out. I've had a word with Tamsin and she'll stamp on the other boys if either of them says anything.'

'Where is he? I'd better have a word,' said Ruth.

'Sure that's a good idea?' asked William.

'Not about . . . *that*. I need to check on his foot.'

Of course, thought William. The blister. Poor lad. No fun. As for the other . . . miserable business. There was a boy at school . . . well, probably best forgotten. William thought he'd hold back a bit, get the car loaded up, before proffering the poles. They might provide a welcome distraction later. Meanwhile, he thought perhaps his granddaughter could do with a kind word. It was all too easy to overlook Beth. He was rather afraid they'd all been doing that for the best part of a decade.

It was going to be a day of contrasts, William reflected half an hour later. The first mile or so took them past the nature reserve that Ruth had visited the afternoon before. And now there was this long – and utterly vertiginous – stretch across the vast Medway bridges, where they walked on a service road, right alongside both the M2 motorway and the railway line that bore Eurostar trains hurtling between London and the Channel Tunnel. Boats beneath them, a long way down. Once an important trade route, but now mostly pleasure craft.

What was that poem? *Quinquireme of Nineveh* ...Ah yes, John Masefield. 'Cargoes'. He'd learned it at school. Recited it in a house competition, if memory served. All about the contrast between the exotic treasures coming in from foreign parts and English vessels, their holds loaded with coal and iron. What was the line? *Dirty British coaster with a salt-caked smoke stack* ...How evocative that was! Rather wonderful to be able to call upon his own treasure chest of poetry all these years later. Would Beth know that poem, he wondered? Or any poetry by heart? Almost certainly not. Probably not part of the blasted National Curriculum. A change for the worse, in his eyes.

As for change, what about the transformation of Kent since Chaucer's day? The contrasts were unimaginable. What would Chaucer's pilgrims have made of the landscape they would see today, scarred as it was by roads, railways and dormitory housing? Not to mention oast houses, and the vestiges of paper mills, quarries and coal mines. And what about their twenty-first-century walking boots, their waterproofs and other high-tech kit? Surely their party would seem as alien to Chaucer's pilgrims as visitors from Mars.

'What are you smiling at?' asked Theo.

'I was thinking about Chaucer. His pilgrims. Different world.'

'Are we on the same route as the *Canterbury Tales*?'

'Not really,' said William. 'I don't think there's any overlap to speak of. Until the very end, anyway. Just musing.'

'There's a whole lot of myth around the Pilgrims' Way,' said Father Stephen, coming alongside them. 'There are some people who claim it's an ancient route that was walked by hordes of medieval pilgrims. And there's another school of thought that says that's wishful thinking, a fantasy, cooked up by a couple of Victorian writers with an overly romantic imagination. But there's certainly evidence of prehistoric trackways along the ridge. They date back to well before the Christian era.'

'But I thought you said pilgrims had visited Canterbury and Winchester for centuries?' said Theo.

'True enough,' said William. 'Canterbury for St Augustine. Winchester for St Swithun.'

'It was the murder of Thomas Becket in the twelfth century that really put Canterbury on the map,' added Father Stephen. 'But you're quite right. There was traffic in both directions. And places like Rochester Cathedral and some of the other pilgrim churches we've passed provided hospitality. It was a hazardous business, being a medieval pilgrim, so safe havens along the way were very necessary. It's whether there was one single route that's in doubt. And no one's quite sure of the scale, the numbers of pilgrims. Could many people really afford to take off for months on end? On the other hand, if the practice of pilgrimage wasn't widespread, why did Henry VIII feel the need to put the boot in and ban it altogether?'

'I've always been rather taken by the idea of pilgrimage as punishment,' said William.

'What do you mean?' asked Theo.

'The medieval courts sometimes sent miscreants off on a penitential pilgrimage. Often to Canterbury. They had to bring back a declaration, a certificate, I suppose, proving they'd made it to the shrine. Had the double advantage of removing a felon from the community for a decent period while also enforcing him to contemplate the error of his ways. Rather a clever idea, I'd say. Think I might write to the Home Secretary.'

As the morning passed, William sensed the members of the group regaining their cheer. There was a slight breeze and the sun shone again, providing almost perfect walking conditions.

Ahead he could see Father Stephen and Theo in animated conversation. Behind him, he could hear the voices of Mary Anne, Catherine and Tamsin. He was glad to observe Sam walking more evenly with the aid of the walking poles. Ruth would miss his company today, but she would be delighted by his recovery. 'How are you getting on, young fellow?' he asked.

'Great, thanks, Grandpa. These poles are *cool*.'

'Helps having something to lean on, doesn't it? Rely on my stick. Always have.'

'Where did you get it?'

'My father — your great-grandfather — gave it to me. Round the time I was at Cambridge. Carved it for himself, but in the end he had to give up walking. Gammy knee. Awful bore.'

'Like Granny?'

'I suppose so,' said William.

'But *you're* OK, Grandpa?' Sam looked anxious.

'Right as rain, old boy. No need to worry about me. Tell you what, though. When — *if* — I slow down, perhaps you'd take charge of my stick? Nice piece of ash. Like to keep it in the family.'

'Yeah. *Wicked!*' said Sam eagerly. William left him chatting cheerfully with Milo and George, who were taking it in turns to throw a ball for Smith. It looked as if Sam's wet bed had escaped their notice. One less worry.

Beth, meanwhile, seemed to have forgotten her indignation and made up with Chloe. 'Honestly, Grandpa, she's such a *retard ...*' she'd told him earlier that morning. 'Why did she have to bring her stupid GHDs, anyway? It's not exactly a fashion moment, is it? Like ... *duh* ... who cares?'

'Anyone can make a mistake,' said William, getting the gist, if not the detail, of Beth's complaint. 'Annoying, yes. But surely not a hanging offence?'

Seeing the ghost of a smile cross her face, he pushed on. 'Do I take it you don't make use of this ... GBH malarkey ... yourself?'

'*GHDs*, Grandpa.' Beth raised her eyes heavenwards in amusement. 'Course I don't. Can you picture me with ironed hair? I'd look *totally* gross.'

Now the two girls were walking side by side, perfectly companionably. How exhausting all that adolescent emotion was! Along with Lucy and Ella, they were singing one of those repetitive songs you might chant round a campfire at guide camp. One girl — no, unmistakably Beth — sang a line, and the others came back with a response. At this distance he couldn't pick out the words, but whatever they were, the song was punctuated by regular bursts of laughter. He could hear Beth's musical ear carrying the tune to perfection.

Really, that girl could sing like an angel. A rich, throaty, jazz tone. Not a traditional choral sound, but a shame nonetheless she'd

126

dropped out of the church choir. She had perfect pitch, like her mother, if he wasn't mistaken. At least she was still playing her saxophone. Rather well, if that last school concert had been anything to go by. He'd been enormously proud of her solo performance in Big Band just before Christmas. How wonderful that Anna had been in the audience, even if the effort of getting there had knocked her for six. William hoped passionately that Beth would persevere with her music. She might not be destined to become a classical performer like Anna. He wasn't entirely sure that she had the ability or the temperament for the professional circuit. But there was a very real sense in which Beth came alive when she played. Just as her mother had done.

He was aware, though, that Anna's legacy was a complicated one. It could so easily be a pressure on children, feeling they had to match up to their parents. Of course Anna wanted them to discover her delight in music, just as William had wanted to pass on the baton a generation earlier. But she'd been very clear that they shouldn't be forced into it, that they must find their own way.

'It's got to be *fun*,' she said, when Beth came back from a piano lesson in tears. 'I'm not at all sure it's her instrument. If she wants to give up, I'm not going to force her.'

Privately William had wondered if this was such a good idea. Like anything in life, learning an instrument required nothing less than sheer grind at times. Practice, practice, practice. Self-discipline and commitment. Not that they'd ever had to push Anna into it. Far from it. Interrupting her playing to insist that she turned her attention to homework had been the battle. Or to run about in the fresh air. But Anna had been quite right. Beth gave up the piano with relief. Not many months later she picked up the clarinet, and a couple of years afterwards the saxophone. And hadn't looked back. He must ask her round, soon, so that they could play some duets. Someone needed to keep encouraging her, and in this instance he wasn't sure Theo was quite up to the mark. He'd sell it to her as doing him a favour, indulging him. Helping him to keep his fingers from stiffening up any more.

It crossed William's mind that this week was the first time for nearly eight years that his days hadn't begun with an hour at the piano. It had been a present to himself, on retirement: a commitment to bring his playing up to the best possible standard he could manage. While he still had all his marbles. Actually, a way of trying to hang *on* to his marbles, too. Essential to keep the brain active. He'd seen too many chaps slide into oblivion as soon as they gave up work. He'd always *played*, of course – and he'd been a church organist for donkey's years – but never to the standard he had achieved as a young man. He'd steeled himself for disappointment and frustration, knowing perfectly well that his brain didn't work as fast as it used to, let alone his fingers. There was something melancholy in the realization that he'd never return to the peak of his powers.

He started cautiously, with a series of daily scales and arpeggios in an attempt to force his synapses into cooperation. Then he moved on to some old favourites: Mendelssohn's *Songs without Words*, a collection of rather lovely Bach Preludes and Fugues, some more manageable Mozart. Somewhat to his surprise, it came flooding back. Bolder, he braved Beethoven and Chopin. He knew that he would never be more than a merely competent pianist – and the showy acrobatics of Liszt and Rachmaninov would doubtless always be beyond him – but he definitely improved with practice. More to the point, playing every day brought him incalculable satisfaction and joy.

He wondered all over again how his life might have turned out if he'd studied Music at university. At the age of seventeen he'd wanted to, so passionately. His music had been the one bright light of his school days, largely thanks to Mr Miller, an inspirational master, whom the boys naturally called Glenn. Although to be truthful, he was considerably more interested in classical than band music. School – a minor public school that made up the numbers by offering generous scholarships to the sons of the clergy – had been otherwise pretty bleak. Britain was creaking under the strains of post-war austerity and William's main memories were of being wretchedly cold and permanently hungry.

During his endless first term – a period clouded by misery, homesickness and an acute sense of betrayal that his brother Richard hadn't warned him quite how grim it would all be – he had somehow found his way to the music school and sought solace in the piano. The little practice room with the tired upright piano became his refuge. A few days later Mr Miller had found him there and put his head round the door.

'Not at all bad,' he said. 'Been learning long?'

'No, sir,' said William, flustered. 'I mean, yes, sir.'

'Which do you mean? And you are . . . ?'

'Meadows Minor, sir. I mean that I've never had proper lessons. Mother taught me. The basics.'

'And are you having lessons here?'

William blushed. His father had made it clear that his scholarship didn't stretch to extras. Piano lessons were out of the question. Mr Miller, sensing his discomfort, nodded sagely and said, 'Leave it with me, Meadows. I'll see what I can do.'

After that, school became marginally better. Every Monday he missed morning break and half of Geography (no great loss) and instead Miss Evans taught him the piano. Although not exactly motherly, she was at least a woman, a rarity in the otherwise ruthlessly all-male environment. Somehow that was a comfort and reminded him of home, his mother and four sisters. More to the point, she was an excellent teacher. She took him back to basics and totally overhauled his technique, and while that had its frustrations to begin with, even at thirteen he could see the benefits of laying sound foundations if he was ever going to make any real progress. And the practice she set him provided a cast-iron excuse to escape the worst horrors of the common room and the rugger pitch.

By the time he was in his penultimate year and considering his future, he was fairly set on studying Music. His father, though, had other ideas. Although he was now a bishop and money was correspondingly a little less tight in the Meadows household, he indicated that if William expected any financial support he would need to study something useful. Preferably a sensible subject such as law or medicine that would lead to a career and a reliable income. William fought as hard as he dared but his father – of whom he'd always been slightly afraid – proved implacable. Eventually he capitulated and agreed to apply to Cambridge to read Mathematics.

The decision granted him the smallest whiff of victory, because his father – for all his mastery of Hebrew and New Testament Greek – was pretty well innumerate and went to great pains to ensure that this embarrassing weakness never came to public notice.

Looking back from the vantage point of his eighth decade, William couldn't really complain. He'd genuinely enjoyed the study of maths (like music, it was full of patterns and puzzles), and his degree had opened the door to a tolerably fulfilling career in the City. He'd been able to provide for his family a level of material comfort that his parents could only have dreamt of. Far more important, of course, Cambridge had brought him Ruth, his beloved life companion, the bedrock on which he had built his adult life. More precious than rubies, as the Book of Proverbs had it. *And all the things thou canst desire are not to be compared unto her.*

Thinking of Ruth drew his attention to the fact that they were almost certainly heading into another nature reserve now. They had left the noisy road behind and were wending their way up a slow-climbing chalky track. Ruth had warned him to look out for orchids. He ought to check in with Sam, involve him a bit in the search. Though he looked happy enough at this distance. It was a shame that Ruth couldn't walk with them, but it was far too demanding. His own knees were beginning to feel the strain after five days on the trot. But he could, he *would*, keep going. No doubt about that.

'Glorious voice, your granddaughter's blessed with.' Father Stephen fell into stride with William. 'Even singing nonsense songs. We miss her at All Saints.'

William grunted, concealing the pride that flooded his chest. He was immeasurably pleased that Stephen had noticed.

'I don't imagine you muster a choir at St Mary's?' continued the priest.

'Hah! Not a hope. We're too few and too old, by and large.'

'Well, Aston's a small village. Bound to be ... challenging. Are you still the organist?'

'Not often needed any more,' said William. He wasn't sure if he was more relieved or saddened to stand down. 'Most services are said, nowadays, not sung. May all change, though.'

'Ah, your new vicar!' said Father Stephen. 'I haven't met Janet but I've heard great things about her.'

So had William. Janet was young – well, under forty anyway – and said to be very lively. Before ordination she'd been a primary school teacher, and his single encounter with her suggested that she brought a schoolmistressy jollity to her second calling. She would certainly be a breath of fresh air after dear old Andrew, who'd been in the post for thirty-seven years. And ran out of steam a very long time ago. William understood that Janet had been appointed on the basis that the powers that be thought that the parishes of Upper and Lower Aston with Netherford needed a bit of a shake-up. The trouble was, William wasn't altogether sure he wanted shaking up. Too long in the tooth. He loved the old *Book of Common Prayer* and the comfort it had brought him since he was a small boy. The ancient liturgy and traditions of the Church of England ran through his very veins. With his head, he knew that the Church was in danger of ossification, particularly in a little village like Aston. Common sense said change or die. But for all that, his heart rebelled. Of *course* he believed in equality of opportunity – look at Ruth, and all she'd achieved. Look at Anna. Let alone Kelly, his somewhat alarming daughter-in-law, who held a very senior post in a US bank. And of course he thought women should be ordained, if that was their calling. But perhaps they could exercise their ministry . . . well, somewhere else. *Listen to yourself, old chap. Anna would tell you, you're an old fart. Pull yourself together.*

'When does she move in?' asked Father Stephen.

'Not sure,' said William. 'But thanks for the reminder. Need to make her welcome in the village. Ask her round to supper and so forth. I'll get right onto it as soon as we're back home.'

Lunch was arranged for the Bluebell Hill picnic area. Looking at the map that morning, William was relieved: it would be ideal for Ruth, because there was a car park right by it.

'Marvellous place,' she told William, greeting him with a kiss. 'Last few bluebells hiding in the shade. And lots to show Sam, too. Salad burnet, bulbous buttercup, hairy violet. All confirming my reputation as a witch. How's he bearing up today?'

'All seems tickety-boo,' said William, smiling. 'Don't worry. Been keeping a close eye.' It truly was a wonderful place for a picnic. There were panoramic views over the Medway valley. Could there be any more beautiful sight than the English landscape in early summer? If only beauty wasn't so ... *painful* to witness at the moment. How *dare* the birds sing, the grass grow, the flowers bloom when his best beloved daughter no longer walked the earth?

Heartbreak was such an apposite word. Sometimes it felt as if his heart truly was shattering, crumbling, falling apart. Literally disintegrating under the weight of the colossal grief pressing down upon it. William closed his eyes and prayed for strength. *Oh God, oh God, why hast thou forsaken me?* In an almighty act of will, he determined not to give into despair. Didn't do, to dwell. He would lay his pain at the foot of the cross and give thanks for the bless-ings of her life. *I have called upon thee, for thou wilt hear me, O God: incline thine ear unto me, and hear my speech.* There were so many things to be thankful for. *So* many. Memories to sustain them all. Her laughter. Her gifts and talents, musical and other. Countless blessings. Smaller things. The day itself: sunshine, bluebells. Butterflies. The pain ... ah! The pain would simply have to be accommo-dated. Prayed through. And lived with.

'I think,' said Father Stephen, 'that we should have our reflection out of doors again. The view's simply too glorious to ignore. So if you've all finished your picnics, could we gather over here, up on the ridge around these benches?'

The area where Stephen was directing them was next to a memorial stone to an air ambulance crew who'd died in a crash, William realized. Later in the day they would use a footbridge over the A249, named after the eight-year-old child who was killed with her grandmother on the self-same spot. Then there had been that poignant Children's Chapel in the Cathedral. As if any of them needed reminding about the fragility of life.

Media vita in morte sumus, as the old funeral antiphon had it. *In the midst of life we are in death.* There was no getting away from it. He was old enough to know that. Had faced enough losses of loved ones, family and friends, to be unsurprised by death. Not that familiarity spared one pain. It was easier when one could think in terms of a life completed, rather than a life cut short, of course. He wondered, as he often did, how the clergy kept on taking funeral after funeral, preaching hope in the face of despair and grief. But that was where faith came in. *The substance of things hoped for, the evidence of things not seen*, as the unknown writer to the Hebrews had it.

He felt the tug of the invisible thread that bound him to Ruth, and looked round for her. Ah. She'd seen the memorial and been pained, too. He could read her like a book. How he wished she shared the consolation of his faith! It didn't take the grief away, of course it didn't. But it gave you somewhere to take it. A framework to live by. Ruth had skirted around the edges of belief for many years, dipping a toe in here and there to test the temperature. Seeing if an adult Christian would emerge from the pupa of her post-war upbringing, when churchgoing was rather assumed to be a form of good manners. Every now and again, she moved a little closer, then drew back when the water became too deep. Then. Well. The killer blow, nine years ago. Understandable. Perfectly understandable. All too often he himself was only hanging on by his fingernails.

William took Ruth's hand and led her up to the gathering spot. He unfolded her camping stool, and took a perch for himself on a corner of the picnic bench. Let others sit cross-legged on picnic rugs. Not as flexible as he used to be, not by a long chalk. On this occasion at least he was prepared to pull the age card. It was either that or risk getting humiliatingly stuck at ground level.

Prayers for the middle of the day. The words came from the modern *Common Worship*, of course. But still. He enjoyed the pause in the day. He'd noticed that it had become second nature now, part of the natural flow of the day. Like cleaning your teeth or eating lunch. He wasn't sure that many of the party were familiar with the liturgy but there was no protest, no gainsaying. Not even the teenagers demurred. Sweet girls, especially those pretty blonde sisters. Respect for Father Stephen? For Anna? Or – and he hesitated even to voice the thought – the work of the Holy Spirit over the days of pilgrimage?

133

Stephen was doing a good job, he reflected. Not easy. Shame about that cock-up on the route the other day! Got everyone's backs up. But they were probably a rum old bunch, if you stopped to think about it. As for that chap Adam . . . curious fellow. Never knew when he was going to pop up. Look at him now, hovering a short distance away, over by the hedge. Head nodding in agitation. Stephen was having a quiet word, and now Adam was settling himself on a grassy hummock, on the very furthest fringes of the gathering. Well done, Stephen.

Stephen might be a bit . . . well . . . *pompous* was probably the only word, but Anna had been very fond of him. They'd enjoyed a strong, if unlikely, friendship. He'd introduced her to opera. Not William's scene, mind you, and certainly not Theo's. But good old Theo, hadn't minded a bit when William had asked if it would be very bad form for him to treat Anna and Stephen to an evening at Glyndebourne. And Stephen was undoubtedly a man of integrity. Deeply prayerful. And *kind*. No idea he was homosexual, till that young fellow turned up the other night. Perhaps that's why Theo had been so relaxed about another man escorting his wife to the opera! William's innocence on that score had caused Ruth no end of amusement.

Natural choice to conduct Anna's funeral, of course. William could remember next to nothing of the service, though everyone said it had been spot on. He'd remembered everyone's names, involved the children and so forth. Encouraged tears and laughter. Lots of music. And this week, William couldn't but notice the effort Stephen was making with each of the pilgrims. The lengths he went to reach out to Theo, who all too often responded like a bear with a sore head. Undeterred, he worked his way round the group, while they walked, and again over meals, but in such a natural way that people scarcely knew it was happening. And he'd clearly put a great deal of thought into his reflections. He was doing his best to take the pilgrims on a spiritual and emotional journey, as well as a physical one.

William closed his eyes as Father Stephen drew the prayers to an end.

> 'God bless you today
> The earth beneath your feet,
> The path on which you tread,
> The work of your hand and mind,
> The things which you desire.
> And when the day is over,
> God bless you at your rest. Amen.

'Now, friends,' he continued. 'Today's silence. Yesterday our word of the day was "weeping". That was a tough one.' Father Stephen's gaze swept around the group, to be met with nods and murmurs of assent. 'I'm sorry if that was painful. Pain is a huge part of the journey at the moment. So today, can I suggest we turn our thoughts in a different, happier direction? How would it be if we think about giving thanks? Thankfulness is so important. St Paul wrote to the Ephesians, encouraging them to "give thanks always for all things unto God the Father". Being thankful doesn't make the hurt go away, but I think what it *can* do is to help us to come at it from a new angle.

'I'm sure we all want to give thanks for Anna, and her part in our lives. But are there other things we can give thanks for, I wonder? Small everyday miracles, maybe. The sun rising. Food in our shops and enough money to buy it. Clean water coming out of the tap. As the psalmist says, "Let us come before his presence with thanksgiving, and make a joyful noise unto him with psalms." Shall we give it a try?'

It was almost as if Father Stephen had a hotline to his own soul, thought William. Had he been able to tell he was praying, trying to find comfort in the memory of good things?

He kissed Ruth goodbye – she was heading into Rochester in search of a laundrette and food for supper – and whispered, 'We have *so* much to be thankful for.' She had smiled bravely back at him, and then left without another word, raising a hand in a half wave, half salute. He watched her go, and worried for her, the habit of a lifetime. He hoped she wouldn't get lost in Rochester. She'd never been there, as far as he knew. Her map-reading was somewhat

135

haphazard, not that she'd admit it. As was her driving, when she had a lot on her mind. Still. She would cope. Be fine. Had all afternoon to sort things out.

Now. To the task in hand. Thankfulness. He suddenly remembered a song from the 1970s. How did it go? 'Reasons to Be Cheerful, One, Two, Three' . . . Not his cup of tea, but their neighbour's son used to play it, too loudly, one hot summer when all the windows were open. Ruth, sleep-deprived from nursing Thomas, had grumbled about the intrusion. But when James and Anna had started joining in with the lyrics every time the long-haired young man blasted out the record, the song had morphed into a family joke. As for the reasons . . . the original lyrics mentioned porridge oats, yellow socks, the Bolshoi Theatre and wine. Among a number of other unmentionables that he was rather glad the children hadn't picked up. It had become a game making up their own lyrics. Sunny weather. Ice cream. Swimming. Chocolate biscuits (Mummy). Gin and tonic (Daddy). The Famous Five (James). Prokofiev (Anna, precocious, who'd just discovered *Peter and the Wolf*).

Was that what this was about? A list of jaunty reasons to be cheerful? A Pollyanna-ish Glad Game, where you found something to smile about in every circumstance? (How his sisters had loved that book! If he remembered, Pollyanna had even carried on smiling when she was run over by a car. Edwardian sentimental clap-trap! Grace, the youngest, had been especially tedious about it, forever asking earnestly, 'What would Pollyanna do if she were here?' He must ask the adult Grace if she still took inspiration from her childhood heroine.)

William rebelled against the idea of relentless good cheer. Too trite, surely. *A time to weep, and a time to laugh. A time to mourn, and a time to dance.* Good to be appreciative of life, to be positive where possible. But true *thankfulness* . . . that entailed something deeper, more considered.

He warily probed the scar tissue around his heart. He loved these silent hours. They were an oasis in the day. Only trouble was, if one indulged in too much introspection, there was a danger that one simply opened up old wounds. Wounds that were just beginning to heal and were better left alone. It was like that terrible temptation to pick a scab, when you were a boy, only to find the blood coursing down your knee and having to go back to Matron for another plaster.

Anna. There was so much to be thankful for. That much was straightforward. From the day she was born and was first placed in his arms, he had adored her. Where James had fretted and cried, discombobulating him as a nervous first-time father, the infant Anna simply gazed up at him out of her dark blue eyes and he was smitten. She had her mother's red hair, and a look of his own father (oh dear!) around the nose. Until that instant he had no idea how passionately he had wanted a daughter. While he loved James, and Tom, of course, when he came along, some elemental instinct rose up inside him when presented with his baby girl that saw him silently vowing to keep her safe for ever.

Had he done that? No amount of paternal vigilance had prevented her death. But how could it? Regrets? Always regrets. Bound to be. Mainly that he'd spent so much of the children's childhood away from home, working long hours, commuting. But – hand on heart – he was as sure as he could be that he and Ruth had given her as happy a childhood as possible. Security, you'd call it today. Materially, she was comfortable. Good education. Lots of opportunities. Enough money to pursue her interests. And above all else, most importantly, she knew she was loved. At the centre of her parents' world. Rather different from his own upbringing. Endless cold vicarages, children seen and not heard, left to their own devices while Father went about his priestly business and Mother ran her committees and visited the sick.

But that was a different era. For one thing, it was war-time, though he barely remembered that, apart from the day when he was three and a tall, frightening stranger with a beaky face suddenly appeared at home, and he was promptly ousted from his mother's bed and banished to the nursery. Overnight, home became an alarming and uncertain place, with new rules that he struggled to understand. To begin with, he assumed that the visitor would leave and they could all go back to normal, eating supper with Mother in the kitchen and running about in the village with no shoes. Everyone kept telling him how pleased he must be to have his father home safely, but he could remember to this day the fear and bewilderment.

Looking back, now, he could see how hard it must have been for his parents, too. How difficult to live through a terrible war, to adjust to peacetime. After their deaths, he and Grace found a box of letters their parents had exchanged while his father was away on army service. He'd served as a chaplain under Monty in the Western Desert campaign, and later in Italy and Normandy. While his father wrote of derring-do on the battlefield and his own advances in the mission field, his mother wrote increasingly plaintive descriptions of the daily grind trying to feed six hungry children on war rations, and keep the house in some kind of running order. *William was naughty today and tipped over his milk. Such a wicked waste*, she wrote in one letter, causing him an agony of retrospective guilt.

His father had not been an easy presence in the family. He was demanding, impatient and irascible, and after so many years in the army, uncomfortable in a household where the females out-numbered the males. He'd clearly been a bit of a rising star as an army chaplain. Now he missed both the company of the men he had served with and the heightened sense of importance that war brought to everything. In response, he poured his considerable energy into his work, and in his rare interactions with the children, ruled with an iron hand.

No, he and Ruth had been blessed to bring up their family in a different age. There was something to be thankful for. Peacetime, prosperity. Hard to appreciate, perhaps, if you hadn't lived through it. All this talk of austerity today – hah! People had no idea! They should try the 1950s for size. Plenty of jubilation when peace was declared, but then the really hard work started, rebuilding a nation. All those lives lost. Families fractured, cities bombed, houses mere rubble. Rationing that continued far longer than anyone had ever believed possible. Unspeakable horror stories that emerged. Prisoners of war. Concentration camps. Untold evil.

So much to be thankful for. What else? Ruth, his own dear heart. His fine sons. Anna, his beautiful, lovely, warm-hearted Anna. She'd been a wonderful daughter in so many ways. They had shared a love of books, a sense of the absurd, a great deal of laughter. He'd been so utterly delighted that she'd been blessed with the gift of music, though he constantly admonished himself against the temptation to fulfil his own thwarted hopes through his daughter. Nonetheless, he couldn't help but notice her early efforts blossom and flower. He tried not to assume too much, to begin with. He thought she was musical, of course, but as Ruth often pointed out he was a little inclined to think that everything Anna undertook was miraculous.

'No, really!' He laughed as he tried to defend himself. '*Really*, Ruth. I think this is something special. Trust my instincts on this one. I know she's only eight, but she's got talent. Her *ear's* so good. I think she needs her own lessons, not these shared sessions she gets at school. Then maybe a better instrument.' Ruth, lying baby Thomas on a muslin square over her shoulder to burp him, wordlessly raised a sceptical eyebrow. 'Not *yet*,' William pressed on. 'In due course, I mean. Let me at least talk to her teacher.'

He had done so, phoning Mrs Blake from the office one lunchtime and catching her, breathless and just about to hit the road on her way to her next class at a neighbouring school.

'I'm glad you've phoned, Mr Meadows,' she said. 'I've been meaning to get in touch. Anna's been ... well, a bit mischievous in class. She imitates the other children. Plays their mistakes back to me. Frighteningly accurately, as it happens. She's clearly bored. Can I suggest she drops out of group lessons? I can recommend a friend of mine who I think would be a good teacher for her. But I should warn you, he turns down more pupils than he takes on. And he's very particular. So it'll take a good word from me, and then Anna will need to be on *best* behaviour if he's prepared to meet her.'

William read Anna the riot act about her behaviour ('But Daddy, they're all so *slow* ...') and she'd approached her trial lesson with Dominic Jenkins with the utmost seriousness. He lived half an hour's drive away, and Ruth immediately protested about the impracticality. Unusually – for domestic matters were Ruth's domain and not his – William held his ground, saying they should at least give the new teacher a go. He didn't mention the eye-watering cost of the lessons. 'After all, he may not take her on,' he said.

He took her to the trial himself, leaving work early especially to do so, on the grounds that Ruth had her hands full with James and the baby. Mr Jenkins lived in a tall, imposing house, and was tall and imposing himself. He was older than William had expected for some reason – sixty-ish? – wore gold half-moon glasses and looked severe. William asked if he should come in, to accompany her on the piano, but was instructed, politely but firmly, to wait in the hall. Half an hour later, Anna emerged with her eyes shining. '*Please*, Daddy. *Please* say I can come back?'

Mr Jenkins had nodded imperceptibly at William, and consulted a beautiful, large red leather diary. 'I can do Thursdays at 5 p.m., Anna. Does that suit?'

Anna, unused to being consulted, turned wordlessly to her father.

'That suits,' said William. 'Thank you. Very much.'

After that, it was all systems go. Anna fell passionately in love with both Mr Jenkins and the cello. She worked her socks off with her practice, and before long asked if she could start proper lessons on the piano, too, 'because Mr Jenkins says I need a second instrument.'

What happiness her music brought him! Something else to be thankful for. And music had given *Anna* joy. Much more important, naturally. Joy and a livelihood. He'd been so proud of her – they both had – when she'd been accepted by the Guildhall. That marvellous quartet! Splendid concerts, all that international travel. Such an exciting time, your twenties, when adult life is just beginning. Shame, the way it ended. Mind you, he'd been glad to see the back of that frightful Laurence. Rotten fellow. He'd made Anna absolutely miserable. Not worthy of her. Not one bit. Such a relief when she saw the light. Theo on the other hand ... Theo was a fine chap. The only man she'd ever brought home that he could contemplate as a son-in-law. He'd seen at once that this one was going to be different. She was happy in her skin with him. She glowed. Another thing to be thankful for. A happy marriage. *Thank you, God*. And for the children. *All* his grandchildren.

Of course, marriage and motherhood meant that her career took a bit of a back seat. Strictly speaking, it was the decision to leave the quartet that scuppered things. Not Theo's fault in the slightest.

Just the way it worked out. Love mattered. Selfishly, he couldn't but be glad that her marriage had also brought Anna back home, a stone's throw from Aston. And she had found her way into teaching, enjoyed it. Regular session work in London till the little ones came along. 'I'm happy to wait and see what comes, Dad!' she told him, the day she announced over Sunday lunch that she was pregnant for the second time. 'I love being a mum, and teaching in between times. That's more than enough to keep me out of mischief for now. There'll be plenty of time to think about my career later on.'

But there hadn't been time. There wasn't time afterwards, and now there never would be. How innocently hopeful Anna had been – they had *all* been – that day. He pictured them all sitting around the dining table at Aston, Beth at Anna's side perched on a pile of Samuel Wesley organ voluntaries so that she could reach the table.

'Should have warned me, old thing. I'd have put some champagne on ice!'

'Ah, but if I'm not allowed a glass, what's the point?' she teased him, as she helped cut up the roast lamb on Beth's plate. Across the table, Theo beamed with pride.

'Well, here's to you all anyway!' said William, lifting his glass of Merlot. 'We're so delighted for you. Congratulations. Live long and prosper, darling girl!'

To think that within two years the world would come crashing down around their ears. Thank goodness one didn't know what was to come. How terrible to be able to see into the future. He thought of the Greek legend of Cassandra, King Priam's daughter, cursed with the gift of prophecy. Not only was she burdened with the foreknowledge of terrible things to come, she was destined to be believed by no one. Treated as an outcast, a madwoman.

A madwoman. If Anna had been born a generation or two earlier, might society have given her that label? The cruelty of it! Thank goodness there was greater understanding of mental illness these days. Heavens above! He was sounding quite Pollyanna-ish himself now. *I'm thankful that we didn't know what was coming. I'm thankful that when my daughter had a nervous breakdown, people were not unkind.*

141

It was Anna's collapse that dealt the true body-blow to her career as a performer. Not Laurence, not Theo, not moving to Farmleigh away from London and the serious action. After the funeral, Anna packed her cello into its case and drove over to Aston, turning up unexpectedly on a Sunday evening just as they were heading for bed. Ruth was in the bath when William heard a key turn in the lock downstairs.

'I can't bear it,' she said, tears streaming down her face. 'I simply can't bear it. If it wasn't for the *bloody* cello . . . and my self-centred *obsession* with it . . . What kind of mother doesn't notice something like that? Not playing. Never again, *never* again.'

William stared at her, quite at a loss. 'Anna, my darling. You're not making any sense,' he said, and hugged her close. She sobbed, trembling uncontrollably in his arms.

'All my fault. *All* my fault. If I'd had my eye on the ball . . .'

'Darling, darling girl . . . Nobody's fault. Certainly not yours. Come and sit down.'

He put the kettle on to make a pot of tea, and poured her a small glass of brandy while the water came to the boil. She drained her glass in one and put it down hard on the table. 'No tea, thanks, Dad. I'm beyond tea. Got to get back. But I need you to take Chuck. Can't bear to have the bloody instrument in the house. Lock it away! I may need to sell it one day if I'm on my uppers.'

And with that she marched out again, and before he could stop her she got into the car and drove away, leaving the cello sitting forlornly in the hall. *She can't mean it. She just can't mean it*, he thought. *All her life, she's expressed every emotion she's ever felt through music. How can she just switch that off now?* But Anna had meant it. For almost two years the cello stayed untouched in her childhood bedroom, the case unopened and gathering dust.

In the end, Anna's route out of her self-imposed musical exile came from an unexpected direction. Among her many travelling companions on the way to Santiago de Compostela was Luisa, a New Yorker who was celebrating her retirement by walking the *Camino*. The two had kept each other company for three days and struck up quite a friendship. Luisa had practised as a psychotherapist for many years before moving into music therapy. She told

142

Anna all about her work with drug addicts and prisoners, explaining how transformational music therapy could be even in the most intractable cases.

'She was absolutely inspirational, Dad!' said Anna. 'But the great thing is, it's not just for adults. We talked about . . . well, everything, really. Me. What happened. And she told me that there's a real need for people to work with babies and toddlers. Little children. That's what I want to do.'

'Are you . . . quite sure about this?' asked William. Even as he spoke, he knew that Anna was set on the idea. More importantly, this new scheme appeared to be part of a recovered, no, *transformed*, Anna. Frankly, if she'd told him she was planning to retrain as a forklift truck driver, he wouldn't have batted an eyelid. The fact that she was fired up about the future was all that mattered.

Somehow, in spite of the fact that the deadline for applications had long since passed, with a little help from her former tutor she talked her way onto an MA course at the Guildhall. And she had taken to it like a duck to water. Loved it. Found work, first through the County Hospital and then a day centre in Farmleigh. She worked with profoundly disabled babies and children. Got quite a reputation for her work with mothers who'd suffered post-natal depression and struggled to bond. And eventually, started playing her cello again.

When Anna died, William had his doubts about whether he would ever be able to return to the piano. He had played throughout her illness, it was true; having something to concentrate on (he was working his way through Beethoven's sonatas at the time) was the only way he seemed able to loosen the cold knot of fear that otherwise clenched his insides. The sheer effort of concentration required provided distraction, and the music itself brought some comfort.

'How . . . can you?' Ruth asked, hearing him play a couple of days after Anna's funeral. She stood leaning against the doorjamb of the music room, nursing a mug of tea in both hands. He was afraid she thought him unfeeling.

'I don't know *how*. Wasn't at all sure I'd be able to,' he said. 'But I think I know *why*. It reminds me . . . connects me . . . to her. Speaks

143

the unspeakable. When no words will do. Does that make any sense?'

Ruth nodded slowly, and came properly into the room. She squeezed his shoulder as she walked past the piano and lowered herself onto the faded red velvet sofa. 'Don't stop. What is it?'

'Beethoven,' he said. 'Allegedly. Tricky chord progression. Want to get it right if I can.'

It had become a treasured part of their routine. Practice in the morning, as before. Scales, arpeggios, note-bashing. The heavy lifting. Then, after supper, when they'd cleared the table and he'd washed the dishes, Ruth would pour them both a glass of wine or a cup of tea, and he would play for a second time. He chose his evening repertoire quite deliberately with Anna in mind. Her presence hovered in the room. Pieces she'd played, composers she'd loved. He was quite clear in his own mind that he wasn't playing *to* her, exactly, but *for* her. In her memory, on her behalf. And above all, for Ruth's pleasure and his own comfort.

Tamsin was talking excitedly on her mobile phone. 'Sure, leave it with me, Ian. I'll get right back to you. No worries. *Ciao* for now, mate!'

'Good news?' asked William. He liked Tamsin. Decorative, of course. But also one of life's can-do people. A godsend with the children when Anna went off to Spain. And at the end. A good friend to the whole family.

'Too right!' she said. 'The Beeb are interested in sending a camera along on Saturday. I was hoping we might get a radio OB but I reckon this is better. Viewing figures for early evening TV news are top banana. It's a great way to boost donations. What d'you reckon?'

'Um . . . OB?'

'Sorry! Outside broadcast. Where we take the programme out of the studio. We might still get something on the radio for Sunday. But some TV coverage would be great. D'you think Father Steve'll go for it?'

'Better ask him,' said William. 'But actually the person you really ought to consult is Theo. What does it involve?'

'Ah. Sure thing,' she said. 'Guess you're right. Well, they'll want to walk for a bit. See the landscape. Get some general footage. Do some one-to-ones. You know, what are we doing, how's it going, tell us about Anna, blah, blah, blah.'

'Don't you think ...' William paused for a second, wondering how best to express himself. 'Your world, not mine. No clue about this sort of thing. But is there a danger it could be ... a tad intrusive?'

'What could be intrusive?' Theo appeared at his side.

'Got the TV on our case,' said Tamsin excitedly. 'Local TV that is. I'm stoked!'

'I'm not sure ...'

'Ah, c'mon, Theo. It'd be great for our profile! We've got a really solid following on Twitter now. Loads of retweets. *#walkforanna's* really taken off. Almost five grand raised. People love us!'

'Us?'

'The story. The concept. The fundraising.'

'I'm not sure I want to be a story. Or a concept,' said Theo.

'Nor me,' said William. 'On the other hand ...'

'Yes?'

'Well, I assume you know these people, Tamsin?'

'Too right. They're going to send Nicky. She's great. Nice as pie. Really knows her stuff.'

'So, would you be able to, I don't know. Control things?'

'Reckon so. Pretty much.'

'What's your point, William?' asked Theo.

'Not up to me. But it strikes me that the children might be tickled by it. Good to up the fundraising, too. Remind people about two fine causes. Presumably Tamsin can set some ground rules. Stage manage things.'

'When do you need an answer?' asked Theo.

'End of play today?'

'Let me think about it, then. And talk to Father Stephen.'

145

FRIDAY

9½ miles
Theo

Theo woke up conscious that he had enjoyed a good eight hours' sleep. Since Anna's death his nights had all too often been fitful, interrupted by vivid dreams and night sweats. He was used to starting his days angrily wrenched into consciousness by the insistence of the alarm clock, apparently only moments after he had finally fallen asleep. He couldn't remember when he had last slept through a night. As a result, his head felt clearer this morning than it had for months. The familiar dull ache behind his eyes was pleasantly absent. So too was the sick dread that always set in the moment he realized – all over again – that he was alone in bed.

Stretching out, he found himself even more surprised that he'd achieved a good night's sleep: at six foot four, he was uncomfortably too tall for the single bed. Other than that, the Priory guesthouse was more than adequate. When Stephen had first proposed it, Theo had had his doubts about staying there, both because it was some distance from the route and also, if he was honest, because he rather dreaded the thought of staying in a religious community. He was afraid there would be hidden rules that he wouldn't know how to obey, that they'd all have to be on their best behaviour. That it would be austere and uncomfortable.

But it hadn't been like that at all. The complex was beautiful – medieval, at a guess – and the welcome unobtrusive yet warm. He'd been admiring the stunning wisteria that entirely covered one side of the pilgrim barn when one of the brothers approached and struck up conversation.

'Beautiful, isn't it? Our pride and joy at this time of year,' he said. 'If you're interested in the glories of nature, you might like to have a wander round the Peace Garden.'

And the garden had been wonderful. A real oasis. It had been established a few years ago thanks to Lottery funding and a great deal of dedication by volunteers. It was made up of a series of smaller, themed gardens, all designed to foster tranquillity through a soothing colour palette combined with delicate floral scents and the gentle sound of running water.

'Life seems to be so pressured these days that people often arrive here exhausted,' said the brother, without judgement. 'This place is designed to be restful. Somewhere we can allow ourselves to be human *beings*, instead of human *doings* for a change. Make yourself at home. Take as long as you like.'

And Theo had done just that, risking the ire of Mary Anne by deliberately losing track of time. Luckily she'd been distracted by the arrival of David with a large Tupperware of cupcakes, beautifully iced in an array of pastel shades. ('A bit *last year*, I know, but such *fun*, don't you think?')

Meanwhile, Theo had simply enjoyed the sensory feast before him, taking time out from the burden of sadness to live for a few moments in the present. He sat on a pretty wrought-iron bench and closed his eyes. His limbs felt pleasantly tired after the day's walk. He could feel the early evening sunshine on his face. He thought of Anna, his dear darling Anna. He felt the familiar tug of agony and longing. He had the sudden image of his grief as a rucksack full of rocks that he was heaving about everywhere he went. Heavy, uncomfortable. Digging awkwardly into his back. Exhausting. If only he could take it off, just for an hour or two!

While he couldn't set aside his grief, could he at least set it *down* for a moment? Could he – what was Father Stephen's expression? – lay it at the foot of the altar? Tentatively at first, as if he was probing a bruise to see how much it hurt, he pictured himself taking off the rucksack and putting it on the bench next to him. He consciously tried to move away from his instinctive thoughts of the loss of Anna to thoughts of love for her. He summoned her memory – oh, where to start! – and simply enjoyed it, without regret. Her laughter. Her freckled skin. Her perfect smell. Words of affection, daily small acts of love. That fundraising concert at All

Saints last year, where she'd played with such passion. A wordless conversation at that awful Christmas party. *Please rescue me. On my way.* He'd been so fortunate to have her in his life. Yes, there had been ups and downs. But so much happiness, so many blessings. Of course he yearned for her. He felt he'd lost a limb. He missed her with every fibre of his being. But as he sat on the garden bench, he felt some of the bubbling anger that for the last few months had boiled within him leak away.

Was that why he had slept? His moment in the garden? Or was it the work of the week's walk? Whatever the cause, he felt *lighter* this morning, if that was the right word. Marginally more human. As if . . . well, as if there just might be better days ahead. Even the tedious tinnitus of his father's voice seemed to have receded. He began to think that perhaps there was room for optimism. That one day this searing pain would fade and be replaced by something more bearable. Oh, heck – the time! Time he was up. He needed to check on Sam; he did hope there'd been no repeat of the previous night's accident. He must find Beth. Put on his public face. Face the day.

Father Stephen allowed them a slower than usual start. There were only nine and a half miles to walk today, so even allowing for the time needed to shuttle the walkers back to the starting point on the Pilgrims' Way, they could afford to dawdle for a change.

Theo was relieved to find Sam's bed empty, but dry. The boys had taken themselves off to the dining room and were happily filling their plates with breakfast. Theo scanned the room for Beth, but couldn't see her anywhere. Probably still in the shower. Mary Anne (as ever) appeared to be in charge. She and David were engaged in an impassioned argument.

'Honestly, David! How can you possibly *loathe* Nigella?'

'Because she's not Mary Berry, that's why! And with *Bake Off* you get the divine Paul Hollywood, so it's two for the price of one. I wouldn't mind being *his* star baker!'

What a relief it was, not always having to be the grown-up! That was one of the things he realized he found hardest to adapt to, as a single parent. There was no one to share even the most trivial of decisions, let alone the big stuff. Theo loaded his plate with breakfast and went to sit down. Afterwards, once he'd helped clear the table and chivvied the boys, he went in search of Ruth. If she and William were here with time to spare, he wanted to make sure she didn't miss out on the garden. They spent a happy twenty minutes wandering around, until she steered him towards the same bench he'd sat on the evening before.

'Theo, we need to talk,' she said, seriously. 'It's Beth. I'm worried about her.'

'Beth?' said Theo, surprised. 'I thought she was doing rather well. Where are we? Day seven and seventy-two miles behind us and she's still with us. I thought she might have bailed out by now. I'd even say she was having a certain amount of fun. Don't you think?'

'Well, yes. All true. But have you noticed what happens at mealtimes?'

'No, what?'

'She disappears. Makes herself scarce. She's as thin as a rake. Wraps herself in layers so you can't really see, but I think we've got a problem.'

Theo thought for a moment. 'It's not that I haven't *noticed*, exactly. But I thought it was . . . well, teenage faddiness about food, I suppose. Shedding a bit of puppy fat.'

'I fear,' said Ruth, 'that it's altogether more serious than that. She worries too much. About Sam. Her exams. About *everything*. I'm rather afraid this has been building for years. Right back to when she was little. We were all so absorbed with the business of getting through each day. Looking after Sam. And she was always so *good* and eager to please, it was easy to overlook her. And now she's lost her mother . . .'

'Oh *God*!' Theo exclaimed. 'Why does *everything* have to be so *difficult*? What the hell I am I going to do?'

'Talk to her,' said Ruth. 'Or better still, *listen* to her. Really listen. Then maybe make an appointment with your GP when we get home next week?'

Theo groaned. One step forward, and two steps back. A good night's sleep and now a horrible new fear on the worry list. How could he have missed what was right under his nose? Was he a neglectful father as well as a worthless husband? Was he really so self-absorbed that he'd ignored his daughter's pain? Or was Ruth wrong? Exaggerating a minor concern into a serious problem?

'But dear Theo . . .' she continued, taking his hand in his. Both were rough, weather-beaten. Gardeners' hands. 'You're not on your own, here. Never forget that. We're all struggling without our darling Anna. But William and I will do anything we possibly can to help.'

It was late morning before Theo managed to catch up with Beth. They'd ended up in different vehicles going to the start of the walk, and anyway he needed to talk to her on her own. The day's walk started in a country park with a steep clamber up a hill to a ruined Norman castle. Beth tore up the slope, easily outpacing the other teenagers, and then proceeded to play tag with Milo, George and Tamsin, sending Smith into paroxysms of delighted barking. *She looks OK to me*, thought Theo. *But she wasn't at breakfast today*, answered another, more worrying voice. *And what about yesterday? The day before?*

There then followed a series of steep steps – up, down, up and down again – which required concentration and care. He finally managed to get her to himself when they were walking along a ridge, alongside a large area of woodland.

'Beth! I've hardly seen you this last week,' he said. 'Walk with your old dad for a bit?'

Beth was fiddling with her phone. He could hear a snatch of 'The Long and Winding Road' played on the saxophone. Since when had Beth discovered the Beatles? He willed her to look up. ''Kay,' she answered finally, shrugging. A couple more taps, and she shoved her phone deep into her pocket.

'So . . . how's it going?' he asked, relieved to have her attention.
'Yeah. All right, I guess.'
'Legs surviving? Managing OK in those boots?'
'Yeah. All good.'

She wasn't making it easy for him. 'I'm sorry you missed that party. Has Natasha been in touch?'

150

'It's, like, *fine*. Sounded majorly *tragic*, if you really want to know. Loser city.'

'Well, that's a relief, then.' Beth shot him a look. 'I mean . . . I thought you were really disappointed about missing it.'

'That was . . . *then*,' she said. Theo detected – what? a secretive smile? – cross her face. *Don't ask, don't blow it.*

'Er, good. So, what else is anyone up to this half-term?'

'God, Dad. Isn't it *obvious*? Revision, of course. Like, GCSEs?'

'Ah! Of course. GCSEs.' How could he have forgotten? That awful parents' evening. 'I always dreaded exams when I was your age. Got horribly nervous. Mind went blank. Not my strong point. Suspect your mother flew through them.'

'Well, she had, like, a system?'

'A system? How on earth do you know that? And what sort of system, anyway?'

'So, Granny told me. Lots of index cards. All alphabetical. Highlighter pens. You know.'

'Sounds like Mum and her lists.'

'Yeah, except one awful time she'd used, like, washable ink for her notes. Like, one of those fountain pens you used in the old days? And the highlighter pen dissolved the writing underneath. Appaz Mum went *ballistic*.'

'Oh, heck! Poor old Mum. I never knew that. Still, she did all right. In her exams, I mean. What about you?'

'What *about* me?'

'Have you got a system? Like Mum's? Maybe not index cards, but something more twenty-first century?'

'God, Dad, what do *you* think?'

'Um . . . do I take it that's a "No"?'

'Fuck's sake, Dad!' Beth was shouting now. Her face was white with rage. 'How do you expect me to *revise* when I'm on this stupid bloody walk? I can't exactly carry my files with me, can I? I don't know why you've got to cross-examine me about my exams anyway! Who bloody *cares*? What does it matter how I do? Who *gives* a shit?' And with that, she marched off.

'Jesus, Mary and Joseph, what was all that about?' asked Tamsin.

'Bloody hell, don't *you* start!'

'Hey, mate! Don't turn on me! Just trying to help, OK?'

'Sorry,' said Theo, turning to her and forcing a sheepish smile. 'Sorry, Tamsin. Completely out of order. Not your fault. Mine. I was just *chatting* to Beth . . . and she . . . well, you heard. She lost it.'

'About? What were you talking about?'

'This and that . . . and then I made the mistake of asking about her GCSEs. She completely flew off the handle.'

'Sounds to me like she's scared,' said Tamsin.

'Scared? Why?'

'Here, Smith! *Smith!* Come here, you mad dog, or you'll have to go on the lead!' Reluctantly, Smith abandoned the pursuit of whatever had taken him hurtling into the depths of the wood, and turned back to rejoin the walkers on the path. He wagged his tail enthusiastically, his pink tongue hanging out of his mouth.

'Well, I don't suppose her mind's been on her studies, the last few months,' Tamsin continued. 'She's probably scared shitless that she's going to come a gutser. Wondering what happens next if it all goes wrong. No wonder she threw a wobbly.'

Oh God. How could I not know that? 'I just don't seem to be able to talk to her any more,' he said. 'And I can't help worrying about her.' He looked at Tamsin, a thought striking him. 'The pair of you seem thick as thieves. Does she confide in you?'

'Well, of course she misses her mum.' Theo sensed that Tamsin was choosing her words with care. 'We talk about that. And girl stuff. All sorts of things. She's only fifteen, remember. She's a great kid, Theo. Guess you just need to keep the door open.'

Lunchtime saw a welcome pause for refreshment at a pub along the Pilgrims' Way.

'Sorry, guys, but there's no argument on this one,' said Tamsin with mock regret. 'I point blank refuse to miss out on a boozer called The Dirty Habit. How great is that?'

Fortunately the pub was as appealing as its name: a solid, red-brick Georgian coaching inn with wooden beams and panelling, an ancient brick floor and a bread oven in the fireplace, along with a tradition of serving pilgrims that apparently dated back to the

Middle Ages. A greengrocer's apostrophe declared one bench *Reserved for Monk's*. Theo gratefully accepted a pint from the landlord, and watched Tamsin work her magic round the lunchtime drinkers. She really could charm the birds out of the trees! How did she do it? Which reminded him: the TV people. A knot of anxiety formed in the pit of his stomach. He'd agreed, swayed by William and finally cajoled by Tamsin, who persuaded him that it was a way of honouring Anna's life. ('Pretty sure she'd have gone for it, if the boot was on the other foot, mate. But your call, obvs.') Well, she'd better not let him down, he thought grimly.

Ruth arrived, late and breathless, but lit up by a visit to another nature reserve. 'It was utterly idyllic!' she told Sam. 'Shame you weren't with me today. It's one of the best remaining examples of an unimproved hay-meadow in Kent. Marvellous meadow grasses! And more green-winged orchids than you could shake a stick at.' How good it was to see her smiling! And how good she was with Sam. Now Theo supposed he'd have to tell her what a mess he'd made of talking to Beth.

'Friends,' said Father Stephen. 'I'm afraid there's rain forecast for this afternoon. Would you mind if we press on? I suggest we head towards the church, and eat our picnics in the graveyard. Then we'll have our usual pause for prayer and reflection.'

Theo drained his glass and headed up the road with the others. 'I really like this part of the day,' he heard Chloe telling Catherine.

'Me too,' said Catherine. 'I'm going to miss it next week.'

Wasn't it odd? reflected Theo. It was the last thing he'd expected, but he felt the same. What was it? The words? The simple act of taking a break in the middle of the day? The community they had formed? Part of the secret lay in the routine: the fact that every day had a rhythm and you didn't have to think too hard. That was restful in itself. Allowing yourself to be carried along by the flow. Like letting out a deep breath you'd been holding too long. Which was bizarre, when you thought about it, because along with the silence came homework. But whatever the reason, the times of reflection, as much as the walking, seemed to be weaving some kind of healing spell.

Father Stephen led them down the road into a large flint church with a square tower. Inside the church was light and bright and smelled of fresh paint. The walkers distributed themselves in the pews. Beth – she was definitely avoiding him – huddled in a corner with Ella and Lucy. Chloe squeezed in next to the sisters. Theo took a seat next to Catherine, and Mary Anne slipped in on his other side.

'This church is associated with the Culpeper family, who owned Leeds Castle, just up the road,' said Father Stephen at the end of the liturgy. 'Some splendid monuments. And in the vestry there's an exquisite piece of embroidery, called the Culpeper needlework. It dates back to the seventeenth century.

'I don't know if you've ever looked at a piece of embroidery, but I've always found it fascinating. On one side you have an intricate pattern or picture. But turn it over, and you can see the embroiderer's workings. It's quite a mess – all the threads woven in, sometimes quite randomly, to keep the front together.

'I think our lives are a bit like that. The world sees the face we want to present. All in order! But those who know us really well understand that there's often another story behind the front. A story of hard grind and disappointment and things that haven't gone so well. Perhaps things we feel bad about. That's certainly true for me. There are things in my life that I'd rather other people didn't know about. As a Christian I believe that God sees everything. There's no hiding from God. Quite an uncomfortable thought! But the good news is that God forgives. There's truly nothing so awful, so shameful, that we can't receive God's forgiveness.'

Oh, *God*. Where was this going? Theo stared unseeing straight ahead. 'So my thought today is that we take some time to think about the knotty subject of "forgiveness". I know it's another tough one. We're all human, which means we all need forgiveness. And when someone dies, it can be particularly hard if there are things we feel we haven't said "sorry" for. Perhaps because we ran out of time, or we didn't realize that it needed saying until it was too late. That's tough.

'Just as tough is the fact that we may actually be angry with the person who's died. Either because of something they've done, or simply because it feels as if they've abandoned us. And then we feel guilty for being angry. So. Our usual task. An hour's peace and quiet, to think about forgiveness, as we walk the next few miles.'

Hell's bells. Where to start? Guilt, forgiveness needed . . . He had a list as long as your arm. Right now, he was feeling guilty for upsetting Beth. For failing her. For having no idea what was going on in her head right now. Was Ruth right – had they all neglected her well-being from the very beginning? It was perfectly possible. Until the teenage hormones kicked in she'd been so easy, really. Anxious to please at school, eager to help at home. Apparently. What had she been bottling up inside her?

The trouble was, Beth had had to grow up very fast. She was only four, not quite five, when the twins were born. A beloved only child who suddenly found that she had not one but two siblings. Anna worked so hard to make sure she felt involved, included. 'I don't know what we'd do without Beth,' she said to visitors more than once in Beth's hearing. 'She's such a wonderful help with the boys.'

And she *had* been. At that age she was old enough to fetch nappies and muslin squares and to watch one baby while Anna was changing the other. She always knew which twin was which, and patiently put the health visitor straight when she muddled them up. Had they got that wrong? Not allowed her to be a baby for long enough? Everything about her behaviour suggested that she relished the role of big sister, enjoyed the sense of importance it gave her. 'Mummy, I think Sam needs changing,' she would announce solemnly. Or: 'Daddy, you should probably give Josh his rattle. He gets very cross when he can't reach it.'

But that was then. Halcyon days, compared with what came afterwards. That awful day when the boys were eighteen months old and first Sam and then Josh fell ill. They were rushed into hospital with terrifying speed, as what appeared to be a routine childhood bug suddenly spiralled into something far worse. At that point his concern – and Anna's too – had been to keep Beth well out of the way for her own safety.

It had been unspeakably frightening. Anna's panicky message on his mobile ('Theo, you need to come to the hospital. *Right now*. Just come. Don't waste a single second!') had him running through the car park to the Land Rover and hurtling through the lanes. On Anna's instruction, he rang his mother from the car to implore her to come and collect Beth. That in itself was a measure of the seriousness of the situation, because Marion was an anxious grandmother and, unlike Ruth and William, rarely babysat. But Anna wanted her own mother at the hospital, to interpret symptoms, to quiz the staff, to fight any battles that might need fighting.

By the time he reached the hospital not only was Ruth at Anna's side but William was there too. Theo was confused; it was the middle of a working day. How could he have got back from London so quickly? He'd entirely forgotten that today, of course, was to have been Ruth's big day. The day when, after years of campaigning and fundraising, Hope House was finally to be declared open by a royal visitor. William had taken the afternoon off to honour her achievement and share the moment when her long-held vision became a reality.

William had been marvellous. He calmly walked Beth to Granny Greene's car and promised to look in to read her a bedtime story, if Granny G wouldn't mind. And then he quietly ferried cups of tea and unwanted sandwiches and messages between them all as they took increasingly anxious turns around the two cots which were – most unfortunately – at opposite ends of the corridor, because Sam was by now in intensive care.

Because at that stage it was Sam who appeared to be more seriously ill. Theo would never forget that plaintive cry, entirely unrecognizable as anything he had ever heard from any baby, before or since. Late into the night, while Anna and Ruth kept vigil at Sam's bedside, and Theo sat with Josh, he must have dozed off, because the next thing he knew, he was jolted out of sleep by the beeping of machines and the swift arrival of a nurse.

And suddenly Josh's breathing was all gaspy and his blood pressure was crashing through the floor as septic shock set in. Anna was running and it was all systems go as doctors materialized out of nowhere and Josh was moved into intensive care and they were warned he was deteriorating. And then ... and then ... by the following evening everything went up another gear still as the medical team fought and fought and failed to save his life.

After that, it was all the most ghastly fog. Anna cradling Josh in her arms, rocking him back and forth, and weeping noisily and messily as if her heart had broken into a million pieces. Josh's little body all cold, his head lolling. Ruth, grim-faced and determined, calmly reporting that Sam's observations appeared to have stabilized, but she didn't think he was out of the woods yet, and asking for the consultant paediatrician to be summoned as a matter of urgency. William arriving with fresh coffee in a flask and the news that Beth was absolutely fine, in the circumstances, and that she and Granny G had spent much of the day happily working on an enormous jigsaw puzzle of the Kings and Queens of England.

As for Theo ... what had he done? What had he contributed? All he could remember was standing about in helpless confusion. And though there were endless questions to answer and forms to fill in and he went through the motions, his brain refused to process the information before him. He felt entirely disorientated, as if he was observing a scene from a long way away involving other people that had nothing whatsoever to do with him. His arms and legs seemed no longer to belong to him. For the first time in his life, he understood the phrase *living nightmare*.

If they had overlooked Beth in the aftermath, was it any great wonder? Was it too late to ask for forgiveness now, all these years later? He remembered Anna's angst, the appalling guilt that had followed. She should have known the boys were ill. That it wasn't just a sniffle. She was so determined not to be an overanxious mother that she'd taken them with her to a rehearsal that morning. Gone out on a chilly autumn day! Had she not dressed them warmly enough? How could she have missed the signs of something so serious? Why hadn't she been watching over Josh in the night? If she had been there, rather than at Sam's bedside, surely she would have noticed his temperature rising, his increased agitation. And if she hadn't been weeping over Josh, would she have spotted that something awful was happening to Sam's feet? Could she have saved his toes by responding more swiftly? Now he was maimed, scarred for life. Permanently disfigured and disabled.

And why had she chosen that day of all days to take the car in for a service, which meant that they had to wait for an ambulance to take them to the hospital? Why was she out at all, let alone encumbered with a cello? Why hadn't she given up work altogether when the children were born? Why wasn't she at home, holding them close, keeping them safe from danger? How had they caught the illness in the first place? Was this punishment for sending them to nursery so that she could work, for trying to have her cake and eat it?

Round and round it went on a never-ending loop. The endless recriminations, the blame, the self-flagellation. If they were thinking about forgiveness ... well, Anna couldn't forgive herself. She couldn't forgive *him* for falling asleep at Josh's bedside. She was a terrible mother. She didn't deserve children. And so on; on and on. Until, forty-eight hours later, she finally slept for a few hours. And when she woke, sank into that ghostly bleak silence. Which was almost worse than the ranting. She'd eventually stirred herself into action for the funeral, played an unbearably poignant piece of music for Josh, and then vowed never to touch the cello again.

If Theo had known then what he knew now, he wondered what, if anything, he would have done – what he *could* have done – differently. Because, of course, that had just been the beginning. While he struggled to come to terms with his own grief and guilt (why *had* he fallen asleep? could it have made a difference?) he had to watch his adored wife plummet head first into the abyss. To begin with, they clung to each other, victims of a disaster that had shipwrecked their lives. But before he knew it, the Anna he knew and loved had become unreachable behind a wall of silence. Unrecognizable.

Nothing he did seemed to help. He felt impotent, frustrated and furious. Perhaps if he hadn't been grieving himself, he would have been less hard on her. But he found himself incandescent that on the scales of public opinion, a mother's mourning appeared to outweigh a father's. She was allowed to fall to pieces. But someone had to earn a living. Put food on the table. Take Beth to school and Sam to the hospital for check-ups. Go shopping, clean the house, do the washing (sod the ironing). Hold everything together. 'How's Anna?' asked everyone, kindness writ large in their concerned expressions. No one asked after him. Or . . . had they? Perhaps he had simply closed his ears to any such enquiries. Brushed them off. He genuinely couldn't remember.

Eventually, of course, she picked herself up. He wasn't sure what the tipping point was, but one day he came home from work to find her sitting at the kitchen table with Beth, who was colouring with felt pens. Sam was curled up on the sofa with his thumb in his mouth, watching CBeebies. Anna had washed her hair – he could smell her shampoo – and was wearing a top he hadn't seen for years. The kitchen was unusually clean and tidy, there was fresh fruit in the bowl, and the table was laid for supper.

'I've made some chilli,' she said. 'And jacket potatoes. Are you ready to eat?'

At the sight of him, Beth wriggled off her mother's lap and ran over to give Theo a hug. 'There's a surprise, Daddy!' she said. 'Mummy's feeling better today and so we've made some cookies.'

'Not such a surprise any more!' Theo teased Beth. 'But that's lovely, sweetheart. Did you help with the washing-up as well? It looks as if you've had a big clean-up here!'

They tiptoed cautiously around each other all evening. 'I'm sorry, Theo,' she said finally, as they went up to bed. 'I am trying. But I've realized I can't do this on my own. I'm not strong enough. I need some professional help.'

That was just the first small step. Things certainly didn't change overnight. He found out later that she'd left the children with her mother and been to see Father Stephen, and her GP. Talked to Ruth, and Tamsin, of course. In fact, she seemed to have sought solace everywhere but with him. Now, he thought, was that so surprising? They had each been so locked up in their own misery that neither had any emotional resources to spare. No wonder couples who lost a child so often split up. At least their marriage had survived. By the skin of their teeth.

159

Theo took a huge breath to steady himself. *Oh God, this is hard. Do I have to do this?* He looked around him. The track stretched ahead, long and straight. In the distance he could see the outline of a large factory, bizarrely out of place in this rural wooded setting. Clouds were amassing on the horizon. Father Stephen was probably right about the rain. The sky was heavy and grey. An incongruous snatch of song floated into his mind: *There may be trouble ahead*, he hummed. Then what? Something about moonlight? Yes. *But while there's moonlight and music and love and romance, let's face the music and dance.*

How appropriate! Well, if he was going to face the music, he needed to be honest with himself. Look himself squarely in the eye. He found himself struck suddenly by the realization that he couldn't have done this a month ago. Before this week, in fact. Somewhere, deep inside, a key had turned in a heavy door he hadn't even known was locked. Where was he? He steeled himself. Six months after Josh's death, Anna was a great deal better. *They* were better. She was on antidepressants and had had bereavement counselling. (He declined the offer; he couldn't see himself sharing his private feelings with a stranger.) But they were at least talking about what had happened. About Sam's feet – he was making steady progress now and, thank goodness, all the signs suggested that his brain was undamaged. They talked about their beloved boy and how much they missed him. Or at least they tried to, although it wasn't easy because whenever Josh's name came up in conversation Beth always interrupted ('Look what Sam's doing!') or created a diversion by spilling a drink or dropping a bowl. But they were more or less on an even keel, Theo thought. A lot better than they had been, anyway, and definitely heading in the right direction.

Then one day, Theo came home after a particularly long day at the end of a punishing fortnight. It was nearly Easter and an absolute peak time for business, crucial for his annual figures. He'd had an unpleasant run-in with a supplier over the non-delivery of his entire order of summer-flowering bulbs. Much worse, he had just been forced to give a member of staff his marching orders, after discovering that he'd had his fingers in the till. Theo felt

160

particularly let down, as he'd stuck his neck out giving a job to Anatole who had only recently come out of a young offenders' unit. He'd wanted to give the lad a chance. Anatole had betrayed his trust, and badly.

With the benefit of hindsight, Theo could see that the day's events had left him drained and defensive, and spoiling for a fight. By the time he got back, he realized that he'd long since missed bathtime and he fully anticipated Anna's reproach. Instead, she greeted him without comment on his time-keeping, and poured him a glass of red wine to drink while she finished preparing the supper. The kitchen was aromatic with the smell of a slow-cooking casserole. There were candles on the table and a plate of French cheese sitting out on the sideboard.

'Do go up and say goodnight, but they've had their stories,' she said. 'I should think Sam's asleep by now. Please don't let Beth keep you chatting. It's time her light was out. And then there's something really important I want to talk about.'

Over supper she told him about her madcap plan to go to Spain and walk the *Camino*. He was completely thrown. The idea seemed to have come from nowhere. He felt a surge of confusion, swiftly followed by anger.

'*How* long?' he asked.

'A month. Perhaps a little less.'

'And how am I supposed to manage? How on earth do you imagine I can run a business *and* look after the children?'

'I've thought about that. Mum and Dad have offered to help. And even better, Tamsin's available.'

'Tamsin?'

'Yes. She's got a short-term contract in Guildford. She needs somewhere to live and I thought she could be a kind of au pair for a few weeks. You know how brilliant she is with the kids.'

'So you've asked her already? And your parents?'

'Well, in principle. I thought there was no point us discussing it unless there was a realistic way of making it happen.' She picked at her salad, and then dropped her fork. 'You've been very busy, these last couple of weeks. There hasn't really been a good moment before now.'

'I'm *very busy* because I've got a business to run, in case you've forgotten. A business on which we all depend for our living, while you're not gainfully employed.' A tide of fury welled up inside him. 'Aside from the fact that I seem to be the very last person to hear of this plan – and I am your *husband*, you know – where on earth has this come from? What's this all about?'

'I guess it's been evolving, slowly,' said Anna. 'I know I haven't been easy to live with. But I'm much better. *We're* much better. We've lost our son and we've been through hell, Theo. I don't suppose our life will ever be the same again. But for me . . . I need some time out. I think if I can get away for a bit, do something totally different, I can have some thinking time. Some praying time.'

'Bit bloody late for praying, isn't it?' Theo shouted. 'If your God had been listening, don't you think he just *might* have done the decent thing and let Josh live? Let alone the minor matter of Sam's toes?'

'Don't be like that, Theo . . . Maybe it's hard to understand but I want to do this in *memory* of Josh. It just seems totally the right thing to do. Stephen says . . .'

'*Stephen* says? Well, what Stephen says goes, I suppose.'

'Please! Forget Stephen. I'm sorry I mentioned him. Though he's been a rock.' By now Anna was crying. 'I really thought you'd understand. This is for me. For *us*. It feels like another step on the journey of . . . coming to terms with losing Josh. It also gives me a chance to think about the future, now that Sam's doing so well. It feels like I've come a long way, but now I'm kind of at a cross-roads. I'm not sure where to turn. My thinking was that this is a way of, well, marking the end of one chapter before starting on the next. Which includes going back to work at some stage, you'll be relieved to know.'

That had been a low blow on his part, Theo thought now. *Gainfully employed*, indeed. What a pompous prick he'd been! They'd always agreed that looking after the children was a vitally import-ant job, and as valid a choice as going out to work. He'd been only too pleased that, provided they cut their cloth accordingly, what he brought in from the business made this more or less pos-sible. Why hadn't he understood what she was driving at? Why had he judged her so harshly? *Thought she was leaving you*, came his father's voice. *And why not? She was always too good for you.* Shut *up*, thought Theo. You know nothing about it. Or her.

In the end, they made up, after the row. Sort of. From Theo's point of view, it still felt like a retrograde step. What was the difference between Anna absent in Spain and Anna emotionally absent at home, as she had been throughout the long winter that followed Josh's death? He half knew that was unfair, but it seemed that – yet again – he was the one left holding the fort. A martyr to Anna's selfish whim. He saw that she was determined to go, and tried to wish her well. But try as she did to include him in her plans ('Lots of maps or a single fat guidebook? Which do you think would be easier, Theo?') he resisted all her attempts to win him over. Instead he clung unhappily to the small patch of moral high ground where he had pitched his tent, in spite of the fact that it appeared to be shrinking daily under the rising tide of support from her wider family and friends. *Oh, Anna, forgive me for not understanding. I think I get it now, especially after this week.*

They coped, of course. Meticulous as ever, Anna made extensive plans and drew up rotas before she left. Tamsin took up residence on the Brew House sofa-bed and threw herself enthusiastically into domestic chores and babysitting in return for free accommodation. After the strains and sadness of the past months, her sunny and uncomplicated presence in the household gave them all a lift. Beth, in particular, adored her. Tamsin never grew tired of playing make-believe with her Sylvanian Families or reading *Pippi Longstocking* (her current favourite). She even got Sam playing lopsided football in the garden.

Ruth, meanwhile, was an enormous help with pick-ups from school and nursery and general quiet moral support. At the time of the crisis, they were so taken up with living from hour to hour that Theo had scarcely appreciated that Ruth had handed in her notice as Director of Hope House. 'Time for the family now,' was the public justification for her abrupt retirement. 'Thought you might need a little extra help,' she added in private for Theo's benefit. How true that had been. Some deep-seated instinct had propelled Ruth into making herself available to stand alongside them all in their bereavement, and guide them through Sam's rehabilitation. Surgery, physiotherapy, regular check-ups. All aided by Ruth's calm practicality and reassurance. Theo's own poor mother, meanwhile, visibly flinched at the sight of Sam's deformed foot and was prone to unhelpful outbursts of sobbing. But he was doing her an injustice: as regular as clockwork, Marion arrived at the Brew House on Saturday mornings with offerings from the farmers' market: scones and jam, home-made cakes, oddly shaped vegetables, and on one memorable day, an improbable bottle of sloe gin.

Anna kept in touch by email and phoned whenever she could. She was getting on fine, and so were they. So all in all, it was OK really. If only ... if only it hadn't been for Beth's birthday, thought Theo. He had no one but himself to blame for what happened. He sighed. He'd successfully buried the memory for years. It had started to rain, in tune with his dark mood.

But. Back to *then*. It was such a highly charged day. Anna had been due home, but was delayed by storms. He'd been so caught up in the ongoing narrative of his martyrdom that he'd done nothing in preparation. Another black mark against him! Ruth had reminded him, of course, and between them they hatched a plan involving presents and a cake and a surprise tea party.

It went wrong almost from the off: he could tell by her face that he'd misjudged Beth's present, somehow, though he really had done his best, checked it with Ruth and everything. Perhaps he should have asked Tamsin, but she was away all week in Manchester. And then Beth dragged her heels about going to school and he almost lost his temper with her, which was unfair, and managed to reduce her to tears. The trouble was, he had to be at the hospital with Sam for a check-up, and he was already concerned about leaving Sharon in sole charge of Greene Fingers because she'd only just joined the staff, and after the Anatole disaster he couldn't afford to take his eye off the ball for a single moment.

By the time he came home from work, though, everything had improved immeasurably. Anna had phoned and said she'd be home within forty-eight hours and Beth couldn't contain her delight. William had taken a half-day off work as a surprise and he and Ruth had clearly spoiled Beth rotten. They'd all had a lovely afternoon together with lots of fun and laughter, eating cake and playing silly games. And he'd almost forgotten that Ruth and William had offered to have the children to stay, as part of the birthday treat. Theo planned to go out for a drink with Jonathan, an old friend from agricultural college, who was now an animal feed rep and was passing through Farmleigh on his way back from a sales conference.

He went to the pub and had a really good time. It was a Friday night and the bar was pleasantly full. Pretty girls and laughing young men. Students who'd spilled out of the FE college round the corner. Office workers winding down for the weekend. He and Jonathan had happily reminisced about their student days before falling into conversation with a spirited group of Young Farmers. Lively company, who laughed at his jokes and made him feel young again. Had a few drinks and just forgot all his troubles for once. A carefree evening. And then ... one stupid mistake. One kiss that led to another. And he found himself doing the one thing he'd sworn he'd never, *ever* do to Anna, having seen the hurt that Laurence's careless behaviour had inflicted on her. He'd broken his marriage vows and been unfaithful to his beloved wife. Just because she was a long way away and he was feeling hard done by and the opportunity had presented itself.

Oh *God*. How could he? No matter that it was once, and once only; that he had had far too much to drink; that it was a complete error of judgement. Never mind whether Anna could forgive him: he wasn't at all sure he could forgive himself. Appalled, he vowed there and then that she must never, ever find out and that he would put it behind him once and for all. When she came home, it would be a new start for them both. What had she said? A new chapter. Yes; that was it. He would make it up to her by being extra loving, extra understanding. Making it his single mission in life to make her happy again, whatever it took.

When she did arrive home – just a couple of days later – it had been remarkably easy for the simple reason that she was so transformed. She was lit up: the old Anna, and something more. A new energy seemed to course through her veins. It was as if power had finally been restored after a long, cold winter endured in darkness.

165

For the first time since Josh's death, she had plans, was looking forward to the future. He was so relieved to see her that he simply held her close and wept into her hair. 'I'm so, so sorry. For everything,' he said when they were finally alone together, meaning far more by his apology than he hoped she would understand. 'I really thought I'd lost you.'

'Me too,' said Anna. 'I'm sorry, too. I just *had* to go. But I'm home now, and we're going to be OK. I promise. Trust me.'

And slowly, they rebuilt their lives, found their way into a new way of being together that encompassed their loss and allowed them to live with it. Perhaps, thought Theo, they were older and sadder than they had been, but maybe a little wiser too. The new intimacy that grew between them was a place of love and kindness again. Theo watched with admiration as Anna researched and made plans to retrain for a new career. They sat down together and agreed that they needed a childminder and possibly a cleaner too, and Anna said that she wanted to ask William for a loan. Theo resisted at first, but Anna was persuasive.

'A *loan*, Theo. Not a gift. I'll pay him back when I'm earning. Don't forget, there'll be fees and train fares as well. It's going to be quite an adjustment for everyone, me being a student. I think we need some practical support, domestically, and we really don't need any extra pressure on our finances right now. Let's not make this any harder than we have to.'

Theo swallowed his pride. He knew she was right. But the most important part of the whole conversation was that they talked it all through as partners, without resentment, and made the decisions together.

And yet, and yet ... although it became easier over the years, Theo could never quite shake off the feeling that he was living on borrowed time. That he'd got away with it too easily; that his transgression would, in the end, catch him out. So that when all those years later Anna's diagnosis came and the horror dawned that he was going to lose her, in the very cobwebby recesses of his mind lay the thought that this was really no great surprise. Rather, it was natural justice. A catastrophe he'd brought upon himself. The punishment he'd always known was lying in store for him, a ticking time bomb.

'Dad, come and *look*!' Sam's cry summoned him out of his self-absorption. He realized he'd been oblivious to his surroundings for the past – how many? no idea – miles. They were almost level with the factory works he'd seen in the distance earlier in the afternoon. But what had attracted Sam's attention was something quite different. He was sitting on a bench next to a stout grey figure. On closer inspection, Theo could see that the figure was the rotund statue of a monk.

'Dad, look! He's called Brother Percival! It says *Pilgrim bound with staff and faith, rest thy bones.* I'm resting my bones! Can you take a picture of me next to him?'

Theo rummaged in his rucksack until he found his camera. Sam crossed his left arm over his body and leaned his chin on his right hand in imitation of the reclining figure.

'Me too!' shouted Milo, and squeezed onto the bench next to him.

'You look like those three monkeys,' said Theo. 'You know, "Hear no evil, See no evil, Speak no evil".'

'OK, Milo, you be "See no evil", I'll be "Hear no evil". Brother Percival can be "Speak no evil" because he's asleep!'

'Maybe he should be "Smell no evil" because of his broken nose,' said Milo, laughing.

'Hey, Milo, mate,' intervened Tamsin sharply. 'Hop off, there's a good bloke. Give George a shot. Not fair to leave him out.'

Milo wriggled, reluctant to cede his spot in the limelight, but Tamsin was insistent.

'He's OK, surely?' said Theo. 'George can have a go in a minute.'

Milo looked from one adult to the other.

'Nah, come on, Milo. It's George's turn now,' repeated Tamsin. 'Don't think we want to hang about in this rain.'

'But it's almost stopped!'

'Milo, mate, don't argue please. Come over here.'

'Fancy a chocolate biscuit, Milo, old man?' asked William. Milo brightened slightly and slid off the bench with a glare at his mother.

What was that about? wondered Theo. But at that moment, Beth appeared at his side.

'Er, Dad? Can I, like, say something?'

'Of course. What is it?'

'So two things? First, I'm, like, sorry I swore at you earlier. Lost the plot. My bad.'

'Um. That's OK. Look . . . do you want to talk about these exams? Anything I can do?'

'Meh. More of a forgiveness thing.'

'Well, if we're talking about forgiveness, I probably need to ask yours for . . . being thoughtless. Not realizing how much the GCSEs are preying on you.'

'Shrugalug. Let's not overdo it, Dad.'

Theo suppressed a smile. Right on cue, the sun came out. Literally and metaphorically. A faint echo of the lightness he'd felt that morning returned. The food conversation could wait: at least she was talking to him again. Treading carefully, he took a delicate step across the fragile bridge that lay between them. 'The other thing?'

Beth blushed, and looked at her feet. 'So, like, a friend, yeah? Would it be OK if . . . someone comes along tomorrow? Maybe Sunday?'

'Of course!' Theo let out his breath. He'd thought perhaps that Beth's apology was intended to soften him up for something, well, bigger. Like going home. 'Who's coming? Natasha? Jade?'

'Um, *no*. You don't, like, know . . . *him*. Just a guy from Big Band. Tenor sax. Um, Matt?'

'Ah. I see. Well, I look forward to meeting *Um Matt*. Of course he's welcome. Will he need a bed for the night? If so, you need to talk to Father Stephen. He can probably give you some tips on handy train stations and so on. Assuming he's travelling under his own steam.'

''Kay. Will do. So Dad . . . one more thing?'

'Uh-huh?'

'You won't, like, come over all Victorian Dad, will you? Be *embarrassing*?'

'I'll be on my best behaviour,' said Theo solemnly. 'Promise.'

'That,' said Beth with a grin as she turned to go, 'is exactly what I'm worried about.'

SATURDAY

15 miles
Beth

'Friends,' announced Father Stephen at breakfast. 'I don't know about you, but I can't believe we're nearly there! Eighty-two miles down, twenty-two to go. And today we should have our first glimpse of Canterbury Cathedral. The end is nigh! In a good way, that is,' he added, and everyone laughed.

Not *that* nigh, thought Beth. Even her rubbish maths told her that the remaining distance was more than a quarter of the miles already covered. So they were, what, three-quarters of the way there? Hang on. That wasn't right. Four-fifths? Bloody fractions.

'Today's a long old day in terms of miles, I should warn you,' continued Father Stephen. Sam groaned dramatically, immediately followed by Milo.

'I'm phoning ChildLine!' said Sam.

'I'm phoning them too!' echoed Milo.

Father Stephen smiled at them both. 'Look, if you've managed this far, I'm sure you can make it to the end. You've both done brilliantly. George, too, before he went home.'

'*And* Smith,' said Milo.

'And Smith. That goes without saying. Anyway, it's pretty flat today. Just one short bit of uphill this afternoon, so that's a mercy. And I'm delighted to say that the weather outlook is fine for the rest of the weekend. We should arrive in Canterbury bathed in sunshine. Now, how are all those feet today?'

Beth considered the question. In their family, the only feet anyone ever asked after tended to be Sam's. The blister that had bothered her after the first day had shrunk and healed. She could feel a sort of stretch in her calf muscles, but they didn't exactly *ache* now, which they most definitely had at the start of the week.

Even her glutes – which she'd *really* felt when she got out of bed on Monday morning after the Box Hill day (*OMG*, the Box Hill day!) – seemed to have settled down. All in all, she felt OK. *Good*, even. Well, good but *scared shitless*. How was that even possible? That you could be, like, *longing* for something – well, some*one* – but kind of *dreading* their arrival at the same time?

She'd agonized about whether she should even let Matt come. For a whole load of reasons. Number one, she wasn't at all sure she could cope with him coming under public scrutiny. The group was such a unit now, that his arrival would hardly escape notice. ('This is *Matt*, everyone. He's my *friend* from school.' Urg!) Would everyone be all *weird*? Totally awkward? But then she remembered that Lucy and Ella were going home on Friday night. Their dad was coming to fetch them, and would be giving George a lift back to Farmleigh too. Some horsey thing the sisters had to do. George had a birthday party to go to. That made it all a bit easier, because Lucy would probably *flirt* with Matt – and she was annoyingly pretty, far prettier than Beth – and Ella would be all giggly and embarrassing.

Beth thought she could probably rely on Chloe to be sensible. She had a boyfriend of her own, even if he was a dead loss. Dullsville Dan. At least Chloe wouldn't be *fazed* by Matt. In fact, she might even be *impressed* that Beth had ... what? Got a Year Thirteen guy interested in her? If he was. How could he be? Oh *fuck*! Presumably he was; of course he must be. He was *Mr K*. He was schlepping halfway across the bloody country to find her, wasn't he? And this morning's song – 'Walking on Sunshine' – was a good omen, surely? Oh God, but what if Sam started being *silly*, along with Mini-Me Milo? Look at the two of them this morning! So immature!

Reason number two was that ... well, flirting by text was one thing, lovely actually, his texts were sweet as, but actually meeting in person? It was a whole new, like, *scenario*. What if he was disappointed when he saw her again? Realized that it was all a horrible mistake and that she was just a poxy Year Eleven? Reason number three ... well, this was the biggie. It wasn't as if he even *knew* Mum, and this week was supposed to be all about remembering her.

Would everyone think he was, like, gatecrashing or something? That it was totally inappropriate, him being there? Was it fair on Matt to expose him to this whole pilgrimage thing? Might he think she and her family were total *freaks*?

In the end, she confided in Tamsin about that one, knowing that she wouldn't make her feel stupid. Tamsin considered for a moment, taking the question seriously. 'Hmm,' she said. 'Fair point. But from everything you've said, Beth-ster, he's a pretty sensitive guy. He's going to get the picture. And if he's going to be part of your life, in *any* way – friend, boyfriend, whatever – he needs to understand what makes you tick. Part of getting to know *you* means getting to know your family. That includes hearing all about your mum. If he can't hack that, I'd say he's not worthy of your attention.'

'So, Tamsin?'

'Yeah?'

'If he *does* come . . .'

'Yes, doll?'

'Can you . . . well, can you be on the lookout? Make sure the boys don't play up?'

'Course I can. Trust me. One step out of line and they're dead meat.'

Working out the business of actually getting him here, there seemed to be a choice between Matt cadging a lift with Ruth and William and arriving first thing in the morning, or catching a train and joining the party later in the day. Beth thought she could trust her grandparents not to, well, *interrogate* him, but it was still a bit of a risk. And a bit *mental*, him being in the car with them for – what? an hour, an hour and a half? – when they'd never even met before. Also, if the whole thing was a disaster – and you just never knew – she and Matt were then *stuck* with each other for the entire day. Maybe tomorrow as well. So although it meant delaying his arrival by a few hours (she couldn't wait! but she had to wait), it seemed overall best to plump for the train. That way he could do some revision for his A-levels, too, and the fact that she was *thinking* about that meant that she was being considerate and no one could accuse her of being irresponsible.

171

After breakfast Beth went back to her bunk in the camping barn to pack her bag. Breakfast! She suddenly realized that she'd been so preoccupied anticipating Matt's arrival that she'd let her guard down and accidentally eaten breakfast. For the first time in, like, weeks. How had that happened? How many calories were there in a bowl of porridge? Not that many, surely? She pulled out her phone, failed to find a signal and gave up on the calorie app. She fought a wave of alarm. But oats were supposed to be, like, a superfood, weren't they? At least she hadn't wavered over those cupcakes. Bound to be *full* of sugar. She'd had chopped apple and apricot, too, because it was just *there*. But that was healthy, too, wasn't it? Cautiously, she put a hand to her stomach and asked herself how she felt. Fuller than usual, yes ... but not uncomfortably so. Still in control. Actually, it was kind of OK, not to be quite so light-headed. She felt sort of *warm* inside. In a good way. Fuelled for the day.

As she came back into the yard with her bag, she heard a car draw up. Assuming it would be her grandparents, she was surprised to see a black taxi. Uncle Tom! She'd forgotten that he was planning to rejoin them. That was good. He was fun. And would help dilute everyone a bit. Even though she wasn't too sad in the circs to say goodbye to Lucy and Ella, she was worried that the party was shrinking. And that was most certainly not fair on Mum. It might look awkward when they did that TV piece. She kept losing count, but she thought they'd started out as a party of eighteen. Was that with or without Ruth? And Smith? She couldn't remember. But at breakfast she'd worked out there would be just ten of them today. With Uncle Tom and Matt too, that meant twelve. Smith made it thirteen. And if it could be somewhere near a car park, and Granny Ruth could be there, they would be fourteen. She must ask Tamsin if it was all sorted out. She did hope it wouldn't fall through. According to Tamsin, that happened all the time.

'Unpredictable as anything,' she said last night. 'All depends if a bigger story breaks. Especially at weekends, when it's usually just one man and a dog in the newsroom. On a good day.'

'So how will we know?'

'I'll give them a call first thing. Need to get it sorted – make sure we're in the right place and the right time. Get everyone teed-up in purple. I'll bring along a few spare shirts, just in case.'

Did anyone know how hard Tamsin was working in the background? wondered Beth. She was getting loads of donations in through her radio reports, and by shaking her tin at pubs and tea rooms. And she was driving the whole Twitter campaign. So Twitter was a bit last year, never mind Facebook (*puh-lease!* rents alert!), but it was reaching a lot of people. And she wasn't sure that any of the other adults had a *clue* about social networking. Honestly, she despaired about Dad sometimes. He was like something out of the Stone Age. Could barely send a text without a major panic. Thank goodness *someone* knew what they were about.

Buoyed by the happy thought that Canterbury was in reach and the terrain was flat, the walkers set off rather faster than usual.

'Happy, Grandpa?' she asked as they strode past a large white cross carved into the hillside.

'Happy indeed, Beth. But at the risk of being a bore, I'm not sure everyone will be able to keep this up. Fair old way, fifteen miles.'

'We, like, managed it on Wednesday, though? Or most of us did. That was the day Sam took off with Granny. What's she doing today?'

'Ah. Today,' said Grandpa, smiling warmly. 'I'll have you know, young lady, that today has something special in store.'

Beth panicked briefly. Did he mean Matt's arrival? 'Today,' continued William solemnly, 'Granny is going to the Wye National Nature Reserve. Which, take it from me, is rather marvellous.'

'So, like, you've been there?'

'I haven't been there, no. And if I'm absolutely honest with you, I'm not entirely sure how and why it's different from all the other nature reserves your grandmama has visited this week. Apart from some remarkable coombes apparently formed by periglacial activity during the Ice Age. My hunch is that orchids of some description are on the agenda.' He winked at her conspiratorially.

'So why didn't she take Sam along, then?'

'Think he's determined to finish the course,' said William. He walked on a few paces, and then added casually, 'He's doing really well, you know.'

'And . . . your point is?'

'Sweet of you to keep an eye out, of course. Little chap's lucky to have a big sister who cares. But I'm not sure you need to be on red alert the whole time.'

Beth was taken aback. Red alert? Was she? She couldn't think of a time when she *hadn't* fretted about Sam. It was just what she did. 'But I can't *help* worrying, Grandpa! *Anything* could happen. I mean . . . what if . . .'

'What if *what*, exactly?'

'If he, like, falls over? Has an accident? Gets ill again?'

'Is that very likely?'

'*I* don't know. I'm not a flipping doctor!'

'I know that, old thing,' said William mildly. He stopped walking, to allow a dog-walker coming towards them to pass, and nodded good morning. The two of them stood back from the group for a few moments. 'But he's *well*, you know. Fit as a fiddle. All the medics who've ever looked after him tell us he's fully recovered. Just look at him!'

Beth turned her gaze in the direction William was indicating with his stick. Sam and Milo were throwing a ball for Smith, who was barking excitedly. Every now and again a throw went astray, and one of them had to run down the slope to rescue the ball to stop it escaping any further into the valley below.

'Where do they get their energy?' asked William.

'Come on, Grandpa. You've got more energy than anyone!' said Beth, suddenly finding she was fighting tears. She struggled to remember a time when she hadn't been frightened. 'It's just . . . I'm so *scared* . . .'

'Of what?'

'Everyone thought Mum and Josh were *well*, didn't they? And then suddenly they *weren't*. And people *forget* that and someone's got to look out for Sam because Dad, well, Dad's in a state, and that means he's a bit useless and doesn't always *notice* things, and anyway I have to watch him too, because otherwise *he* might die as well and then I'll be like an *orphan* . . .'

174

By now the tears were streaming down her face. *Oh fuck, why did this keep happening?* William silently handed her an immaculately ironed hanky embroidered with a W. Those hankies were practically his trademark. He said nothing until she had herself under control.

'I can understand it's a worry,' he said eventually. 'But I think perhaps if you stop and think about it, you'll find that you're rather assuming Armageddon's just around the corner. Not really very likely. On the scale of probability. Another thing to bear in mind ... I'm not sure that you *worrying* about it would actually prevent the apocalypse anyway.'

He paused, and then added, 'Rather a good bit in the Bible about that, actually. "Which of you by worrying can add an inch to his height?" or words to that effect. Sound advice. Old as the hills, but still true. Look it up sometime.'

Beth pondered for a moment. Her vigilance was so hard-wired into her that she never stopped to ask what it achieved.

'It's not all your responsibility, you know,' said William. 'Apart from the fact that I imagine it's somewhat exhausting. Carrying the weight of the world on your shoulders. Like Atlas, in Greek mythology. Had to hold up the sky. Very tiring. And he was a Titan. Had colossal shoulders. A lot bigger than yours. Oh, and Beth ...'

'Yeah?'

'In the highly unlikely event that you're orphaned, you can still count on us, old thing. May be a bit creaky, but we're entirely at your disposal.'

Beth looked up at her grandfather. 'Before we catch up with the others, can I ... like ... have a hug, Grandpa?' she asked thickly.

Father Stephen was right about the weather. The day was fine and increasingly warm. By mid-morning Uncle Tom, Tamsin and he were in animated conversation about the wisdom of stopping for a drink at a suitable pub.

'My guidebook says that Charing's very scenic,' said Uncle Tom. 'Lots of pilgrim history. The old archbishop's palace? Thirteenth-century church? Side trip to the Royal Oak? What do you think?'

'I had no idea you were so interested in ecclesiastical history, Tom,' said Father Stephen serenely. 'The only trouble is, your guidebook's sadly out of date. I believe the pub is closed. But if you can hang on for another hour or so there's an equally charming pilgrim church in Westwell. And at Boughton Lees. Pubs in both villages, you'll be glad to know.'

'Whaddya reckon, Tom? Can you hang on?' asked Tamsin.

'Not sure we have a choice,' said Uncle Tom. He was hovering around Tamsin like a wasp round jam, thought Beth. He'd done the same last weekend. Tom and *Tamsin*? Was that why he'd rushed back?

'Good. We have a plan,' said Father Stephen. 'Mind you, there's another interesting church we might look in on later.' Beth spotted Uncle Tom wink surreptitiously at Tamsin.

'Tell us more, Father Steve,' said Tamsin, ignoring Tom.

'Well, it's another ruin, like the archbishop's palace at Charing. St Mary's Eastwell. Haunted, supposedly.'

'Haunted? Strewth! Spill the beans!'

'I'm sure it's stuff and nonsense. People always like a good haunting, especially when a church is in ruins,' said Father Stephen. 'St Mary's has been derelict for sixty years or more. It's right next to a lake. Something to do with seepage into the foundations. Then the estate was used for tank manoeuvres during the Second World War, and that weakened the structure more than ever. The roof finally fell in during the 1950s.'

'But what about the ghost?' asked Beth.

'A monk who lurks, apparently. But the other interesting thing there is the association with Richard de Eastwell. The last of the Plantagenets.'

'Sorry, Father. I don't know my Pommie history. Can you elaborate?'

'Well, this Richard was the illegitimate son of King Richard III.'

'Ah! Heard of him. King Richard of the car park!'

'Well, yes. After the Battle of Bosworth, the Plantagenet star waned, and this Richard ended up working as a craftsman here in Kent. He died in the 1550s and his tomb is in the graveyard.'

'So he could be the one haunting the church?' asked Beth.

'No idea,' said Father Stephen. 'A bit of a tall story, I'd say.'

'Richard III had a whole load of bastards, did he?' asked Tom. 'Those royals! Honestly. They had a fine old time of it.'

'Three, I think. Not all acknowledged in his lifetime,' said Father Stephen.

'Well, all right if you're the king, I guess,' said Tamsin pointedly. 'But you can bet your bottom dollar that there's a whole other yarn to tell if you asked those women for their side of the story. No fun being left high and dry with a sprog, if you ask me. Royal or otherwise.'

In the end, it was almost two o'clock by the time they reached the pub. A traditional country inn in dark red brick, it was ideally positioned overlooking the village cricket green.

'Isn't this just perfect?' said Tamsin, setting a tray of drinks in front of the walkers who had gathered round benches in the sun. 'An English village scene right out of Hollywood. And the sun's even shining for a change!'

'I can tell already that I'm not going to want to leave,' said Catherine. 'This is utter bliss. My legs always protest horribly after a break.'

'I know,' said Mary Anne. 'It's almost easier if you just keep going.'

'Almost,' said Catherine. 'But not quite!'

'Well, I'm afraid we can't hang about too long,' said Tamsin. 'We need to be up the road by three o'clock for this TV piece.'

'So tell us, Tamsin, what's the plan?' asked Mary Anne.

'Father Steve?' called Tamsin. 'Do you want to run us through the batting order?'

Father Stephen wandered over, pint in hand. He explained that once everyone had finished their lunch, they would walk the mile or so up the road to All Saints where the reporter was due to meet them.

'It's a rather special pilgrim church, thirteenth century, so it seems a good setting for our reflection if we're going to be on TV,' he said.

'You always say that!' said Sam. 'That where we're going is *special*.'

'Well, I do my best to take you to memorable places,' said Father Stephen. 'The Pilgrims' Way is littered with fine churches. In this case, it's *extra* special because according to tradition, this church was the last overnight stop for pilgrims on their way to Canterbury. Remind me to show you the porch where they used to gather so that they could gang up before the long walk through King's Wood. That was dangerous because it's acres deep and was full of robbers and bandits. Safety in numbers. So we'd all better be on the lookout!'

Beth saw him wink at Sam and Milo, whose eyes lit up at the prospect of danger. 'The only other thing that's different about today is that we won't have our silent time until later in the day. I'm not convinced that it would make very good television. Tamsin – do you want to tell everyone what to expect?'

'Sure! Well, it's just local TV. Early evening regional news. There'll be a single reporter with a camera. Nicky, she's a friend of mine. We used to work together. She'll film us at our devotions, and then I guess she'll want to talk to one or two of us afterwards about what we're doing and why. She'll also walk on with us for a bit after that, get some long shots of the terrain. Look, there's no pressure, anyone. No need to speak to camera unless you want to. But what I do want, please, is for everyone to wear their purple T-shirts. It'll look much better. And it's important for driving donations.'

'I'll do it! I want to be on TV!' said Milo, immediately.

'Me too!' said Sam, a little less certainly.

Well, I'm bloody not, thought Beth. Oh *no*, would Sam be OK? Might he dissolve into tears, talking about Mum? He'd certainly *look* cute. Not that she'd dream of telling him. But it could still go horribly wrong.

'Let's just see how we go,' said Tamsin.

Beth went in search of her father, who was eating his sandwiches on the village green. 'You OK with this, Dad?' she asked.

'The TV thing?'

'Yeah. I just, like, wondered . . .'

'Thoughtful of you,' said Theo. 'I admit it goes a bit against my better judgement. But, well, Tamsin persuaded me.'

'As she does.'

'As she does. What about you?'

'I'm not doing it. No *way*.'

'Because . . . ?'

'So . . . totally embarrassing, Dad? Someone I know might actually *watch* it, and then what? And I don't want to be like this *poor-little-match-girl, let's-all-feel-sorry-for-her* loser, thank you very much.'

'Ah, I see,' said Theo. 'Sandwich?'

Beth hesitated. 'Um . . . any fruit going?'

Theo reached into his bag, retrieved a banana and gave it to her. 'Actually, Beth, I wanted a word. I've been thinking about those GCSEs.'

Beth groaned. 'Urg. Must you?'

'No, hear me out, sweetheart. I've got an idea.'

Beth wavered for a moment, and then sank down on the grass next to him. 'OK,' she said cautiously.

'Well, look. I know this year's been a disaster.' He laughed. 'OK, so that's the understatement of the century. I meant, it's entirely understandable if your mind hasn't been on your exams. I find it difficult to concentrate on anything at the moment.'

'You do?'

'Too right. It's hard enough just putting one foot in front of the other, some days.'

Beth finished her banana. She was actually quite hungry. She reached out her hand for a sandwich, and then changed her mind. 'So . . . ?'

'So I was wondering. What are your plans?'

'*Plans?*'

'When you get your results? Still thinking about science A-levels and then Physiotherapy?'

Beth sighed. 'I don't know, Dad. I've got literally no idea. That's been the plan, like, *for ever*.'

'Because of Sam?'

'What on earth do you mean?'

'Well, Mum and I always rather thought your interest might have something to do with Sam. Going to the clinic with him. Seeing him learning to walk again. Adapting to circumstances. You wanting to help people.'

Beth pondered. First Grandpa, now Dad. Why did everything always come back to Sam? 'I'd never thought of that. I am, like, *interested* in it, you know.' But was she? Of course she was, at some level. But the idea had also become a bit of a, well, *habit*, if she was honest.

'But that's not the point,' continued Theo. 'If that's what you want to do, brilliant. Useful profession. Follow your heart, if that's where your passion is. I was just thinking, though, that this is a bit of a crossroads for you. Choosing A-levels and so on.'

'And?'

'And it's probably not the easiest time in your life to be making big decisions.' Theo wiped his mouth on a paper napkin. 'Actually, I never think it's quite fair that we have to make all these decisions as teenagers. There's enough else going on as it is.'

'So what am I supposed to do?' said Beth.

'I did wonder,' said Theo hesitantly. 'Well, you might hate the idea. But however your results turn out, might it be a good idea to have some time out? A bit of breathing space? Some life experience, while you make up your mind? I could easily find you a job at Greene Fingers. Sharon goes on maternity leave in September, so it would work well for me. You could go back to school or college when you're ready.'

Beth was gobsmacked. She literally didn't know what to say. 'No need to answer now,' said Theo, gathering up the lunch things. 'Take some time to think about it. We can talk again when you're ready.'

The church, as Father Stephen had promised, was quite special. Even Beth could see that. For a start it was grand – far too grand for the middle of *nowheresville* – and looked almost like a castle, with its chunky towers. Inside, opposite the main door there was the promised porch with its fireplace and a stack of logs. And it was all light and open; chairs, not pews. Ruth was already sitting in the front row. Tamsin was in conversation with a slight, blonde woman who was setting up her camera and tripod in the hexagonal pulpit. She waved Beth over.

'Hey, Beth, this is Nicky. Nicky, meet Beth, my favourite goddaughter.'

'Um, your, like, *only* goddaughter?' said Beth.

'But still my favourite!' said Tamsin. 'Look, would you take charge of the T-shirts for me, Beth-ster? And "no" is not an option. Even from Father Steve.'

Beth happily took the bundle of T-shirts, glad to have something to do and an excuse not to talk to the reporter. For all she knew, Nicky would be as persuasive as Tamsin. Maybe you had to be, to do that kind of work. Mind you, she looked OK. She hadn't done that rubbish, head-on-one-side fake sympathy thing that some of the teachers at school seemed to think was called for. She distributed the T-shirts and then took a seat next to her grandfather. She wondered if she should talk to him later about the conversation with Theo. Ask his advice.

Just as Father Stephen stood to begin the service, she heard the church door open. Looking round, she saw it was Adam, the odd man who seemed to have hovered on the fringes of the pilgrimage since the beginning of the week. He had a habit of appearing unexpectedly once or twice a day. Today his hat was decorated with bright red poppies. Where had she seen him before? She hesitated for a moment, but Tamsin had been quite clear. Everyone was to wear a purple T-shirt. She slipped out of her seat and tiptoed to the back of the church.

'Before we start, can I welcome Nicky?' said Father Stephen. 'But I'm sure she won't mind if I also say please do your best to forget she's there for now! This is one of my favourite pilgrim churches. It's really good to be here, with the feeling that Canterbury is almost in reach. This time tomorrow, we'll be there, God willing. We'll have a period of silence later today, as usual, and our theme then will be "letting go". Letting go of the past. Letting go, perhaps, of some of the heavy load of sadness we're carrying. Maybe letting go of Anna, just a little bit.

'But that's for later. Now, let's have our short act of reflection. You've all got the words. Let's begin with a moment of quiet to still our hearts. Let us pray.'

Beth closed her eyes and let the rhythm of the words wash over her. She listened to William's deep voice beside her, Ruth's quieter tones just beyond him. She could hear Sam and Milo behind her.

181

Her dad on the other side of the church. Tamsin, Uncle Tom, Catherine, Chloe and Mary Anne. She felt an unexpected surge of affection for them all, even Mary Anne. *And Matt, Matt, Matt was coming. Already on the train, on his way to see her.* She opened her eyes and joined in with the words.

Afterwards, they gathered outside in the sunshine. Nicky set up her camera, and Tamsin looked round for interviewees.

'Think we'd better give the boys a shot,' she said to Beth. 'Nicky can always edit them out, if it goes belly-up. But we'll start with Father Steve. He should know what he's doing. And your grandma. She did loads of TV when she was campaigning for Hope House.'

Beth planted herself on a bench under a tree, so that she could watch from a safe distance. Father Stephen went first. Tamsin was right; he was a good choice. Even knowing nothing about it, Beth could see that he was a dream interviewee, speaking fluently about the tradition of pilgrimage and how that still made sense in the twenty-first century. God, he almost made it sound like a *normal* way of spending half-term. Ruth followed, and spoke calmly about Anna and how Hope House cared for whole families.

To her surprise, Theo put himself forward next. Beth watched with interest, laced with anxiety. He stumbled awkwardly over his words, and broke off mid-sentence, shaking his head.

'Hey, Theo, no worries,' said Tamsin. 'That's a great phrase, about the two charities that helped make Anna's last days more comfortable. I'm sure Nicky won't mind doing another take.'

'Of course not,' said Nicky. 'In your own time, Theo. I can see it's not easy.'

And then Dad kind of got his act together and had another go, and it all came out much better. Mary Anne was next, and funnily enough, for all her brisk and sensible teacher act, she came over all emotional, talking about what a lovely person Mum was and how they all missed her. Then Milo and Sam wriggled their way in front of the camera, but in the end they couldn't really think of anything much to say, and Smith started barking, but Nicky took them seriously, and they calmed down a bit, and actually their bit was very short and *kind of* OK.

'Are we done?' asked Tamsin. 'Got enough, d'you think, Nicky?'

At that moment, Adam shuffled forward and mumbled something to Tamsin.

'Sorry?' she said, uncertainly. 'Hey, Father Steve, can you spare a moment?'

There was a brief flurry. Father Stephen came over to see what help Tamsin needed. Beth realized that Adam wanted to say something to camera. She could see that Theo was frowning, and looked as if he was about to intervene. From his frantic body language, Adam himself was becoming increasingly agitated as people crowded around him.

'Is that entirely *appropriate*, Tamsin?' asked Mary Anne sharply. 'I mean, *really* ... He may be wearing one of our T-shirts but what on earth has this man got to do with any of us?'

And all of a sudden Beth realized why Adam was so familiar. Almost before she knew what she was doing she stepped forward from her hiding place under the tree and launched herself into the conversation. 'It *is* appropriate, actually, because Mum, like, *knew* him,' she said fiercely to Mary Anne. 'In fact if you bother to *ask* Adam, you'll find out that he once did Mum a massive favour. When she really needed it.'

'Friends, please,' said Father Stephen. 'Could you give us some space? Why don't you all go and wait on those benches by the wall for a few minutes. Bethany, Adam. Let's sit down for a moment.'

With outstretched arms he shepherded the two of them away from the group towards a crudely made seat underneath a yew tree. Beth, scarlet with embarrassment, sat down. Adam hovered a few feet away, his ragged carrier bags at his feet.

'So, Adam. I didn't know you knew Anna. How was that?'

'The music lady,' he mumbled. 'Walking for Anna.'

'Yes, I know that. But how did you two know each other?'

'The Cathedral.'

Father Stephen turned to Beth with barely concealed exasperation. 'Can you help?'

Oh, God! It was all a bit hazy. 'Um. It's, like, a long time ago. But when ... when Josh and Sam were babies ... Well, Mum was doing these, like, lunchtime recitals. Wednesdays. We all used to go. I mean, not Dad, obviously, he was at work. But because it was the holidays, I was off school so I used to look after the boys. And then we had ice cream afterwards as a treat. It was meant to be *easy* because they were supposed to be asleep and the concerts were really short. Half an hour, I think. Although that felt like *for ever* if one of them woke up and I had to push the pram round the Cathedral. I was only, like, six.' She laughed shakily.

'And you used to come, didn't you?' she said to Adam, who nodded furiously. 'You were there every week, in the front row.' She remembered being slightly afraid of him, daunted by his eccentric appearance, his yellow-brown teeth and the all-pervading smell of unwashed clothes. He had a beard in those days, but no flower-bedecked hat.

'Music. I liked the music,' he muttered. 'And the music lady always smiled. Said hello.'

'I remember. She said you were her Number One fan.' Adam nodded again, and let out a curious sound that Beth realized was a laugh.

'Number One fan! That's me!'

'And then ...' Beth felt the tears well up. Could she *bear* to remember? '*That* day. The day the boys fell ill. I could *tell*. I knew something was wrong with Sam. He didn't look right. But I couldn't tell Mum because she was on stage.'

She remembered the interminable wait. It had been a cool day, for summer, and drizzling with rain, which was one reason why she'd noticed that Sam was unusually hot. She sat swinging her legs, which didn't quite reach the floor, one hand on the cool metal handle of the pram. The audience was made up of the usual handful of visitors and shoppers enjoying a free recital. Some music brightening up a damp day. Little puddles were forming on the floor under rain-sodden umbrellas. How long was half an hour? How many more minutes? Perhaps if she counted to fifty? To a hundred? She willed the programme to end, so that she could attract Mum's attention.

When Anna finally finished playing, and stood up to take a bow, Beth waited for as long as she could bear, but still found herself on the dais before the applause had quite died down. As she tugged at her mother's sleeve, she heard a collective 'Ah!' from the audience. She hoped Mum wouldn't be cross. 'Sam looks *funny*,' she whispered urgently, and then *at last* Anna came and looked in the pram and all of a sudden there was a mad scramble to pack up her cello and get out of the building.

'What happened, Beth?' Theo had joined them at the yew tree.

'The car! We didn't have the car. We usually parked right by the entrance.'

'It was in for a service,' said Theo. 'Mum was going to take you to the park, collect it at the end of the day.'

'I just remember . . . a big *panic* because we didn't have the car. And Mum had left her mobile in the glove pocket. We had the double buggy and her cello and there were all those steps by the Cathedral, and we looked for a taxi, but there weren't any. And you . . .' She turned to Adam. '*You* were the one who . . . who got someone to call an ambulance.'

Adam nodded, or she thought he did. It was hard to tell, when his head was bobbing up and down anyway. 'The music lady always said hello,' he mumbled.

'So that's why you came to find us?' said Father Stephen.

'It was on the radio. Walking for Anna.'

Father Stephen looked at Theo. 'Thank you, Adam,' said Theo. 'Thank you for helping Anna that day. And for joining us this week. If you want to talk on camera, you'd be very welcome.'

But Adam shook his head. The moment seemed to have passed. He muttered something inaudible to Father Stephen, picked up his shabby carrier bags and turned to leave. After walking a few steps, he turned back, towards Beth. 'I like my Anna T-shirt,' he said shyly, not quite meeting her eye. He stroked it reverently. 'Number One fan!'

Nicky followed them for another mile or so after the church, so that she could get her long shots. They walked away from the little clutch of houses, crossed a country lane, and then made their way up the hill and onto the Downs. It was all very well, Father Stephen telling them to forget she was there, but Beth felt acutely self-conscious knowing that the camera was on them. Finally, after a word with Tamsin, Nicky waved goodbye and headed back down the slope towards her car.

'Well, that went OK,' said Tamsin. 'Happy, Theo?'

'Yes, thanks. You were right. She didn't intrude.'

'See, Dad? Tamsin knows best,' said Beth, and Theo laughed.

'I'm just glad it was Nicky,' said Tamsin. 'She's great. I knew she'd be sensitive.'

'When's it going to be on?' asked Theo.

'Tomorrow night, with a bit of luck. Which means we'll all be home and can watch it.'

Theo groaned. 'Not sure I want to see myself on TV! I made a bit of a hash of it.'

'Harder than it looks, huh?' said Tamsin. 'But don't worry. You were great.'

'Yeah, Dad, and they'll probably edit out any bits that make you look a *total* plonker.'

'Thanks, Beth! But I suppose that's true. It'll only be a tiny item, won't it?'

'We'll see,' said Tamsin. 'We've got Father Steve doing the radio tomorrow morning too. With a bit of luck and a fair wind, I'd say there's a head of steam building.'

Father Stephen had suggested a pause at the top of the hill.

'It's what I call a breathtaking view,' he said, panting slightly. He looked round. 'Bethany – a quick word?' He led her a few metres away from the group.

'Thank you for that,' he said quietly.

'For, like, what?'

'For standing up for Adam. For helping to tell his story. Honouring his humanity.'

''S'OK,' she muttered, with a slight nod. 'Oh God, I sound like him, now, don't I?'

'I think you've a way to go yet,' said Father Stephen. 'But well done. Not always easy to stand up for the oddball. Especially against adults.'

'You do it, though. All the time. Look out for oddballs, I mean.'

'Ah,' said Father Stephen with a grimace. 'Occupational hazard, I'm afraid. Give house room to strangers, and just occasionally you find yourself entertaining angels.'

'And it's Beth. Please. No one calls me Bethany.'

'Noted. I stand corrected. Shall we join the others?'

The rest of the group had now reached the clearing at the top of the hill. 'Now, friends,' said Father Stephen. 'Thank you for your flexibility today, and thank you, Tamsin, for looking after that little media moment for us. I thought we might begin our silent hour now, as we head into the woods. I must say I can see why pilgrims found this a daunting spot. It's very scenic, but it seems to go on for miles. Like something out of *Sleeping Beauty*. What have we got here, Theo?'

'Beech, Corsican pine and Douglas fir, at a glance. And sweet chestnut galore,' said Theo. 'Managed by the Forestry Commission, I think. There's a sculpture trail buried somewhere in the depths. As well as Sleeping Beauty and Snow White, for all I know.' *Good for Dad!* thought Beth. He really knew his onions. Would she learn all this *stuff* about the natural world, if she went to work for him?

'I think that might have to wait for another day,' said Father Stephen. 'I really don't want to lose anyone. Or wear you out more than necessary. Though we haven't got very many more miles to go today. Somewhere along this woodland path you should find a milestone that tells us it's only another ten miles to Canterbury.

'But back to our silence. Earlier I suggested we might think about letting go today. I'd like to add another thought that struck me this afternoon. I talked about letting go of our burdens. But I think sometimes we also have to let go of our preconceived ideas. Be open to the fact that we might have misjudged things.

'It's so easy to leap to judgement. I know I do it. I suspect that some of us may have misjudged our friend Adam. Thanks to Beth, we've discovered something important about him that none of us knew before.' Beth could feel her cheeks burning. At least he'd called her *Beth*. She stared at her feet. Mum's walking boots. The dusty forest track.

'So can I suggest we all do a bit of soul-searching? Ask ourselves if there's anything any of us need to let go of today?'

Letting go ... where to begin, wondered Beth. That really did seem to be the, like, *wallpaper* for today. There was Grandpa suggesting that she should be letting go of her worries about Sam and Dad. Then Dad came along with the idea that she let go of her studies for a while. And now Father Stephen was going on about it, too.

She felt knocked sideways by Dad's proposal. At one level, the thought, the *thought* of someone pretty much saying *no need to worry about your GCSEs any more* made her feel light-headed with relief. But what if she did as he suggested and went to work at Greene Fingers? Number one, what if it was a nightmare? She knew next to nothing about plants and gardening. It was *so* not her thing. Would she make a total idiot of herself? Would the customers walk out, disgusted, because she was so pig-ignorant? Would the other staff laugh at her for being stupid, or *resent* her because she was the boss's daughter? Suddenly it seemed impossibly high risk, for Dad as well as for her. What if she let him down?

Objection number two. Would it be like what Catherine said at lunchtime? That it sometimes feels almost worse if you take a break from something, because starting up again is such a shock to the system? Would she ever be able to get back to her studies? Because you kind of *had* to get exams and grades and stuff if you were going to get anywhere in life. Deep down, she knew that, even if she had cocked up spectacularly this year.

Thinking about it, depending on the hours she had to work, she could probably keep some subjects ticking over. Maybe do a couple of retakes if she needed to. Which she would. Probably. No, definitely. And she wouldn't want to give up her music, either. Argh! Saxophone lessons outside school might be possible, but would Mr Shepherd let her play in Big Band? Was that even *allowed*? The head teacher would probably say it was against some *law* or something. Oh *shit*! The one person who could probably answer that question – whether they'd let her leave school but keep one foot in the door on her own terms – was *bloody* Mary Anne, and Beth had the nasty feeling she'd been a bit rude to her earlier. Not that she wasn't *fully* justified in what she'd said. But Mary Anne might not see it that way.

Mind you, if Matt wasn't there any more, would she still love Big Band so much? Actually, yes, she would. She'd miss him when he went to university, but Big Band wasn't *only* about Matt. *OMG! He'll be here in, I don't know, an hour? Two?*

Beth's heart began to race. Her mouth was dry. Oh *God*, what was it going to be like when he arrived? *Calm, calm, calm.* Long deep breaths. Breaths! Arg! she rummaged in her backpack to find some chewing gum. She *so* couldn't afford to have bad breath when Matt arrived. Briefly she contemplated turning round, and heading as fast as possible in the opposite direction. But *no.* That was *ridonc.* She was *not* letting go of Matt, thank you very much. The thought of Molly O'Riordan's cheesy grin was enough to put a big fat lid on that idea. Actually, thinking about it, if she was working for her dad, she'd have a salary, wouldn't she? Even if it was minimum wage? And he might not be *quite* that stingy. That would mean she could afford to go and visit Matt for weekends and stuff at uni. Maybe even, I don't know, go Interrailing next summer or whatever. If they were together. *If, if, if.*

But the best thing about working for a bit was that it really did, as Dad said, buy her some time to think about her future. This year had been so topsy-turvy, when you stopped to think about it, so *fucking* awful with Mum being sick and everything, that she really was all over the place. Some time out might be, well, good. Better than rushing into the wrong A-levels and finding herself on the fast track to nowhere. A year out would actually give her time to think what *she* wanted for a change. Not what other people thought you should do. The trouble was that school was like some fucking conveyor belt sometimes. You got on and kept going until the system spat you out the other end, and as long as you got the stupid results everyone wanted for their flipping league tables, no one asked too many questions. Like whether you were actually *happy* or doing the right thing for your life. Maybe she didn't even have to stick with school. She could go to college, or something. When *she* was ready.

Now, the other part of letting go. Grandpa had really unsettled her with his *red alert* comment. Worrying about Sam, especially, and more recently about Dad, seemed as natural as breathing. It was like having red hair or blue eyes. Something she didn't know you even had any, like, *choice* over. Although if you thought about it, that was a silly comparison, because you could dye your hair. Or wear coloured contact lenses. Was the *red alert* thing something you could change, too?

But actually. *Actually* . . . Grandpa was kind of right. Sam was, like, doing OK. She looked ahead to where he and Milo were walking together, Smith between them. They were doing a sort of funny slouchy walk, dragging their feet theatrically as if they were wading through mud, and trying to make each other laugh. Honestly, they couldn't seem to take this silence thing seriously. They were so . . . *silly* . . . sometimes, so *immature*. All of a sudden she laughed out loud. Of *course* they were: they were children! But Grandpa had a point. Sam was to all intents and purposes a healthy, happy boy.

And Dad? He was beside himself, howling with agony at the loss of Mum. Obviously. But *really*? He seemed to have loosened up, somehow, this week. Look at the banter with Tamsin earlier. As Grandpa said, what did worrying achieve anyway? Mind you, that just made her feel cross. If she knew how to turn off the worry tap, just like that, she *would*. Fuck's sake. But maybe, just *maybe*, it was progress that she was even contemplating the possibility of letting some of this *stuff* go.

Oh, Mum, I wish you were here. You'd tell me how to do this! What *would* Mum say? 'Let it go' was actually one of her, like, stock pieces of advice. If Beth fell out with her school friends – remember that horrible time with Jade? – Mum would listen, and give her a hug, and say, 'Just let it go, Beth. Life's too short to hold grudges.' Perhaps she could adopt that as her own catchphrase. *Let it go, let it go, let it go.* Now she sounded like flipping Queen Elsa out of *Frozen*. Oh, shit!

So deep in thought was Beth that she failed to see a figure ahead on the path. By the time she spotted Matt sitting on a low wall at a break in the line of trees they were almost upon him. Behind him stretched a grassy slope, a rare glimpse of open countryside. Luckily, she was at the front of the group, with only William for company.

'Matt!' she said, her nerves suddenly melting away. It was just, like, *Matt*. Gorgeous Matt, with his easy smile, looking all *studious* with a book in his hand. 'You're earlier than I expected!'

'Hey, Em,' he said, and gave her a big, friendly bear-hug. 'I thought I'd walk up from the station and surprise you. Guess what? Jane Austen's brother used to live in a big house, somewhere over there. She even wrote some of her books when she was on a sleepover.' He turned to William and held out his hand in greeting. 'How do you do? I'm Matt,' he said.

Beth felt the joy spread across her face like a shaft of sunlight. How *could* she have been dreading this moment? Nothing awkward about it. He was, like, *awesome*. Most definitely pleased to see her, but super-polite to Grandpa, too. He'd called her *Em*. Their secret. And he was here.

SUNDAY

7 miles
Tamsin

Tamsin stretched. She'd be glad to be back in her own bed tonight and no mistake. Although she generally slept like a log wherever she fetched up, bunking down in a different bed each night was beginning to take its toll. Bloody hell! She must be getting *old*. It was the kind of thing people's parents said.

It would be good, not living out of a backpack. But, hey! That meant the end of the journey. *Canterbury here we come*, she thought. *Not sure I really believed we'd make it*. Hadn't the boys been total stars? Good for Milo. He'd come up trumps. And so had Sam, feet and all. Fair play to him. How many other kids their age would have plodded on, day after day, without complaint? They'd even gone along with the silences.

She checked her watch: 7.30! She really ought to make sure that Father Stephen was up and ready for his radio interview. On the other hand, he was an early riser. Reliable. And if anyone was used to getting up on Sunday mornings, it was Father Steve. Not likely to forget ... surely? Strewth, she couldn't risk it. The final hurdle, media-wise, and her reputation on the line if she didn't deliver. Reluctantly she dragged herself out of bed and off to the shower.

Interview over – and Father Steve was a pro, the real deal – Tamsin went in search of Milo and breakfast. She found both in the foyer of the camping barn where they'd eaten supper the night before. Milo had piled a bowl high with cereal, while Sam was about to tackle a mountain of toast. Smith was sitting under the table at Milo's feet, gently wagging his tail. Matt and Beth were just slightly removed from the rest of the group and, if Tamsin wasn't much mistaken, holding hands under the table. There was a detectable buzz of conversation around the room.

'Demob happy, d'you reckon?' she said to Father Stephen.

'There's certainly something in the air,' he said.

'Relief that we've just about made it, I'd say! And by the way, great job back there,' she added. 'Some great storytelling and just the right tone. Beaut! Wish all the interviewees I had on my show were that well versed.'

'Thank you!' he said, visibly pleased. She found herself wondering how often people paid him a compliment. Maybe his was the kind of job where the only kind of feedback you ever got was when you messed up.

'Let's hope that gives the fundraising a good final boost,' he added, helping himself to cereal and fruit. 'I'm assuming you're off the hook now? Allowed a break from media duties?'

'Time off for good behaviour, you mean? Yeah. Reckon I've done my bit. Almost fifteen grand raised! The station have been really good, but I don't think I can push my luck after today. Now, what's our schedule?'

'A laid-back breakfast,' he said, with pleasure. 'I'm relying on Mary Anne to have worked her magic and produced something approaching drinkable coffee.'

'Friends, this really is the final leg of our journey,' Father Stephen announced. 'Just seven miles today. A week ago perhaps even that distance sounded daunting, but now – well, it's a stroll in the park, to coin a phrase! The route's all reasonably easy, too. We'll be in Canterbury in time for a late lunch.

'My intention is to hold our final reflection at St Dunstan's church, within the city. It's a traditional point for pilgrims to pause, ever since King Henry II stopped there to pray on his way to the Cathedral. While he was here, he stripped off his finery, put on a hair shirt, and walked on to the Cathedral in bare feet in penance for the murder of Archbishop Thomas Becket. So a tradition grew up that pilgrims walk the last half-mile into the city barefoot. It's not quite such a penance these days as we have pavements and clean streets, but on the other hand our feet tend to be pretty soft.

I don't know whether that's something any of you want to do? Have a think. Entirely optional, of course.'

'You said it's our last reflection, but I thought we were going to a service in the Cathedral?' asked Catherine.

'Quite right,' replied Father Stephen. 'There's Evensong at three-fifteen. But while I'm sure we'll be made very welcome, there'll doubtless be lots of other people there. Locals, visitors from all over the globe, maybe other pilgrims too. Which is symbolic of our return into the world, back to our everyday lives, of course. But St Dunstan's will be our last gathering as a group.'

'When do you think we'll be away?' asked Mary Anne. 'It's back to work for most of us tomorrow. I need to work out what train to catch.'

'If you're staying for the service, soon after four, I'd say.' Father Stephen glanced in Theo's direction. 'Some of us have one last engagement before we head for home, but that's the general idea. Now, half an hour till the off, everyone?'

There were murmurs of assent. Time to check that she and Milo had everything. At that moment she saw Ruth crossing the room towards her. She and William had stayed with friends just outside Canterbury for the final night to avoid yet another long journey to and from Aston. Luckily the barn had been dog-friendly.

'Morning, Ruth!' she said. 'Good night? Survived without Smith?'

'Yes, thank you. Very comfortable. But Tamsin – may I have a word?'

'Sure, but can it wait? I need to round up the troops. Sort my stuff. That OK?'

Ruth appeared to consider for a moment. 'I suppose it will keep.'

'Catch you later, then,' said Tamsin.

The day, as Father Stephen had promised, was a gentle one as far as the terrain was concerned. They left the chocolate-box village of Chilham, with its historic castle – actually a stately home – and church, crossed a busy road, and took a tarmac lane up the hill towards the next village. Once through the village, they headed out into open countryside.

Tamsin felt her heart lift. The sun was out, the end was in sight and there was a festive atmosphere among the group. Conversation and laughter rippled along the line of walkers as they passed through a great swathe of apple orchards. William and Tom were at the head of the group. Not far behind them, Beth and Matt were walking side by side. Matt was singing 'Climb Every Mountain' in a funny falsetto voice and Beth was joshing him playfully. No worries there. Theo was playing catch with Sam, chucking a tennis ball between the two of them, aided and abetted by an overexcited Smith. Milo, whose catching skills were not quite up to the mark, had seized the opportunity to use Sam's walking poles and was milking the moment to great success. Catherine and Mary Anne were deep in conversation and Chloe was talking earnestly to Father Stephen.

It was odd that they were all so cheerful, because the end of the day meant the end of the pilgrimage. They'd all be going their separate ways. Well, kind of; of course, their lives were all intertwined, but there had been something uniquely bonding about the walk. It had been special. Healing, somehow? *Knew what you were about, huh, Anna? Good thinking, Batman.*

She was surprised to realize how much she was going to miss everyone after today. Not to mention the routine, where you just got up and got going. Partly that was about being surrounded by other adults. Good to share the load. Tamsin sighed. It was great that single parenthood no longer carried the stigma it once did, but she missed being part of a family unit. It wasn't just the companionship, but the sense of solidarity that gave you. You and me against the world, and all that. But better by far to be on her own than with the wrong man.

She'd had a pretty awkward encounter with Tom that morning. What was it with Anna's family? First Ruth, then Tom, coming over all serious and wanting a *word* with her. In his case, there was no avoiding a conversation. He caught her just as she was stowing her luggage in the boot of the car, but before anyone else was ready. And, just as she feared he might, he asked her out. True, the invitation was couched in slightly vague terms about meeting for a drink in London, but one thing that recent history had taught

Tamsin was to listen to any alarm bells that took the trouble to ring. And bells had been clanging like billy-o around Tom ever since he'd turned up in the car park a week ago. All very charming and handsome, but your classic commitment-phobe. Probably thought he was doing her a favour, imagining she'd jump at any sign of male attention, just because she was single. One thing when you were footloose and fancy free to have a bit of fun, but she knew where her duty lay and that was with Milo.

'Sorry, Tom. It's been fun getting to know you, but I don't think it's such a good idea,' she said. 'I've got my hands pretty full with the little bloke. I'm not up for a relationship right now and I don't do casual.'

And Tom, to his credit, had taken it fine. He hadn't pushed it. Or maybe that *wasn't* to his credit? Maybe it just proved that he was only ever after an opportunistic shag. Or had she just become horribly cynical? Bloody hell! She had to remember that not all men were monsters. They weren't all like Frankie. Look at William. He was a true gent, old school. Surely some of that would have rubbed off on Tom? Anyway, she wasn't interested, she was clear about that. It would take someone pretty special to risk jeopardizing the security she'd worked so hard to create since her return to Britain.

'Hey, Milo!' she called. 'Where's your Aussie pride, doll?'

'What?'

'The ball game. Not playing?'

'I kept dropping the ball!'

'I could see that. You just need a bit of practice. Can't have you letting the side down!'

'If you're so good at catch, you show me, Mum,' said Milo crossly.

'Well, I might just do that. But I can't quite see how we'll manage that with Smith and those walking poles.'

'We can take Smith, if you like,' said Beth.

'Or I could give Milo some catching practice,' Matt added. *Bless!*

'Good bloke!' said Tamsin and winked at Beth, who grinned from ear to ear and blushed a furious pink. Tamsin handed Smith's lead to Beth and took the walking poles from Milo. She retrieved an old tennis ball from her backpack. An old hand with both boy and dog, it was a case of *have ball, will travel.*

Now she knelt down so that she was eye level with Milo. 'Remember, mate, national pride is at stake here,' she said with a wink. 'You get to work on that hand–eye coordination and then you can knock the socks off the Poms!'

'So, Tamsin, I thought you were supposed to be, like, a Pom yourself?' said Beth, as Milo and Matt set to work.

'Only when it suits me!' she said. 'That's the joy of dual nationality. Now then. Far more important. All well with you and Mr K, do I take it?'

A pause in the ball game became necessary as the party passed through another village. The first sign of civilization was a pub. Tamsin and Tom exchanged a rueful glance (well, that's what she would call it) and a friendly bit of banter as Father Stephen hurried them past.

'They even do a Pilgrims' Lunch special,' protested Tom.

'I couldn't agree more – it looks very appealing,' said Father Stephen. 'But trust me, there are plenty more pubs in Canterbury. You'll have to take my word for that. We do need to press on, because we're going to be met when we get there. We're really not far off now.'

'I can't wait to see the Cathedral,' said Tamsin to William. 'Talk about ancient history!'

'One of the wonders of England,' said William. 'But if it's history you're after, look over to your right for a moment.'

'Up the hill?'

'Yes. Bigbury Fort. Iron Age.'

'Which means?'

'Well, the Iron Age traditionally begins in around 800 BC, when we started using iron instead of bronze to make weapons. But rather later than that, when old Julius Caesar invaded Kent in 54 BC, the ancient Brits holed up at Bigbury. You can see the walls.'

'And how did that turn out? Not well, if I know the Romans.'

'Spot on. Two days later, the Brits were comprehensively routed. At which point half of them retreated north to lick their wounds

197

and regroup. And the other half saw which side their bread was buttered and decided it was less trouble to throw in their lot with the Romans. Not the end of the story, though. Old Julius Caesar had other things on his plate.'

'Hear that, Milo? Was that in *The Rotten Romans*? He's slightly obsessed,' she added to William.

'I came, I saw, I conquered ... but only for the weekend!' said Milo. 'That's what Julius Caesar said.'

'Did he, indeed?' said William. 'Well, it took another century or so before the Romans really got us in order. Good to think our ancestors put up a struggle.'

'Rule Britannia?'

'Something like that,' said William with a smile.

Half an hour later, they were on the outskirts of the city, and in another twenty minutes, approaching a flint church with a tall, square tower. Ruth was standing outside.

'St Dunstan's, friends,' announced Father Stephen. 'Are they expecting us, Ruth?'

'All ready and waiting.'

'Excellent. Come in, everyone. They've kindly opened up, especially for us.'

Inside the church was uncluttered and simple. A large, rough-hewn wooden cross hung over the main altar. Tamsin, casting around for Milo and Sam, caught sight of Ruth approaching her with a determined look on her face. What the heck did she want? At the same moment, William appeared behind Ruth, carrying a large terracotta bowl and a white towel.

'Where would you like me to put it, dear heart?' he said. For no reason that she could quite put her finger on, Tamsin took advantage of Ruth's momentary distraction to slip outside again in the guise of giving Smith a drink of water. Whatever Ruth wanted would just have to wait.

She put off coming back into the church until everyone else was inside and she was as sure as she could be that Father Stephen was ready to begin the reflection in the small side chapel. She sat near the back where Milo, bless him, had saved her a seat.

'Well,' said Father Stephen, beaming. 'Here we all are! One hundred and three and a bit miles after setting out. Marvellous! I know that not everyone has walked every single mile but what an achievement! I hope you're all pleased.'

'Pleased and relieved!' said Catherine.

'As I said this morning, this is our last gathering on our own. Because we're going to attend Evensong later, I thought we'd do without formal liturgy here. Instead, there are three other things I want to do. First, I thought this might be a chance to share with each other what you've got out of this week.'

'Tired legs!' said Milo.

'I'm sure you're not the only one,' said Father Stephen as everyone laughed. 'The good news is that tonight we can all put our feet up back home. Second, although it's less than a mile to the Cathedral, I thought we might do that in silence. I'll come on to the third thing in a minute. But let's start by talking about what this week has meant. Apart from tired legs, that is. Perhaps there's something you've enjoyed or discovered. A memory you'll treasure. One small thing you might try and do differently when you get home. No pressure, but if there's anything you'd like to say, now's a good time.'

There was a pause, quite a long one. People were shifting uncomfortably in their seats. Funny how everyone had been chatting so easily earlier, and now appeared to be struck dumb. *Well, I've always been gobby*, thought Tamsin. *Better help him out and go first.*

'Well, I—' she said at the precise moment that Father Stephen began to speak.

'After you, mate,' she said.

'I'll begin, then,' said Father Stephen. 'I've found myself thinking about all sorts of odd things this week. Some I suppose I knew I was bringing with me. Others have just bubbled up along the way. I've found myself thinking a lot about Anna, as I'm sure you all have. And in particular, that when she came back from Spain, she embarked on a whole new career. That must have been a big decision, and a brave one, because she had a lot on her plate already. I'm not planning on a new career. But I have made a decision about something in my personal life. A change I want to make, that will take some courage. I won't say any more now, because there are private conversations I need to have. But that's something I'm taking home with me.'

'Follow that!' said Tamsin. 'All I was going to say was that Milo and I've really enjoyed being part of the gang. It's been a whole lot of fun. Cheers to Anna for a great idea!'

'I was really nervous about the walking,' said Catherine. 'But I've surprised myself! The thing I'm going to try and do at home is go for regular walks.'

'I've valued the quiet,' said Mary Anne. 'My life's pretty hectic. Well, I'm sure we all have a lot on, back home. You know, busy working mum of teenagers, the lot. If I'm honest, I rush about like a scalded cat sometimes. Even when I'm supposedly relaxing I'm listening to music. I'm going to try to find more silence in my life.'

Bit of a turn-up for the books, thought Tamsin. I'd have had Mary Anne down as listening to classical music on the treadmill and learning Mandarin in her sleep. All organized on a colour-coded spreadsheet. Good on her.

Tom spoke. 'I thought I knew all about Anna. After all, she was my sister. But by spending time with you guys . . . I've seen a whole new side to her. That's been great.'

'So I'm going to, like, come back to choir, maybe?' said Beth unexpectedly. 'If that's cool with you?' she added to Father Stephen.

'Of course. Anyone else?'

'I'll remember the orchids,' said Sam. 'And Milo falling in the water!' The two of them guffawed. Tamsin exchanged a despairing look with Theo.

'My journey hasn't been quite the same as yours,' said Ruth. 'I've had to dip in and out, as you know.'

'We couldn't have managed without you,' said William loyally.

'Thank you, darling. But what I wanted to say is that I've been thinking about St Christopher.' She said nothing for a moment or two, and then carried on. 'I looked him up the other evening, and like many of the saints, St Christopher's story is a bit hazy. Legend has it that he carried an unknown child across a river on his back. Only afterwards did he discover that the child was Jesus. It all sounds a bit nonsensical to me. I think it was probably an ancient Greek myth that was appropriated by Christians for their own nefarious ends.'

She gave Father Stephen a beady look and then smiled. 'But the point is that because of this he became a patron saint of travellers. Like your St Botolph. Because he carried a child on a hazardous journey. The reason for my particular interest is that St Christopher is also associated with the hospice movement. You've probably heard of St Christopher's Hospice in London, founded by Dame Cicely Saunders, who was a pioneer in the hospice movement. Interestingly, even the word "hospice" dates back to the days when the early Christian monastic orders welcomed the sick and needy. And travellers and pilgrims.'

'All the same word,' said William. '*Hospes* in Latin means guest, host or stranger.'

'Thank you again, darling. I suspect I'm rambling somewhat. I suppose what I'm trying to say is that I've been reminded this week that we all need a bit of accompaniment on life's journey. Sometimes, like St Christopher, we carry others. And sometimes we need carrying ourselves. That's not always easy to admit. And I suppose I'd just add that there are all sorts of different ways of . . . of being of *service* to other people.'

Tamsin watched as William took Ruth's hand in his and patted it. At the same time, Ruth exchanged a look with Father Stephen in which Tamsin read – what? Respect? Understanding?

'Thank you, Ruth,' said Father Stephen with a little bow. He glanced in Theo's direction. 'Anyone else, before we move on?'

Theo twisted slightly in his seat. But then he cleared his throat and spoke. 'I'd just like to add . . . Well, thanks for coming. I wish Anna had been here . . .' He let out a slightly strangled laugh, then rallied. 'Of *course* I wish Anna was here. More than I can possibly express. What I'm trying to say is that she'd have been touched . . . *I'm* touched . . . that you've all given up this week to do this for her. It's been a memorable . . . no, a *good* week.'

'Too right,' said Tamsin, meeting his gaze with what she hoped was an encouraging smile. Theo smiled briefly, and sank into his seat, as if exhausted by the exertion of speaking. Which he probably was, she thought. Not a man who found it easy to talk about his emotions. But actually, he looked better. Or better than when they'd set out, at least. Less *crushed*.

'Thank you, everyone,' said Father Stephen. 'Now, our final collective silence. Strangely, one of the things that can be difficult at the end of a pilgrimage is going home. It's an adjustment, getting back to the everyday. Before we know it, we'll find ourselves swept up in the ordinary busy-ness of life. We've been a group and now we're going our separate ways. So, there's our word: "scattering". The opposite of gathering. The other bookend to our week of themes, if you like. Also chosen because at the end of the day, the immediate family are going to scatter Anna's ashes.

'So. It's a short silence, just the time it takes from here to the Cathedral. Perhaps while we walk we might think a bit more about what we're going to take home as we scatter.

'Now, for the third thing I mentioned. Ruth's just reminded us of the long history of hospitality to pilgrims. One of the kindnesses that those early hospices offered travellers was the washing of their feet. That's a lovely thing to do for anyone. There's the straightforward, practical reason that walking long distances takes a toll on the feet. But it's also offered as an act of Christian service, in imitation of Jesus. You'll remember that he washed the disciples' feet before the Last Supper. I thought we'd do that here. Obviously, we're not quite at our destination yet, but it might be rather more difficult to manage at the Cathedral. Has anyone thought about walking barefoot?'

'Me!' said Milo. 'It'll be cool. Can I, Mum?'

'Don't see why not,' said Tamsin. 'Is anyone else?' As she spoke she caught sight of Beth's face, which was clouded by anxiety.

'Is it hygienic?' asked Mary Anne. 'There could be dog mess. Broken glass. Anything . . .'

'Then we just need to watch where we walk,' said Tamsin. 'Should be easier in silence. But each to their own. No worries.'

'I'm up for it,' said Matt. 'If that means I'll qualify as a fully fledged pilgrim. Otherwise I feel a bit of a lightweight, only doing the last few miles. What about you, Beth?'

'Um, like, OK?' said Beth, looking uneasily at Sam. 'But . . .'

A penny dropped noisily in Tamsin's brain. 'Theo? You OK with this? We can call a collective halt if you like. But that should be *now*, I reckon. Before we all get caught up in the idea.'

'Ah,' said Theo. 'I think—'

'I want to do it,' blurted out Sam, before his father could finish his sentence. 'Only . . .'

'Only what?' asked Theo gently.

'Can we walk *slowly*, please?'

'In that case, might we hobble along together, Sam-I-Am?' asked Ruth. 'We can always go at the back.'

'Actually,' said Father Stephen, 'I think it would be preferable if you led the way, Sam. Set the pace for us, and we'll follow.'

'And a child shall lead them,' said William quietly.

'If you like,' said Father Stephen. 'Now, can I suggest we begin our silence? If you plan to walk barefoot, now's the time to take off your shoes and socks. If you'd like to have your feet washed, come up one at a time. If that doesn't feel comfortable, you might like a prayer of blessing. Or simply stay quietly in your seats. When we're ready, Ruth and Sam will lead the way and I'll bring up the rear.'

Tamsin watched as Father Stephen poured water from a thermos into the bowl, and placed a chair in front of him. William went first. He looked oddly vulnerable as he walked barefoot towards the altar. As Father Stephen knelt before him, Tamsin had to look away. It felt too intimate. She concentrated instead on Ruth, who after a momentary hesitation edged out of the pew and followed him, still wearing her shoes. She stood by the chair, and inclined her head for a blessing.

As first Catherine, then Matt and Beth got up from their seats to take their turn, William moved to the piano and began to play softly. Tamsin had no idea what he was playing – she didn't have a musical bone in her body – but the notes seemed to flow as effortlessly as the babble of a stream. The sound washed over her in a beguiling wave of emotion. As she bent to undo her laces she realized that her face was wet with tears. *Hail Mary, full of grace, the Lord is with thee.* The words came into her mind unbidden. *Blessed art thou among women, and blessed is the fruit of thy womb, Jesus.*

Everyone, she thought, went up to present either feet or bowed head to Father Stephen. Tamsin was the last, and waited just behind the boys. At the last minute, Sam pushed Milo in front of him. His feet washed, Milo walked back to his seat with a cheeky grin in her direction. Then it was Sam's turn. She watched as he half slumped onto the chair, looking intently at Father Stephen as if daring him to flinch. Father Stephen smiled reassuringly, and then took Sam's feet tenderly in his hands, one at a time. He poured water over them and gently patted them dry. As she took the seat herself, Tamsin's vision blurred with a fresh flow of tears. *Holy Mary, Mother of God, pray for us sinners, now, and at the hour of our death.*

They must have looked a strange sight, reflected Tamsin as the silent procession wound its way slowly through the streets. They were almost all barefoot, carrying their walking boots: only Mary Anne and Ruth had resisted the invitation. Mary Anne looked more self-conscious than the rest of them, as if she was walking fully clothed through a nudist colony. But a glance around suggested that by and large no one was giving them a second look. Well, if Father Stephen was right and this was traditional practice for pilgrims, maybe the people of Canterbury had seen it all before.

Scattering, thought Tamsin. Her thoughts were certainly scattering. She was all over the place. Needed to pull herself together, get a grip. She wasn't at all sure what had gone on back there at the church. She wasn't someone who cried, let alone prayed. Safer to put a lid on things and get on with the task in hand, whatever that was. Yet there she was, saying *Hail Mary*. Sister Bridget would be turning in her grave.

Music could do that, though. That's why soldiers marched into battle to the sound of pipes and drums. You could whip up a mood with music. Or was it the other way round? She suddenly remembered a quotation Anna had taped to the fridge in their London flat. '*Music is an outburst of the soul.* Delius.' Tamsin had remarked on it the day she moved in, but Anna just laughed and said, 'Pretentious? *Moi?*' Not long afterwards a tidy-up consigned the yellowing scrap of paper to the bin, but Tamsin had never forgotten it.

Smith was tugging at his lead. Probably couldn't understand why they were walking at a snail's pace. And now they'd practically ground to a halt. Beside her, Father Stephen was looking anxiously ahead. But no: there was no problem. Sam, flanked by William and Ruth, had simply reached what looked like the vast gate to a castle and they were navigating their way carefully through the narrow passage around it.

'Halfway there,' murmured Father Stephen. 'The next bit should be easier because it's pedestrianized.'

She nodded, and tried to return to silent contemplation. Hopeless! She was bombarded by distractions. Sounds, smells, sights. Perhaps she should give in to them. Use her senses to experience the moment, to identify with pilgrims from the past. The hubbub of the city. Shops, tourist tat. Presumably traders had always done well out of the sea of visitors. Smells of food and drink to tempt the passing pilgrim. She could detect a whiff of coffee, hot pastries, the ubiquitous reek of fast food, cooking oil. The sound of conversation. Someone yelling into a mobile phone. A street musician, singing rather badly to his own guitar accompaniment. The bustle, the press of people was quite overwhelming. Was that because she was worried that a heavy boot might land on her bare feet? Or just the contrast with the past eight days which had been spent largely in peaceful countryside? How quickly you got used to a different pace of life. That rhythm ... she was going to miss the rhythm of the days. And the silence – she should treasure it while she could. Tomorrow she would be back in the relentless routine: get Milo up and off to school, go to work, dash to pick him up, cook dinner, do the chores, collapse into bed. Where was the space for silence there? *Note to self: Find more space in my life.* Another chore for the list.

At last, it seemed, they were in the heart of the city, surrounded by ancient buildings. God, it was so easy to take all this history for granted if you grew up with it, thought Tamsin. But you only had to raise your eyes from street level to see the most amazing architecture. She wished she could ask Father Stephen to give her a guided tour. Explain what was what, and when was when, for that matter. They turned down a narrow lane into the Butter Market towards another great gate. Above them towered the Cathedral. Their little group clustered to one side of the gate into the Precincts, jostled by tour groups. A cacophony of different languages assaulted Tamsin's ears. Father Stephen, meanwhile, made his way to the front of the group, and after a word with the man on the gate, shepherded them through the entrance.

'Come through, everyone, this way,' he said. 'As pilgrims we enter as guests. Well done, everyone, over here.' He steered them to the right, away from the crowd, towards the Welcome Centre where a grey-haired priest was waiting.

'Stephen! Welcome! How very good to see you again,' she said, kissing him on both cheeks. 'Pilgrims, you're all very welcome here at Canterbury after your long journey. Many congratulations!'

Stephen's face lit up. 'Everyone, meet my good friend, Jane. We were at college together, many years ago. Now, we have a choice. It's an hour or so before Evensong. Jane has kindly offered to take us down to the Crypt, to offer prayers for our safe arrival. Others of you, I know, prefer to mark the moment with a pint of beer. So that's another option. Or you might just want to enjoy your picnics here in the Precincts. Can I suggest we gather again at about three o'clock?'

Tamsin looked round for Milo. He and Sam had collapsed onto the grass with Matt, Beth and Chloe, and were digging into their backpacks to find their sandwiches.

'Pint, Tamsin?' asked Tom.

'Ah, think not, thanks, mate,' she said. 'Reckon the kids have got the right idea. I'll stay here with them. The others might, though.'

'Tamsin,' said Ruth. 'That conversation. If you please.'

'Sure thing,' said Tamsin. 'You and William going to the Crypt? Because I'm not sure I can really sneak Smith in.'

'William will want to go, I'm sure. And if everyone else is going to the pub, I suggest we ask Beth to take responsibility for Smith and the boys. Because you and I are going into that café over there for a cup of tea,' she said firmly. 'I need to take the weight off my feet.'

Tamsin, comprehensively cornered, submitted as graciously as she felt able and allowed Ruth to steer her into a tea shop. As she stood in line to order the drinks at the counter, she watched Ruth purloin the last remaining free table from a couple of Japanese tourists, by playing the fragile old lady card. You had to admire the woman. She got what she wanted. She wondered uneasily what Ruth wanted from her.

'There!' said Tamsin, feeling the need to reassert herself as she put down the tray. 'Earl Grey for two, with a choice of milk or lemon. D'you need sugar?'

'No, thank you,' said Ruth. 'Would you pour, please?'

'Sure thing. Now, what's up? How can I help?'

Ruth took a sip from her tea, found it too hot, and put the cup carefully back on its saucer. After all that, she seemed reluctant to begin. 'I've been wondering about your ex-husband,' she said at last. 'Are you still in touch?'

'I *beg* your pardon?'

'Your ex-husband. You never mention him. Nor does Milo.'

'Strewth, Ruth! Where the heck's this come from?'

'Bringing up a child on your own can't be easy,' said Ruth, gazing into the middle distance. 'Now that my grandchildren have lost their mother, I'm more aware of that than ever. So naturally, I found myself wondering what part Milo's father plays in his life.'

'None at all,' said Tamsin shortly. 'And he was never my husband, as it goes. One thing I did get right.'

'Is that entirely fair on Milo? Have you thought about the long-term impact on him?'

Tamsin felt her temper flare. 'Have I *thought* about it? Good grief, Ruth! Milo's well-being is my first and last thought, morning, noon and night. If you must know, that's the whole reason I left Frankie!'

'What do you mean?'

'I reckoned that if Frankie was prepared to beat the living daylights out of me it wouldn't be long before he raised his hand against Milo. That wasn't a risk I was prepared to take.' She was shaking now, and realized that she was almost shouting. But how *dare* Ruth question her care of Milo? What did *she* know about anything?

'I apologize,' said Ruth, fiddling with a teaspoon. 'I had no idea about any of that. It sounds ... ghastly.' She took another, longer sip of tea. 'I suppose ... well, I have a more general concern. About the bringing up of boys, I mean. I think, on balance, that it's good for boys to know their fathers. And that fathers deserve to know their sons. Even if the circumstances are ... less than ideal.' She looked directly at Tamsin for the first time since they had sat at the table. 'Wouldn't you agree, Tamsin?'

Tamsin felt the blood drain away from her face. She felt suddenly, violently sick. 'Excuse me,' she said, getting up so abruptly that her chair fell backwards to the floor with a crash. Blindly, she barged her way through the crowded tea room towards the Ladies, shoved open the door and retched. *Jesus, Mary and Joseph!* How the *fuck* had she ended up in this mess? Mind you, that was a pretty stupid question. It was no big mystery. The usual story of one stupid, *stupid* mistake and the regret that she'd live with for the rest of her life. Except how could she possibly regret having Milo in her life? Trouble was, she'd spent so long letting it be understood that Frankie was Milo's father that she'd practically convinced herself it was true. Allowed herself to believe her own story.

Well, it was bound to happen at some point. She'd become gradually more uneasy about the physical likeness between the two boys recently, more so than ever this week. Seeing them on the bench together next to Brother Percival! They were like peas in a pod. In her heart of hearts, she knew the facade was becoming increasingly fragile. But did it have to come out now? In a twee English tea shop? *Today?* What was she going to do? Would she and Milo have to move away, start all over again? And *Ruth*, of all people. Anna's mother! Oh *God*, what must she think of her? Tamsin leaned over the basin and splashed her face with cold water. There was a small window, just big enough to climb through. Tamsin allowed herself a brief fantasy of clambering out, scooping up Milo from the Precincts, running for the airport, fleeing the country. Again. But how the heck would that help anything? She needed to speak to Ruth, find out what she planned to do with her knowledge.

Reluctantly, then, Tamsin made her way back to the table by the door where Ruth sat waiting, with every appearance of tranquillity. Tamsin brushed off the concerned enquiry of the waitress with a rueful wave – let them think she was mad, or, heaven help her, *pregnant* – and sat down. For a minute or two, neither spoke.

'It's not what you think,' said Tamsin eventually.

'And how, exactly, do you know what I think?' Ruth tone was icy.

'Well, of course I don't. But you probably hate me. I would in your shoes.'

'I'm not sure that's quite the language I'd choose.'

'Look, all I mean is ... it wasn't an *affair*, or anything.'

'Oh?'

'No. I'd never ...'

'But you did.'

Tamsin sighed. 'Yeah. I did,' she said flatly. 'We did. *Both* of us. *Once*. One bloody idiotic mistake.'

'And?'

Head in hands, Tamsin considered how to reply. Beth's birthday. She'd been away all week, due back on the Saturday morning, but bailed out a day early. She arrived in Farmleigh late on Friday night with her tail between her legs because she'd been turned down for a presenter's job that she wanted – *really* wanted, had been led to believe was in the bag, in fact – and fuming because she'd missed out to mediocre Mike. Everyone knew that he wasn't a patch on Tamsin – absolutely no personality – but the station manager had told her in no uncertain terms that her Aussie accent was too pronounced for BBC local radio. For goodness' sake! It was jobs for the boys; they'd had it all stitched up before the interviews. Her temporary contract had come to an end and she was high and dry, out of a job. So she'd been sore as anything, and there was Theo, tipsy after a good night out and sweetly affronted on her behalf. They opened his mother's sloe gin and had a high old time putting the world to rights. And before she knew it, unforgivably, she found herself in bed with her best friend's husband.

'And I left the bloody country,' she said. 'Got on the first plane possible home to Oz. You might just give me credit for that.'

'Did you tell Anna what happened?'

209

'God, no!' Tamsin was appalled. 'I was far too ashamed. And how would it have helped Anna to know? In Theo's defence ... I think they'd been going through a very bad patch. I get the impression that when Anna came home from Spain they finally sorted things out. Got back on track.' Certainly, by the time she and Milo moved back to the UK the whole shameful episode seemed like a bad dream, from another life.

'Does William know?' asked Tamsin. Ruth shook her head. 'And now what? What are you going to do?'

Ruth let out a long deep breath. 'I don't know,' she said. 'I think the main question is, does Theo know?'

'Does Theo know what?' asked Theo, as he and William walked through the door.

The next couple of hours were a blur. Looking back at the end of the day, Tamsin could remember only jumbled snapshots of the afternoon. For all its splendour, Canterbury Cathedral might as well have been a bus shelter as far as she was concerned. She took in nothing. After a brief but excruciating conversation with Theo, she made her way back to the Precincts, and sent Milo in to Choral Evensong under Matt's special care on the grounds that Smith wasn't allowed in, and she was feeling crook.

She watched Ruth – who looked smaller, somehow – make her way unevenly across the green to the Cathedral doors, leaning heavily on William's arm. Theo looked simply shell-shocked. Everyone else – remarkably – seemed to have hung onto the morning's good cheer, oblivious of the bomb that had just been detonated.

'You do look peaky,' said Mary Anne with a frown. 'Are you sure you're OK?'

'I'm good!' she said with false cheer. 'Think maybe I ate something. I'll stay in the fresh air and meet you guys later. No worries!'

She did remember walking round and round the perimeter of the Cathedral, with a slightly bewildered Smith. She could just make out the sound of singing. Briefly, she tried to picture their group inside. Would Theo be looking askance at Milo? Would the others notice? Her head began to swim again. Nothing seemed to make sense any more.

When they emerged, one small group among a crowd of visitors, Milo came running up. 'Hey, Mum, they read out our names. All of us, even Smith!'

'That's great, doll. Shame I missed it! You behave yourself?'

'Of course I did,' said Milo indignantly. 'I was as good as gold. Wasn't I, Matt?'

'Top marks,' said Matt.

By half past four, Tamsin and Milo were in the back of the school minibus with Beth and Smith. Father Stephen sat in the front, chatting animatedly to David. Theo and Sam were travelling with Ruth and William. There'd been a round of affectionate goodbyes to the others who were heading for the station and home.

'You must *promise* to let me know what you think of my Red Velvet cake,' said David to Mary Anne as he pressed a cake tin into her hands and kissed her on both cheeks. 'I *adore* baking with vegetables, but beetroot? *Really?*'

'Must you go?' Ruth asked Tom.

'Sorry, Mum, but yes. I'll ring you.' He kissed his mother and turned to Tamsin.

'You've got my number if you ever want that drink,' he said.

'Yeah, sure,' said Tamsin distractedly. 'Matt not joining us?' she added to Beth.

'So he offered to come,' she said unhappily. 'But I put him off. It felt . . . like, too much, too soon?'

Now Milo was sulking because she wouldn't let him ride with Sam, but Tamsin had put her foot down. 'Give them some space, mate,' she said. 'And look, when we get there, you and I stay in the background. This is a family matter.' Oh *God*, the irony!

'Then why are we even *going*?'

'Because there's something I've got to do. Something for Anna.'

Once they'd cleared the city, it was only another twenty minutes' drive to the coast. David pulled into the car park, next to Ruth's Volvo.

Theo took Tamsin's elbow, and steered her away from the family. 'Look, I'm sorry,' he said with a frown. 'I'm struggling to get my head round this. I still can't quite believe it.'

'I know,' said Tamsin, her eyes swimming with tears. 'I've had nine years to get used to the idea and it still seems pretty unlikely.'

'But you're quite *sure*?'

'Look, mate, I'm sure. And even if I had any doubt at all . . . well, there's the evidence . . .' She inclined her head towards Milo, taking turns with Sam to throw a stick for Smith. Theo shook his head in disbelief.

'Look, Theo. I'm not asking you for anything. Today's not the day for this, anyway. Take some time to get used to the idea.'

'Theo?' Father Stephen approached, a round white box in his hands. 'Are you about ready?'

For a fleeting moment, Theo looked blank. Then he appeared to collect himself. 'Ready,' he said in a clear voice. 'Time to go. Everyone?'

They walked up the hill, slowly for Ruth, towards the ruined towers of the medieval church. The day was still warm, and there was a light breeze coming off the sea, sending little wisps of cloud scudding across the sky. In the distance, gulls swooped shrilly over the surf. Waves crashed onto the beach, noisily dragging the pebbles into the undertow. All around them, families were playing games, walking dogs, eating picnics. A nearby clutch of caravans made it a popular place for holidaymakers. Tamsin wondered how easy it would be to find a quiet spot. But maybe it didn't matter. *Life goes on*, and other clichés. She reached out for Milo's hand, glad that she'd left Smith with David in the car park below. He looked up with a little smile of surprise, but made no resistance.

'Here, I think,' said Theo, fifty metres or so beyond the ruins. 'Ruth – would you like the bench?'

They clustered around her, in silence, unsure quite what to do. Tamsin took off her backpack and put it at her feet. Father Stephen lowered his head and draped a purple stole around his neck. At a nod from Theo, he stepped forward.

'Dear friends,' he said. 'It's good to be here together. It's tempting to say that we've reached the end of our journey, but of course, that's not really true. But we have reached the end of our week's pilgrimage. We have one last but important task left to us. When we scatter Anna's ashes, we'll be marking another step on your journey as you say goodbye to her.

212

'Theo's chosen this place because of the happy memories he has of coming here with Anna on their honeymoon.' He smiled encouragingly at Theo, who was visibly struggling to control his emotions. 'I must say, the view is magnificent. I can't think of a better choice,' he continued. 'But just before we begin, there's one more thing. Tamsin?'

Tamsin took out a small fabric bag from her backpack. 'I've got something for each of you,' she said, her voice trembling slightly as she unzipped it. She cleared her throat, and when she spoke again, it was in a firmer tone. 'A present from Anna. She asked me to give these to you at the end of the walk.'

Starting with Theo, she went from person to person, putting in each hand a tiny MP3 player. Green for Theo, pink for Beth, blue for Sam, silver for William and orange for Ruth; the bright shades of a bag of boiled sweets. 'Anna chose a special piece of music for each of you. Something she loved and wanted to pass on to you. She also said a few words about why she picked it. And how sorry she was to be leaving you. I recorded the messages with her the day before she died. It's a way of sending you her love, now she's not here any more.'

The tears were welling up again. Milo gave her hand a little squeeze. Bloody hell, she hoped they all worked. But she'd spent hours in the studio, getting hold of Anna's specified recordings, adjusting the sound levels on her voice, charging the batteries, and checking them all a hundred times over to make sure everything worked like clockwork.

'Thank you, Tamsin. I thought perhaps you might like to stay up here for a while afterwards, to listen. Theo, shall I begin?'

Tamsin closed her eyes, and felt the tears spill down her cheeks from under her eyelids. She tuned in and out of the words as Father Stephen spoke them. 'Though we are dust and ashes, God has prepared for those who love him a heavenly dwelling place. At her funeral we commended Anna into the hands of almighty God. As we prepare to commit her remains to the earth, we entrust ourselves and all who love God to his loving care.'

And now Theo was speaking. 'Goodbye, Anna. I'll always love you.' She opened her eyes to see him shaking the urn to scatter a cloud of ashes to the breeze.

'Bye, Mum,' whispered Beth.

'Bye, bye, Mum,' said Sam.

'Rest in peace, darling girl,' said William. Ruth's words, if she spoke any as she shook the urn, were lost to the wind.

Then Father Stephen caught Tamsin's eye, and raised his eyebrows. She glanced at Theo, who nodded his permission. She let go of Milo's hand to take the urn.

'Goodbye, Anna,' she said softly, as she cast out the last few particles of ash. She fixed her eyes on the horizon, and breathed in the sharp tang of sea air, determined to fix the moment in her memory for ever. 'I miss you, doll. You were one in a million.'

And now Father Stephen was speaking again.

> 'May the road rise up to meet you.
> May the wind always be at your back.
> May the sun shine warm upon your face,
> and rains fall soft upon your fields.
> And until we meet again,
> may God hold you in the palm of His hand. Amen.'

Tamsin summoned up every atom of her being to send thoughts of joy and gratitude and apology, but most of all her love, to Anna, wherever she was. Then she took Milo's hand, and started back down the slope.

Epilogue

Anna hovers in the vestry, adding rosin to her bow. In just under ten minutes, she will walk out into the chancel and take her place centre stage. Her chair awaits, the black hole endpin holder precisely placed to prevent her cello spike from slipping on the shiny tiled floor. Her music stand is just where she wants it, although she hopes to play from memory. But after such a gap since her last public performance, having the notes in front of her feels only wise.

She's wearing her favourite green dress, with its swishy skirt, sufficiently wide to encompass the instrument. The fabric has just enough sheen that it will catch the light and sparkle slightly while she plays. All set, ready to go. A lollipop programme of well-known pieces that might not challenge the audience but seems appropriate for a fundraising event. Nothing to frighten the horses, in Father Stephen's words. Classic FM, not Radio Three. And they are beautiful pieces, hackneyed only by their overuse in film scores and TV programmes. Bach's First and Third Cello Suites are two of the most immediately recognizable pieces for the cello, and she knows they'll show off the natural resonance of her instrument to full advantage. Even she has to admit that it sounded rather wonderful resounding round the church when she rehearsed this afternoon, although the frightening number of people in the audience will undoubtedly dampen the acoustic a little.

Oh, horrors! The nave is almost full. She hopes they've all brought cushions, because she knows from experience that those pews are horribly uncomfortable, prone to catch you in just the wrong place halfway up your back. No wonder Stephen wants rid of them. An ongoing battle with the Victorian Society. There are the great and good of Farmleigh, the chain gang, dressed in their best, sitting in the front row. Special seats to encourage generosity, hopes Stephen. A few rows back, the seats reserved for the family are as yet empty. And there on the far end sits Dominic, nearly ninety but commanding even in his wheelchair. Blind as a bat these days, and pretty immobile, but his ears (oh, help!) still in perfect working order.

After the Bach, her former flatmate Neil will accompany her in Beethoven's glorious Third Cello Sonata. William, bless him, has had the piano tuned specially. They'll end with a soupy bit of Rachmaninov, his *Vocalise*, a final tug on the audience's heartstrings. She's so glad that Neil is here. By some serendipitous miracle she's caught him in a rare gap between professional engagements and he's agreed to accompany her. She started the rehearsal full of stumbling apologies: she's horribly out of practice, she'll probably mess up, she's terribly afraid of letting everyone down.

'Anna, shut up, will you? Just get on and *play*,' he said, with just enough briskness that she pulled herself together. And actually, it was OK. Fine. That tingle of excitement at the prospect of a live performance. That moment when you find your way into the place where it's simply you and the instrument, working as one, wholly inhabiting the music, where nothing else matters. Not perfect, not brilliant. But good enough. Probably.

She's always been nervous before performing, but never cripplingly so, thank goodness. There's always that lurking terror that you'll go on stage and find yourself dumbstruck, unable to play a note, or even hold the bow. Like those anxiety dreams when you're about to take an exam for a subject you've never studied. Some performers suffer so badly from stage fright that they vomit before playing in public, or turn to drink or drugs to get through the ordeal. Or give up live performance altogether. The worst thing for her has always been the long walk from the wings to the stage. But she recognizes that she needs a sliver of fear, a kick of adrenalin to give of her best.

And this time ... Can she do it? It used to be her bread-and-butter, but it's years, aeons, since she's performed in front of an audience. Part of her old life. The last time she played in public was at Josh's funeral. Here, in this very building. A tide of sadness

216

threatens to engulf her. *But you knew that,* she reminds herself as she submits to the emotion. *You knew that when you agreed to this.* Of course she did. It's partly to thank Stephen for his loving support over the years since their loss that she's accepted his invitation, so tentatively made, to give a recital in aid of his project to remodel the church. Partly that, and partly to put down a marker. A quiet comeback from the wilderness years, when she thought she'd renounced the cello for ever. She will play for him, her darling lost boy. For her family. For herself.

She sees that they have just arrived. Her father's brow is furrowed. He so hates being late. Her mother (so often the cause of his lateness) is soothing him, steering him towards the reserved pew. Theo brushes his hair out of his eyes in a harassed gesture and shepherds Beth and Sam into their seats. Good; he's remembered the cushions. Blue and white ones from the kitchen. A hasty dash back into the house? Beth looks around for her, and gives an exaggerated thumbs up with both hands. Anna smiles and raises her own hand in reply.

She hopes that Sam will last. Ten is still quite little to sit through a grown-up concert on uncomfortable seats. He looks wriggly already. Ah, but that's because he's casting his eyes around for Milo. Tamsin has said she'll try and come, and has promised to creep out if Milo's patience wears thin. Anna watches Sam scan the church. When he spots Milo, he grins and waves, whispers something to Theo, and slips out of his pew, cushion in hand, to join them on the other side of the building.

There was no single moment when Anna worked it out. With the benefit of hindsight, she thinks she's probably always known. Tamsin's sudden flight, Theo's inexplicable remorse on her return from Spain, the casual care the two of them took to avoid each other's company when Tamsin reappeared in their lives. Meeting the six-year-old Milo for the first time in the flesh provided the final piece of the jigsaw, bringing the picture fully into focus. He has Theo's jaw, Sam's frame. Seeing the two boys together now, she wonders how long it will take other people to put two and two together. Theo clearly has no idea, bless him. At first the sense of betrayal cut her to the quick. These days, distress has given way to

217

something approaching forgiveness. Compassion, even. Whatever it had been, it's long since over, she's sure of that. Part of an unbearably harrowing chapter in their lives that should be consigned to the past, where it belongs.

'You ready, Anna?' asks Neil behind her. 'I think it's time.'

She takes a deep breath and closes her eyes for a moment to focus her attention. Then she steps forward with her cello, and the audience begins to clap.

Acknowledgements

Knowing Anna is set on the real Pilgrims' Way from Guildford to Canterbury, although I have taken one or two small liberties with details for the sake of the plot. For further information on the route, see:

<www.nationaltrail.co.uk/north-downs-way>

Lots of kind people have provided encouragement and support as I wrote this book. I'm hugely grateful to Alison Barr, Lorna Fergusson, Tabitha Gilchrist, Paul Handley, John Pritchard and Wendy Robins for comments on the text while it was still in draft. Heartfelt thanks, too, to Nick Gethin, Shauni McGregor, Phoebe Mead, Melanie Patton and Sally Welch for helpful conversations during my research. Any mistakes are of course my own. Thank you, too, to K. T. Bruce and Lucy Gordon for the cover photo.

Finally, my thanks above all to my companions on the journey, Imogen, Jack and Ben Phillips.